Praise for Matthew Salesses

Advance Praise for *Disappear Doppelgänger Disappear*

"How to live in a world that refuses to see you? Matt Kim's intoxicating battle with his mysterious doppelgänger moves him deeper and deeper into the vast and urgent sea of this question—and towards a possible answer. *Disappear Doppelgänger Disappear* is inventive and profound, mordantly hilarious and wildly moving. Matthew Salesses is one of my all-time favorite writers, and this is his most thrilling book to date."

—Laura van den Berg, author of *The Third Hotel*

"Brilliant, unsettling, and wholly original, *Disappear Doppelgänger Disappear* is an astonishing exploration of identity, violence, alienation, double consciousness (and quadruple consciousness!), family, and love. Spiraling out into parallel worlds and intersecting lives, and raising questions about what we owe the ones we love and how we can survive a place that renders us invisible, the plot dazzles at every twist and turn with the kind of revelatory grace that feels both shocking and inevitable. This is a book of breathtaking depth and scope. A miraculous achievement."

—Catherine Chung, author of *The Tenth Muse*

"Matthew Salesses has written the quintessential novel for these troubled times. Outrageously inventive and flat-out hilarious, *Disappear Doppelgänger Disappear* probes our obsession with individualism and what it means to be truly free. An absolute masterpiece from a stunningly singular voice."

—Kirstin Chen, author of *Bury What We Cannot Take*

"A brilliant, existential detective story in which the mystery is the truth of oneself. Disturbing in the best way, Matthew Salesses's *Disappear Doppelgänger Disappear* throws you off-balance but never lets you fall. A haunting, dreamlike tale for anyone who's ever feared they're living the wrong life."

—Mat Johnson, author of *Pym*

"Like everything Matthew Salesses writes, this book grabbed me on page one and didn't let go. Salesses has written a wild, propulsive, and sometimes startling novel about learning how to live in the body; how to inhabit an identity; how to confront a fractured, perplexing world even as one is forced to confront the confusion and conflict within."

—Nicole Chung, author of *All You Can Ever Know*

"*Disappear Doppelgänger Disappear* is a Kafkaesque, Murakamiesque, dreamlike novel of alienation and duplication, oftentimes quite funny, and all the times quite strange. A remarkable, entertaining, disturbing achievement. Look out for it."

—Viet Thanh Nguyen, author of *The Sympathizer*

Praise for *The Hundred-Year Flood*

A *Millions* Most Anticipated Book of 2015
A BuzzFeed Pick for 19 Awesome New Books You Need to Read This Fall
A Refinery29 Pick for Best Summer Reading
A Gawker Review of Books Pick for 9 Must-Reads for the Fall
An Adoptive Families Best Book of 2015
A Thought Catalog Pick for 10 Essential Contemporary Books by Asian American Writers

"Salesses's novel dramatically documents how longing can turn, painfully, into love."

—*The Millions*

"What carries us through the novel is Salesses's gift for language: here is a meditative, poetic, modern fable crafted in haunting bursts of impressionistic prose."

—*Kirkus Reviews*

"Through dreamlike language, Salesses toys with our human need to control forces that are larger than us: the flood, secrets, the past, disease, the inevitability of the reality one creates for one's self. The novel holds a meditative, reflective pace."

—*Kirkus Reviews*, feature interview

"Salesses delivers an immersive novel about identity, myths, and ghosts . . . This is an engulfing read."

—*Publishers Weekly*

"The novel is not only a well-rendered exploration of identity, pain, and love, but also an expertly paced story, incredibly engaging throughout."

—Askmen.com

"*The Hundred-Year Flood* is admirable for what it tackles, for the depth of its subject, for the risks it takes with structure, for the love triangle it quickly establishes and charges with tension, for the questions it raises about what we inherit from our parents, known or unknown, and how we ground ourselves when we've been living on top of lies and murky beginnings—on rising, threatening waters, you might say."

—*The Rumpus*

"Tee is in Prague. He is running away from memory. He is running toward myth. He is searching. In Prague, Tee meets an artist and the artist's wife. Before long, the three are drawn into a fateful series of events as Prague is laid bare by a flood that only comes every hundred years. This beautiful debut novel by Matthew Salesses is much like that flood—epic and devastating and full of natural majesty."

—Roxane Gay, author of *An Untamed State* and *Bad Feminist*

"*The Hundred-Year Flood* yanks you off your feet, whipping you along on a brilliantly crafted adventure. You can't fight the current and you don't want to, either. Matthew Salesses is a new force of nature."

—Mat Johnson, author of *Loving Day*

"A filmic, fast-moving, disjunctive ride, *The Hundred-Year Flood* rollicks through an exquisitely constructed plot to arrive at a surprising destination. Matthew Salesses writes taut, intelligent, lyrical sentences. He is definitely a writer to watch, and *The Hundred-Year Flood* is the novel to read right this moment."

—Robert Boswell, author of *Tumbledown* and *The Heyday of the Insensitive Bastards*

"How artfully Matthew Salesses transports his reader between Prague and the States, past and present. I fell under the spell of his lovely novel as thoroughly as his protagonist, Tee, falls under the spell of Prague and, in particular, of one of its inhabitants. *The Hundred-Year Flood* is a vivid, cunning, compelling narrative about inheritance and forgiveness. A wonderful debut."

—Margot Livesey, author of *The Flight of Gemma Hardy*

"*The Hundred-Year Flood* is a beautiful, transporting novel that lays bare the heartbreak and loss of the world while never forgetting its magic. A dreamlike exploration of how the myths and stories we tell— and those that we choose to keep to ourselves—forge our identities, this book will swallow you whole."

—James Scott, author of *The Kept*

"In this spellbinding novel, Matthew Salesses artfully weaves an intricate tapestry, shifting effortlessly between time, place, and identity while exploring all three subjects in the process. He succeeds in transporting the reader to a ghost Prague—a timeless, kaleidoscopic city layered with wonder and devastating sorrow."

—Kenneth Calhoun, author of *Black Moon*

"*The Hundred-Year Flood* is an incredible literary achievement. It's not often you find a novel that is capable of accomplishing such conceptual sophistication while maintaining the narrative force of compelling fiction. At times poetic and emotional, at times brutal and devastating, this intricate tale about identity, loss, love, and purpose is a force to be reckoned with and an absolute pleasure to read."

—Mario Alberto Zambrano, author of *Lotería*

"Like the water that threatens to consume everything in its wake, the narrative is lyrical and winding, but if you have an affinity for soul-searching sagas, *The Hundred-Year Flood* is for you."

—Gawker Review of Books

DISAPPEAR

DOPPELGÄNGER

DISAPPEAR

ALSO BY MATTHEW SALESSES

The Hundred-Year Flood

I'm Not Saying, I'm Just Saying

DISAPPEAR

DOPPELGÄNGER

DISAPPEAR

A NOVEL

MATTHEW SALESSES

Text copyright © 2020 by Matthew Salesses
All rights reserved.

Published by Little A, New York

www.apub.com

Amazon, the Amazon logo, and Little A are trademarks of Amazon.com, Inc., or its affiliates.

ISBN-13: 9781503943261 (hardcover)
ISBN-10: 1503943267 (hardcover)
ISBN-13: 9781503943254 (paperback)
ISBN-10: 1503943259 (paperback)

Cover design by Isaac Tobin
Cover illustration by Lauren Nassef

Printed in the United States of America

First edition

To my kids, in loving memory of 나옥경.
사랑해. 보고싶어.

For us—

AN ABBREVIATED LIST OF DISAPPEARANCES

1875 Page Act

1882 Chinese Exclusion Act

1907 Gentlemen's Agreement

1917 Asiatic Barred Zone Act

1924 Immigration Act

1934 Tydings-McDuffie Act

1942 Executive Order 9066

CHAPTER 1: DISAPPEARING

EARTHQUAKE

One night my girlfriend asked what was wrong with me and I couldn't explain. We lay on my black sheets between my blank white walls, on the bed that was the room's only furniture. We had bared ourselves—we had a connection when we were naked—but Sandra wanted more than full exposure. It was three a.m. after her late shift waiting tables at The Cave, and she smelled like fry oil and strangers, and still she talked. Who was I to prefer silence? I told her how I blacked out as I watched the news, ate my microwave dinner, wrote, how I woke to find my status update a string of *g*'s with no likes, nothing to account for the time between. "It's not just loneliness, I mean. I'm pretty sure I'm disappearing. People walk straight into me on the street. When I'm alone in a bathroom with ten urinals, some white guy will come in and pee right next to me."

She twitched her mouth from side to side. This was a habit I envied. She was always doing things equally on either side of her body.

When her lips parted the smack echoed off the empty walls.

"How long you been feeling this?" she asked. "Like you're disappearing?"

I couldn't tell whether she was being sarcastic.

Well. These were the facts: My cat was dead. My wife and daughter had left me. At some point in the last three years I had stopped going out or having friends. After the divorce I had kept the walls blank because the echo was a kind of company.

"Just to clarify," Sandra said, "you've felt like disappearing the whole time you've been with me?"

"Just to clarify," I said, "what I mean is you're all I have left. Maybe you're the only reason I'm still here." I felt quite smart about this line.

"Try again," she said.

Above us the popcorn ceiling seemed about to shed its puffs. "Okay. Today I went to the butcher shop for bulgogi. I stood in line thinking about how to tell the guy to slice it, and he served everyone else inside and then every new person who came in. He didn't even look at me."

Sandra held her finger in front of me, showing off a new burn on her fingertip. She must have gotten it from work that day. The ceiling blurred in the background.

"Tonight," she said, "one white boy pinched my ass and another tried to tuck his tip under my apron string. I would settle for no bulgogi."

The room spun.

"After a while," I said, "my daughter walked into the shop with her mom. They didn't see me either."

"I'm trying to tell you something—"

All around us rose the smell of raw beef, the sound of chopping and flirting—a butcher shop was a place of zero subtlety—and then there was my daughter with her lips purple and her hair spiked, in black leggings and silver boots and a camo T-shirt, like this was normal.

Sandra sighed. "You're in a rough patch," she said cruelly. "You'll get out of it."

I could tell she wanted to say something more. When she turned her head away I thought I had to look on the bright side. After all in the scheme-of-things, disappearance was literally *no* thing. I was thirty-six, and I was dating, and my body still functioned, even if my left foot was slightly bigger than my right. I could afford $1,600 a month to rent the first floor of a duplex in a white Boston suburb. It could be worse, etc. "Plus," I added, "my agent called. She couldn't sell my novel. Plus my savings are almost gone. You were right, I shouldn't have quit my job."

Sandra sat up and let her hair down over her face like a ghost. "Boo," she said. "Don't try to blame me. You're depressed."

Why were other people always telling me what I was?

"Anyway"—she waved her hands in my face—"did you forget I went to city hall today to change my name? I want you to say my name correctly when we're having sex."

She had my full apprehension now.

"I'm done answering to two masters," she said. "I mean languages."

I had known of her plan to take one official name instead of one English name and one Korean—I had just lost track of what day today was.

"Yumi?" I said.

Yumi brushed back her hair, and the ghost shifted to her eyes.

"Do you feel like a single person now?" I asked.

"I never felt like two people," Yumi said. "It was only other people who acted like I was."

I wondered whether *what was wrong with me* was that I was other people.

———

Once Yumi left, clacking her lacquered nails against the doorframe for luck, I showered and put on the purple tracksuit that I used to wear for my daughter. She had claimed it made me look cool. I met my desk in the purple office that used to be my daughter's bedroom. I had added as little as I could, only a desk, a chair, a computer. I felt closer to Charlotte in her old space. Regret plus writing was a little like time travel.

From my desk I texted Yumi that I would love her better, I needed to figure out how to do that. I knew "love," I knew "better." Somehow their combination stumped me. Before she got dressed Yumi had said I wasn't disappearing, I was choosing not to be present. I could see how she could see it like that.

I touched the keyboard and the keys felt hot, as if someone with a lot of excess body heat had just been typing. My fingers felt hot. Maybe I felt hot. I wondered what kind of book people would buy. Two characters who hate each other fall in love? Plus the apocalypse? Plus they're of different races? I decided to write a new novel. All I needed was three thousand words a day for a month. Ten thousand words a day for a week? I'd just make something weird happen.

I muffled my mouth with my hands and screamed for a while into them. Then I coughed until I could breathe again. My chair poked into my spine, though nothing stuck out of it. A note on my desk said *buy a new chair*.

In my failed novel a straight cis able Korean American guy woke, drank coffee, made toast and eggs, hacked into his company's website, ate a grilled cheese sandwich with four lactose pills, took notes to protect his company from other hackers, microwaved his dinner, watched the news as he dined, slept dreamlessly, again and again—and desperately wanted a different life. He was at an age of dwindling options: Each choice he made limited the choices he had left. In the end he settled for what he had, and his desire vanished. He was finally everything he could be. It was a happy ending.

I was still at my desk, massaging the sore spots on my back and thinking about my options, when my computer shut down. In the apartment upstairs something crashed. The floor swayed. Gravity got confused. My photo of my ex-family danced off the desk, and when I reached out, my hand didn't go where I intended it to go. I couldn't make my intention action. My head seemed to float on liquid, and yet I was more aware of the ground than I had ever been. The ground was always in motion—I'd only just noticed. I hugged my knees to my chest and squeezed my eyes shut. I prayed for my daughter in her bedroom across town, yanking her blanket over her head—or was she in school by now, huddled under a desk?—when had the sun come up?—had she eaten?—either way I couldn't reach her—

This was how I disappeared.

———

When the floor returned to normal I rubbed the soles of my bare feet over the hardwood. I stomped, paused, stomped a few times more. For the first time the blankness of the walls looked wrong, like something on them had been shaken down. I stomped again, then shuffled out to the TV to hear another human voice.

The living room was the same—what used to be typical was now strange. On one side was my cheap TV, on the other side the red couch my ex-family hadn't wanted. Beside the TV stood the electric keyboard. Behind the couch a cardboard shipping box.

The whole room looked very haphazard. Only the keyboard seemed intentional. I had bought it after the divorce.

The news didn't mention an earthquake. Even the local news covered a presidential candidate who kept refusing to denounce the KKK. One pundit said he never condoned the KKK either. How could you tell a person's stance? My phone got no emergency alert. The movement of the earth went unacknowledged. I googled "earthquake Boston" and learned that tremors in the greater metropolitan area are more frequent than people think. Usually they're too small to be felt. Once I saw a show about people who vacation wherever they think the next "big one" will hit: Either they hoped the earth would swallow them or they hoped to discover a new earth.

I cracked the front door, and the same old earth eked through the opening. Disappointing. No Minotaur slammed its horns into the house. No hand descended from the sky. No wolf huffed. The world held the same unremarkable terror as ever. The older white straight couple across the street caressed each other on their porch with their terrier barking at their feet. I called out to see whether they had felt anything, and they ignored me. They were your typical neighbors.

In the kitchen I corkscrewed a bottle of Chardonnay, and I drank a quarter, and then another quarter, and then another quarter, until I felt less tired. I tried to keep myself awake, aware. I shook the bottle, and the liquid inside it shook. With each sip the bottle lightened, its weight proportionate to the wine I *hadn't* drunk. Consumption was lightness.

I took the wine back to my office and lifted the photo of my ex-family back onto my desk. This time action matched intention—what was different? As always, in the photo, Charlotte wore a purple sundress and chewed her brown hair and clung to her mother's sunburned leg. As always I wiped my thumbprints off the glass with my thumb. The next time I would have to do it again. I drank the last quarter of wine and then wrote three thousand words about the earth shaking a person's sense of the earth.

It wasn't until I returned to the living room, with the empty bottle in hand and the cardboard box behind the sofa staring back at me, that I realized why I was pacing. It was the box: There was something off about it. In that box were toys my daughter had wanted that I never got the chance to give her. I had bought them, one by one, over my last three years alone. It occurred to me now that the line earthquakes make between the past and the present is called a *fault*.

I knelt, and the flat wood dug into my knees, which were still indented from the many pews I'd knelt at after my parents died. My adoptive parents had not been the kind of Irish Catholics who went to mass out of faith: They had based their devotion on an hour per week of corrective behavior. I had based mine on wanting to be loved. They had adopted me, and then they taught me how to be adopted—and how to be Catholic and how to be white—and then I left for college, and then they stopped talking to me, and then I got married, and then Jennifer and I had a child, and then I was afraid of myself, and then I could never tell what my family wanted from me, and then the divorce happened, and then my wife and daughter moved to another house and asked me to leave them alone.

Soon I am going to disappear.

How to explain? Maybe it started one Saturday six years ago when I woke Charlotte early and we drove out to farmland to stargaze. As the moon set and the sun rose she said the stars made her sad and she didn't know why. "Stop taking me here," she said. "I need to sleep. I'm not five anymore." She was six. She pulled her hood down over her face, and I thought the reason the stars make us sad must be that some have already burned out and we don't know which. Since light takes time to reach us, the stars we see are those stars as they shone years earlier. The sun we see is the sun as it shone eight minutes and twenty seconds earlier. No matter how close I got to Charlotte, she would always see me as I *used to be.* Vision is an impression of the past.

That was the intuition I had as I opened the box and found that inside . . . was nothing. All of the toys were gone. And yet, at first, I still thought I'd been robbed. Why take the toys, I wondered. Why not the TV or electric keyboard or computer? I pressed my palm to the cardboard bottom. The cardboard felt hot as if someone had just been inside. My hand left a faint sweat print. It looked like the back of a throat. The longer the box yawned open and empty the more I wanted to step into its mouth.

WHAT I DID

When my family left me (two years, 296 days earlier) I had to figure out how to spend all that time alone. In order to pay child support I went freelance in IT security. I achieved some success hacking into companies and recording my path so that it could be closed behind me. I did this for about six hours a day. I had the rest of the day to do something else.

At first I tried cooking, but I hated how it made me shop—planning ahead ingredients for an entire week. I would end up cooking for only the first few days and then panicking and eating everything that looked like it might spoil. Also I had no talent. Recipes never revealed themselves to me as code did. Jennifer, my ex-wife, had never liked me to cook, and I realized finally that this wasn't because she had liked cooking. Eventually I bought a lot of frozen food, which only left more time to kill.

What could I do? I didn't like movies, and people frowned when I went alone. I hated the mall. I hated organized sports. I had quit going to church. I kept a goldfish alive for eleven months and twenty-nine days. I learned to watch the news.

I bought an electric keyboard and retaught myself what I had known as a boy. My parents had sent me to lessons they couldn't afford, and after their deaths I had stopped going. My adoptive parents wouldn't pay for lessons that wouldn't turn into a career. It was their life philosophy to treat everything as an investment. Either on earth or in heaven. I was a failed venture. Now I went back to spending an hour a day practicing a skill I used only in practice. I imagined my mother's scowl inside me. This relaxed me.

When I started dating Yumi that filled one or two nights a week. It also made the other nights feel worse. I spent fifteen minutes a day looking through my phone contacts for someone to call. Somehow I didn't have any friends left? I had cut them off when I got married, though Jennifer had kept hers? I must not have been close to mine? I looked up old classmates on the internet and direct messaged a couple of them. One said he didn't remember a Matt Kim and I must be trying to scam him.

From time to time I had to restock the freezer. I taught myself to appreciate wine. After a month I went to the nearest animal shelter and bought a cat. It was an older tabby, a domestic American shorthair. I thought an older cat would help me understand how my adoptive parents had felt, taking me on at twelve. But later I found out the cat was something like seventy in human years.

The only place I felt like myself was the toy shop. Once a week I went to the Curious George store in Harvard Square and everyone assumed I was a generous parent. That was how I made sense there, and how you make sense to people is how they treat you.

Eventually I started going by my ex-family's house every day, between 3:30 and 5:15 p.m., after Charlotte got home from school and before Jennifer got home from work. I dressed up and parked down the street, watching carefully. Sometimes I barely saw anything but the glow from the TV. On Tuesdays Charlotte wore her mom's clothes and makeup and strolled around the neighborhood, I didn't know why. She never had other kids over. She never seemed to study. From time to time she made paper models of animals or buildings or monuments, and tore them up after she built them. This was a hobby I had never seen when we lived together.

One day the house filled up with boxes, and then they moved again, and soon Jennifer's lawyer sent a letter with a new address for the child support checks. Then Jennifer emailed and apologized for using her lawyer and described her new job and Charlotte's new school, where she seemed to be fitting in. After that one last email came, saying they were happy and to stop texting and emailing unless it was an emergency. I didn't know what had changed. I went by their old house and pictured my daughter powdering on her mom's pale foundation. Whose fault was it that I couldn't imagine my little girl as a popular kid? I sold my fancy computer stuff for a simple laptop, and I wrote a novel about a hacker whose ability to disappear was his only strength.

———

The last time I saw Charlotte was just after the second move. The secretary at her new school called and said my daughter was acting out. I asked why he hadn't called her mom, and he said he had, with no answer. The guy wouldn't accept excuses over the phone. I got there in fifteen minutes. In the principal's office a nice older white lady with nice round glasses and nice impersonal manners asked me about my family. I told her what I had told her secretary: that I had agreed not to see my family anymore, so couldn't they cut Charlotte some slack, she was going through a lot? I said I had heard that Charlotte was fitting in.

"Usually kids who think acting out can make them popular," the principal said, slowing her words as if I wouldn't understand, "are kids who feel they are acting at home."

It was a line you gave someone who didn't know his whole life was an act. Maybe you could only recite it if you didn't know this about yourself.

I told her I would give up everything, even my daughter, if it meant a better life for my daughter.

Afterward Charlotte was waiting in the hall. She knew about adults, what could hurt them and where they were going next, like a ghost or a shrink. "Do you not get it?" she said. "You're making everything harder on me. Now everyone will know you're my dad. How can I be normal?"

She guided me to an emergency exit. She had a ten-year-old's brutal eye for what was an emergency and what was not.

THE CAVE

I needed to update Yumi on my situation, I would present the box as Disappearance Exhibit A. I had filled that box with objects of Charlotte's unfulfilled desire—wasn't that loving better? Now those objects were gone, and the unfulfilled desire was mine. How could I make myself *not* disappear, when disappearing and not disappearing were both acts of nothing? The one thing my parents and my adoptive parents would have agreed on was that you didn't control your fate (your personality is an aspect of your blood type, God never gives you more than you etc.). What I wanted to hear from Yumi was that she still believed we held our lives in our own hands. She was everything pro-choice! Earlier that month she had shown me a line from one of her grad courses: *To want is to realize what we don't have . . .* I was still thinking about that and about what it meant I lacked.

She had described the whole scene. She was taking notes on autopilot, the professor was bio-ing some French psychoanalyst, then suddenly class was over and she hadn't moved in ten or fifteen minutes. When I asked about the last note she took, she got her pad out of her bag. It was the same pad she used for work.

To want is to realize what we don't have.

To love is to give what we don't have.

Then some letters that probably meant food orders.

Dude at table 2 is a groper.

Etc.

Several times she had called this course "White Men Obsessed with Their Penises." The more I thought about her notes, the more I worried about who I was.

I parked on Mount Auburn Street and walked to clear my head. The short stretch of trees before the university could almost fool you into thinking you were in a small town. In the peace between traffic I could hear birdcalls. Then I got to the quaint shops made loud by students. Soon I regretted coming. Halfway to Harvard Square the footsteps behind me grew threatening—they kept a beat. My senses expanded in an invisible circle around me. I walked a little farther, and the footsteps kept coming. Finally I spun on my heels. Twenty feet back, at the edge of my sense-circle, two white dudebros pretended to chat. They wore hats that said something about this country we all lived in, that it wasn't great anymore.

Sweat dripped from my palms. I had suffered some damage to my nervous system. I wondered how long the dudebros had been following me. The other day the news had reported a white man raping and strangling Asian women in New York's Chinatown. Black males kept getting shot by police. This was the menace we lived with—I wasn't lucky enough to disappear from menace. It was a menace you could sometimes barely see. I stopped to check whether the dudebros would pass, but they stopped too and honked their hands at a student in a headscarf. In other words they made convincing dudebros, and this didn't comfort me.

I turned right on JFK Street. The dudebros turned right on JFK Street. They talked about bikes with zero gears, difficulty as a trend. The world wasn't hard enough for them. I tried to walk like JFK, the president: chin level, good Catholic posture, as if going to greet God. I clasped my hands devoutly in front of me and turned into an alley. In my head I recited, *Ask not what your country can do,* etc. I dropped a ten in the bucket of a brown woman with no legs. When no one followed I portioned my breath into consistent measures. I listened over my noisy heart. Then I took a series of rights back toward The Cave, telling myself there was no reason dudebros would follow me, and two red hats came around the bend.

Unless they too had parked on Mount Auburn Street with the plan to walk from there to The Cave to get a little air because earlier the toys they had bought had disappeared, they were following me. What was the connection between disappearing and following? I swung my head left as if something fascinating had appeared, and one of them nudged the other.

We stood in front of The Cave. In the window my reflection had come an unknowable distance of time and space to meet me. I felt extremely tired, like my reflection's effort had been mine. Before I could censor myself I asked why the dudebros had followed me.

One of them twisted his hat back and forth like who was I talking to. The other said, "What? You mean us?"

"Do you see me?" I asked.

"You think you're invisible or something?"

I wondered whether that was it, I had mistaken disappearance for invisibility. "Then why are you following me?"

The first dudebro touched the second's arm and nodded to go inside, but the second held back. "Wait. This dude is pissing me off."

I pressed my fingers to either temple.

"Okay," I said. "Never mind. Maybe it was just in my head. I get carried away sometimes. I've been told I'm not a good judge of people."

"No, tell us more, Charlie Chan," the second dudebro said. "Tell us about your purple tracksuit."

He was a hulking specimen, exactly the kind of person who would follow someone. The kind of person who prepared his body to harm another.

I looked down at my skinny limbs and frowned.

"Charlie Chan was a white person," I tried.

"You make me want to punch you."

Make America punch again, I thought.

The first dudebro pulled the other's arm and said, "Come on. He's mental."

I stared at my hands. They rubbed each other like two newborn animals. My reflection twitched: One side of my lips lifted higher than the other.

The angry dudebro said, "Dude, this is not over."

I never expected anything to be over though. My hands knew this. I only wanted the world to play by its stated rules. If you minded your own business, why should anyone bother you? Where was the freedom I was promised? When I stopped seeing my family, when I left my job, people called me a quitter, a coward, too proud or ungrateful. But the world could destroy itself on its own—why did it need me?

Suddenly the angry dudebro turned and spat at my feet. His friend pulled him into The Cave. Three drops of saliva fizzled on the purple velour of my pant leg. I had worn the tracksuit to feel better about myself. I waited for the spit to dry and thought about my cool air-conditioned home. Why do we leave our homes? To be with other people, for better or for worse, for richer or for poorer, in sickness and in health.

As they passed me people kept to the edge of the sidewalk or stepped down into the street. I was marked contagious. I rubbed the fur of my tracksuit on a lamp pole and followed the dudebros inside, pretending to be fine. Fake it until you make it to heaven.

In the desert someone else's saliva is a shower.

My girlfriend was not at work.

The perv who owned The Cave said, "Sandra isn't answering her phone. She didn't ask for a night off."

I told him that wasn't her name anymore, her name was Yumi, and maybe that was why she wasn't answering.

"The fuck are you talking about?" He pointed at my chest. "Don't you know where she is? What are you even good for?"

CO-HALLUCINATION

Yumi didn't answer my calls either, so I ordered the house red, a Merlot, and waited. It was a test: If she appeared, then she hadn't disappeared. I thought about Charlotte in the butcher shop, in an outfit her nine-year-old self would have scorned. I picked at the shellac on the bar, and a chip lodged under one bitten nail, drawing blood. My mouth dried with the urge to suck my finger, but The Cave wasn't the type of place to put in your mouth. Was that urge to lick your own blood about reincorporation, like gods eating their children? Was it about secret-keeping? You want to keep what is inside your body inside your body—that was clear from the moment Charlotte first wailed to get her hands on her poop. What babies know is you let one thing get away from you and then another and another, and eventually you are only what you have not yet given away.

The shellac covered alternating red and white tiles, the kind you find on a 1970s bathroom wall. I imagined an ongoing checkers game I was winning and had to find a way to lose. That had been typical with my daughter. How to love better? I was just trying to keep the people I loved from disappearing on me.

I wanted Yumi's comforting side, the side she had shown the last time I was truly afraid. That time my cat had kept running into walls, chasing nothing that I could see, and maybe because the cat did it, I started bumping into things too. At home this made no difference, but in public people ogled my bruises, shuffled away. In the grocery store a woman who worked for a domestic abuse shelter slipped me her card. "It happens to men too," she whispered. The humanity she gave me made me feel less human. Other people's pity insisted I should be pitied. Other people's fear insisted I should be feared. Someone *must* be trying to hurt me. My cat *must* be chasing something.

But Yumi had called it *co-hallucination*. For school she had read about a schizophrenic and his partner: The schizophrenic went off his meds and saw bugs all over the house, and instead of confronting him, his partner imagined them too. Because their stories matched, their friends didn't know what to believe. Finally someone set up a camcorder. Together the couple pointed at nothing, sprayed chemicals at nothing. To ease the schizophrenic's suffering, his partner had adopted his delusions. When the pain exists, but its cause does not, how do you fight it?

Yumi had said co-hallucination usually happens among people, but for a person like me maybe it could happen with a cat. It was true I never thought of myself as above the animal kingdom. At first I argued that a blank recording didn't mean nothing was there—I had gone through puberty eating the body of Christ. Then my cat died (not from hitting a wall, from a disease possibly related) and my accidents stopped. My body healed. Once again in public people either ignored or insulted me. After a while my dead cat began meowing in the ceiling. Because of what Yumi had said, I understood that the meows were in my head. I understood that I would rather be haunted than alone.

———

Someone's weeping broke through my thoughts like another co-hallucination. In the corner of The Cave a thin black woman hunched over her hamburger, her back shaking, despair strung like a spiderweb around her. The night was early—later the rich white Harvard boys would show up to drink, to make themselves less human before they went out on the prowl. The two dudebros who had followed me were overeager, pregaming. One of them ordered the woman a cocktail. She continued weeping and stuffing her face with meat.

I was panicking. I didn't want to check the time, but it had a scientific appeal. My phone said Yumi was one hour and nineteen minutes late. In the back they were probably doing her prep work, resenting her for skipping the unprofitable part of the night. On the TV cops ran around solving a heinous murder.

"You're into that?" one dudebro asked the other. He nodded toward the weeping woman.

"Come on, don't act like you aren't."

I moved my wine to her table and sat with her, not speaking, offering my meager protection. She cried and chomped her burger and fries, her eyes turned inward, backward. The dudebros passed their meanness back and forth.

Finally the woman looked up at me and said, "The hell is wrong with you? Fuck off."

What could I do? I picked up the cocktail and downed it in one gulp. I waited for the disappearance of the cocktail to make something else disappear. I didn't feel the effects of any kind of roofie. I was more or less the same amount of tired.

The dudebros laughed.

I remembered what Yumi had said about The Cave, that the appeal of such a shithole was about the limited male imagination. She got paid to let men underestimate her: She waited for the moment to pull out the rug from under them. All of her tips were either amazing or terrible. When I asked her why she liked me she said I *mis*-estimated her, not over or under. The way I got things wrong could be charming. She said it was something we shared, that our expectations were different from other people's.

I didn't believe in our similarity. She had dropped out of her last year of med school to get free of her parents, but she continued to study the body. My parents had died and I had followed through with what they'd wanted for me, keeping my head down and being promoted now and then when it would have looked racist not to promote me—I only quit when I discovered that somehow I had traded my small successes for my family. Yumi was confident; I was something else. She could change her name on a certain day because the weather was nice or not nice, she didn't care that people might have trouble correcting themselves. I had feared for my name from the moment I was adopted. All my life people had told me my face was a square; Yumi's was a heart. I gained and lost bulk like a hibernating mammal, in seasons. Her limbs stayed so thin it was hard to know how she balanced her hair, which was thick and luxurious and hung past her waist. I wore outfits like the tracksuit that no one else seemed to like. She wore black clothes, black nail polish, black eyeliner, despite that it matched her uniform (the pervy owner made his staff dress like the staff at Foot Locker, like they would feel up your foot while serving your Mac and Grilled Cheese—consumption for other hungers).

The weeping woman glared at me, and I fucked off because she was right and Yumi was right too. It was typical to co-hallucinate: This was the menace we lived with, but also *how* we lived with it. We co-hallucinated each other's bugs because we wanted to be loved. Whether the toys were gone or had always been gone, the end result was the same: For three years I had filled a box with something that existed only in my imagination.

I ordered whatever cocktail the dudebros had ordered for the woman, and I sat at the bar across from the perv and sipped, trying to taste what it was. A cocktail wasn't something you could identify without the proper training. I appreciated this.

"Are tracksuits some kind of new trend I don't know about?" the perv asked.

I let him think what he wanted.

He rubbed his mustache and asked how I got Yumi to date me. This was a frequent line of questioning. My skin thinned to the consistency of smoke.

"Is this a Tom Collins?" I asked. "I've always wondered who a Tom Collins is."

"It's not a who. It's a what."

"I'm trying to be precise."

"That's what I mean. Who the fuck would say something like that? What is it she sees in you? You're good-looking only to Asians? You look like an ordinary asshole to me."

"I'm completely ordinary," I said.

"You can say that again."

"I'm complete and ordinary," I tried.

He shook his head, but there was no one else to talk to. "You shouldn't just say whatever comes into your head. In fact maybe you should do the opposite. Say the opposite of what you think."

"I'm going to stay alive for a long time," I tried. "I'm totally justified in keeping away from my daughter. It's definitely what we both want."

He shook his head again and moved to the empty end of the bar. When his eyes flicked back at me he poured himself a glass of Bulleit. Then he poured one for me too and slid it across the wood.

By the time Yumi arrived I could hardly see straight. I could hardly recall why her appearance relieved me. The door banged open and the humidity came in with her, like she carried a locker room in her arms. I remembered vaguely that I was supposed to ask her whether I had disappeared. The bar was crowded now, dudebros clinked glasses and slapped backs. Yumi walked straight through them.

"You're free hours late," the perv said. "And what's this about your name?"

Maybe he said *three*, I couldn't hear well. It was like I had water in my ears, the pressure outside matched by a pressure inside. Yumi bit the left side of her upper lip and then the right side of her upper lip, and then the left side of her lower lip and then the right side of her lower lip. Her left leg shook a stool. I had never seen her so shaken.

"Where were you, Sandra?" the perv asked.

She flattened him with a frown.

It wasn't strange that Yumi ran over him though—he was afraid of her—it was strange how nervous she was. She didn't frown *at* him, but *past* him. It was a frown that said she was serious about something *out there* and The Cave was barely a nuisance. She didn't seem to follow her advice about being present.

The perv took a step backward. I took a step toward her.

She said, "Find someone else tonight. I'm here for a drink. Pour."

I flexed one muscle at a time, starting with my toes and moving upward, trying to sober faster. Something was happening.

"I called you," I said. "I texted you. The disappearing—"

"Matt," Yumi interrupted. "Why are you here?"

I was still visible.

Yumi finished my drink, then reached over the bar and poured another double shot into my glass and downed that too. She strode back out of The Cave before I could manage a reply.

———

I stumbled outside. A blue convertible idled on the curb, a make and model I had never seen before. The chassis curved over the wheel well like a feline hip, the paint as thick as fur. Yumi ducked into the passenger seat, and the tires whined. Dust shot up into my eyes. Yumi drove past so fast her red cheeks streaked the air. I tried to note which way she headed. But twenty feet away the car stopped as suddenly as it had started. Everything happened so quickly it was difficult to sort out what exactly confused me. I had seen Yumi get into the passenger seat, and then Yumi drove past me.

My system had been thrown out of order. I could barely breathe—my heart breathed and my lungs beat. Alcohol soured and burned in my throat. Yumi drove like that, hard starts and hard stops, but she couldn't be in two seats at once. The car seemed to wait for me. I walked slowly. It stayed where it was. Yumi sat in the passenger seat, exactly where she had gotten in. On the other side of her, in the driver seat, was also Yumi. There were two of them, I mean.

I cupped my hands over my eyes, trying to see better through the window. Drinking had never made me see double before. I had thought seeing double was the movies, not life.

Two Yumis.

The Yumi in the passenger seat muttered under her breath, refusing to look at me. The Yumi in the driver seat gawked. Her eyes widened and squinted, widened and squinted, focused and refocused on me, like she kept seeing me *more* somehow than she had seen me a moment before. Being seen like that I felt extremely alert, exhilarated, solid . . . I was really losing it.

It was the look Charlotte had given me as a baby: certain of who I was. That certainty was the thing I could give her that I didn't have. The door locks clicked open. In a daze I grasped the handle. I cleared my throat, which had filled with mucus. My jaw ached from clenching my teeth. For the first time I seemed to see Yumi *as she was*—I had thought she was somehow more whole than I was, but together the two Yumis made it clear the rest of us must be no more than halves. The

Yumi in the passenger seat shook her head and clacked a nail on the window. The Yumi in the driver seat continued to stare. As I opened the door something on the street almost stopped me. The car was leaking. A bright yellow line trailed from the door to where I had stood on the sidewalk. But the line didn't spread, it wasn't liquid. It was as solid as yarn. I got into the back seat, ignoring it, and the car sped off with the two Yumis and me inside.

THE OTHER ME

We sat on floral-upholstered armchairs in a fancy hotel room, the two Yumis and me, and I thought, so this was how a fancy hotel room felt, like another life. At my feet a bear's former skin clawed toward me. A fireplace flickered without heat. A faint cinnamon scent lingered, as if someone paced outside with an expensive candle. Yet I only felt *less* present. Life doubled, I stayed the same, it was simple math. Yumi's presence was more difficult to calculate. She didn't have a twin. One Yumi wore The Cave's uniform and rested her hand on my thigh— while the second wore a navy skirt suit and eyed me as in the car, like ants bit me all over.

I checked my reflection in my phone. No ants.

"Sandra," the second Yumi said, extending her hand to me. "That's my name, I mean." She squinted again and leaned closer to me, then closer still.

I resisted the urge to recheck for ants. "You're sure?" I asked. "Maybe that was a slip of the tongue?"

The first Yumi pinched my leg.

But their faces were exactly the same . . . It was as if Yumi's name change had been a kind of preparation, as if she had known another her might appear. Which seemed unlikely. Or—Yumi's name change had *made* another her appear. Which also seemed unlikely, but which caused a strange buzzing between my shoulder blades.

Sandra, who I was meeting for the first time, who was not my girlfriend Yumi, told us the story of how she had ended up outside The Cave. The story started a week earlier—Sandra knew how to spin a tale. She had gone away on a business trip to pitch an ad campaign to a makeup company (the campaign would sell beauty not as *everlasting* but as *everchanging*, a slogan that would, ironically, last longer), and when she returned, triumphant, she was surprised to find her boyfriend had moved out without warning. He had taken everything he owned. The next day he didn't come back. He wouldn't answer his phone. Sandra spent an entire week trying to get in touch. She did everything except call the police, who would only say he had left her. His parents either wouldn't tell her where he was or didn't know. After a week of binge eating (and binge drinking) Sandra decided that for the sake of her health, she had to move on. She had always had an iron will—she had quit smoking cold turkey, on a dare—so she set her mind to it. That same night she dreamed that she was driving through a tunnel supposed to take her to another world—a tunnel so long and dark that after a while it seemed more like a deep cave, as if she were driving into herself—and before she found the end she woke up, dripping with sweat. Once she had gotten hold of herself she packed two suitcases and took off in her actual car, bursting with some kind of leftover determination.

Sandra said she left with only the desire *to leave*, as her boyfriend had left, no thought about where she would go. After several hours the desire began to fade. She didn't know what to do, she had already put in the effort of leaving. That was when the earth shook. Sandra took the nearest exit and, as if with the last of her dream energy, seemed to come upon a sudden city. She said the skyline had seemed to pop up out of nowhere. She didn't remember it being there before the quake. She chose one random side street after another, trying to find somewhere to eat, until she saw the sign for The Cave. It was a symbol from her dream. A parking spot opened right in front of her—she tried to wake herself, she was awake—and as soon as she got out of her car, up walked her mirror image in prison stripes (as Sandra described Yumi's uniform). In other words, while I was in The Cave, at the exact same time, Yumi and Sandra had been just outside, huddled in the car, having a conversation that eventually required drinks.

I knew the rest. It was an unbelievable story—even staring at the evidence of their same bodies I could barely believe it. And yet, to me, the most unbelievable part was what came next.

First the ants returned, all over me, and then Sandra leaned in so close that our noses nearly touched. "You're seriously not you?" she asked. "You're seriously freaking me out. What's with the tracksuit?"

"Matt's got some stuff to work out," Yumi said, pulling me backward.

Sandra hunted in her purse and took out a photo.

I moved closer. Yumi didn't stop me. She moved closer too. I moved closer still. Yumi moved closer still. Neither of us knew what to tell each other. It was the first time in a long time that I had seen Yumi completely silenced.

"This is a photo of my boyfriend and me," Sandra said. She pointed. "That's my boyfriend, Matt. Who went missing. And that's me. Now do you get what I'm saying?"

Matt was my name. The boyfriend in the photo was me.

———

I didn't remember living with another Sandra. I didn't remember taking my things and leaving her. It occurred to me that this other Matt was a me who had disappeared himself—myself—as if unwilling to wait for someone else to do it. The universe had a terrible sense of humor (Exhibit A2: the shared names). On the other hand humor was a matter of context.

29

The other Matt had my same slightly wavy black hair, my same prematurely balding forehead, my same flat nose, my same wide cheeks, my same square chin, my same fat lips that had always seemed to belong to someone else. But the really creepy part wasn't that we shared facial features. It was that those features which never seemed to come together on me . . . they all seemed perfect on him.

How to explain? I had seen myself in a mirror thousands of times and yet barely could have described myself. At one glance you would remember the other Matt for the rest of your life. He was a person whose presence you knew would be instantly missed, someone you would regret not getting to know. It was obvious that people loved him, that he was clever, successful, generous, authoritative—it was like he glowed while I stayed dull. The glow in that photo was impossible to look past. It was a glow that made everything else appear. You could see by it. No one ever got that impression from photos of me or me.

Sandra said the other Matt had started out writing copy for travel magazines and ended up the one Asian on a team that coined slogans for entire cities and states. Of course someone had written "Virginia Is for Lovers" and "What Happens in Vegas Stays in Vegas." Matt's ultimate achievement was adding all four words of "Home of Your Now" to the eight-word slogan "City of Your Future, Home of Your Now." Sandra said Matt was famous in the industry, often invited to speak on panels with his white peers.

He was the me who had succeeded at being the Matt we were both capable of being.

I did some quick calculations: It wasn't fair, etc.

Sandra said she had dated Matt for six years until the day she came home to find every last one of his possessions gone, photos of him cut out of every single album and even cropped out of every JPEG on her computer, as if he had never been with her at all. In other words the perfect me had not only disappeared but erased all evidence of himself—so who was I?

I was fucked.

"Did his things vanish first?" I asked. "Or did everything go at once? You didn't know he was going to disappear? There weren't any signs?"

"Wow," Sandra said. "That's definitely not what Matt would say."

"This is not going well," said my girlfriend.

But it was just like in her lecture notes: We wanted what we didn't have. I wanted to glow, so I knew I didn't glow.

"You and Matt were very happy?" I asked.

"You look just like him," Sandra said with such desire it shook me. She stood and went to the window, turning her back to us. A car honked for two seconds, tires screeched, doom marched on.

"I know what you're thinking," Yumi whispered to me. "Don't think like that." She went over to her doppelgänger and rested her hand on that same arm. They mumbled to each other lovingly. They comforted themselves. They had words I couldn't speak, Yumi/Sandra words. Like me Yumi asked questions, but the difference was she could still be satisfied by answers. What did Sandra do for fun? For self-care? For exercise? What were Sandra's parents like? Where was she ticklish? What Yumi wanted to know was complete and different from what I wanted. She wanted to know what other lives she could have had. I wanted to stay alive.

THE UPSTAIRS
NEIGHBOR

In nature doppelgängers exist because of evolution. Edible grapes
evolved to look like poisonous fox grapes. King snakes evolved to look
like poisonous coral snakes. Their safety is in the appearance of a deadly
other. On the other hand it is wrong to talk about evolution as if a species can choose its path. The real reason for its change are predators.
A snake resembling a coral snake survives because its predators fear to
eat it. Under those terms of survival two different species sometimes
evolve to look the same in two different places, like two butterfly species both with spots resembling owl eyes. In either location predators
mistake those spots for owls, and so those butterflies survive to have
sex and birth butterflies whose spots even more resemble owl eyes, and
so on and so forth, until separate species appear the same because their
survival has appeared the same. Scientists call this *cryptic biodiversity*.
Doppelgänger species can look so similar that only DNA testing can
tell them apart.

I found all of this on the internet as soon as I got home. In human
history—the internet suggested—doppelgängers often foretell death.
Soon after his first election President Lincoln saw two reflections of

himself in a single mirror. He described one self as "a little paler" than the other; the First Lady described it as a bad omen that her husband wouldn't live through a second term. English poet Percy B. Shelley saw his doppelgänger point out to sea not long before Shelley died on a sailing trip. English poet John Donne saw his pregnant wife's doppelgänger holding an infant at the same instant his live wife suffered a stillbirth many miles away. Before her death Queen Elizabeth I saw her doppelgänger inert on her royal bed. In Scottish legend fairy creatures give birth to sickly babies that look the same as healthy human babies, and thereafter try to swap out their kid for yours.

These were stories of surrender to an outside force—but an outside force in the shape of the self. I found plenty of stories about people who killed their doubles in order to take their identities. I had read that 36 percent of murders go unsolved. How many of those cases might be explained by a doppelgänger asserting his right to who he is? According to the internet, superstition holds that should you see your doppelgänger, you will want to kill it and it you. Only one of you can survive as you—this is evolution to the extreme. The other you is your most dangerous predator.

On the other hand these were all stories about white people, who aren't used to being mistaken for someone else. How much did their reflections haunt them? After my adoption I used to stand at the mirror every night and slap my cheeks, trying to make them as red as my new parents'. What happened to the Other People in those stories? To answer this question took a little more digging.

In the 1600s a Spanish priest went on a mission to New Mexico and found the Jumano people carrying crosses and saying Catholic prayers. He wrote home, asking who had gone before him. But he was the first. The Jumano described meeting a "lady in blue." Upon his return to Spain the priest found a blue-habited nun who claimed she had visited New Mexico—in her dreams. She never left her convent, yet she knew the landscape and people in perfect detail. She had colonized reality with her imagination.

And yet the story that really hit me wasn't that one. It was the story of Emilie Sagée, a white schoolteacher in the 1850s whose students often saw another her beside her (though she never did). While Ms. Sagée wrote questions on the blackboard, her double would walk in and write the answers in the same handwriting. The second Ms. Sagée's appearance physically depleted the first. Thirteen students gave the same account. Once Ms. Sagée was inside and they spotted her outside. They gathered around her double. The second Ms. Sagée started teaching them everything other teachers refused to touch: shortcuts to answers and sexual innuendos and what other religions said about God. One boy tried to touch the double's arm: He felt nothing. As soon as the lesson ended the first Ms. Sagée collapsed.

———

Maybe that was what I felt—my energy draining out of me and into someone else, someone who lived a life I could not, someone with the answers to my life. I guzzled a bottle of Pinot Grigio on the sofa by the empty box, searching the internet on my phone. Then I called the operator and asked for my ex-wife's number. The operator said the number was private. After a second bottle of wine I got drunk and rang the upstairs doorbell.

My upstairs neighbors were a cis straight able couple in their midtwenties, an Asian woman and a white man who used to have friends over late at night and now never did. For some reason, maybe because my cat died, I couldn't enjoy the change; I felt sorry for them. In their silence above me I heard my ghost cat meowing. More than once recently I had woken in the middle of the night to find the man's moonlike face outside my window, mouth and eyes gaping like craters.

I tried knocking on the glass and waving him away, but he ignored me. I almost thought he was an illusion, until it happened when Yumi was over. She hid under the covers. Later she didn't want to walk to the bus, and as we got in my car the man stared down from his own window—at Yumi, it seemed. "Maybe he has Asian fever," Yumi whispered. That time, after I drove her home, was the first and only time I saw her apartment. She collected dolls. That was what I remembered, a collection of rag girls that she never talked about and that didn't seem to fit with what I knew about her.

Upstairs I knocked on my neighbors' door until a deep radioperfect voice demanded patience. I waited for four minutes and fiftythree seconds. The sun was setting, and artificial light came on beneath the door. Shadows passed between the light and me. Shuffling noises started and stopped. It sounded like someone moving stacks of paper. Finally the door cracked, and the man slipped through and shut it behind him. Immediately I wished I had stayed in my apartment. I wondered what the other me would do in this situation. Why did I do things I didn't want to do?

We faced each other at the top of the stairs. My neighbor kept one hand on the doorknob. After plenty of time to change he had come out of his apartment in a tank top and floral shorts. He must have been trying to intimidate me. I almost tripped down the stairs. I caught the railing, and wine rose up my throat. Before he had shut the door I had noticed photos of women strewn across my neighbor's living room. Though it occurred to me that my perceptions were probably only half-reliable.

His weight shifted to his back leg and he said in that radio voice: "Aren't you the dude from downstairs? What are you doing up here?"

I asked whether his girlfriend was in. He sniffled.

I tried again. "I would just feel more comfortable talking with her?"

"I guess you'll have to feel uncomfortable then."

35

Well. That was typical.

"Nice tracksuit," he said.

"Did you feel an earthquake?" I asked him.

"Huh?"

"Did anyone break in recently and steal some toys?"

"What?"

"Have you seen anyone around who looks exactly like you?"

He opened and closed his mouth a few times, like a fish. "Okay, restart. Try making sense this time."

"What exactly," I asked, "are you hiding in your apartment?"

When he sniffled again I realized he was smelling me. I had a strong impulse to sniff my armpits. The other Matt was probably scentless.

"Give me a break," my neighbor said finally. "I opened the door because I know you, but we've really never known each other, have we?"

I wondered. He slipped back inside and shut the door in my face.

He and his girlfriend had lived above me for two years, and I had listened to them come and go so many times I could tell the difference between the growl of their Volkswagens, I didn't even have to look. Wasn't that as well as anyone knew their neighbor? It was easy for him to never think of me.

Inside a smart speaker beeped, and the voice of an older woman crackled. "Not right now, Mom," my neighbor said. "Mom, not now. I had a bad day that just got worse. No, I don't mean you."

I was not the other Matt, but I was alive. Slowly I descended. Having been spat on earlier, having learned I was a lesser me, what could a shut door hurt me? In other words why did it hurt so much?

When I reached the bottom of the stairs I heard a loud click—my neighbor had checked to make sure that the door was locked. To him *I* was the suspicious one.

———

I sank again into the couch my ex-wife hadn't wanted in the divorce, my heart overworking itself. Funny how labor brings us into this world and rest is what we get when we leave it. Trying not to disappear would be the end of me—maybe that's what happened to the other Matt. I pushed the empty box in front of my door and slid the safety lock. Two could play at this shame.

In my office I tried to write three thousand more words of the new novel. My protagonist lay on his couch trying to *feel* the world spinning. In the apartment above him someone screamed. It was a scream on the edge of what was and what wasn't real. To him the scream sounded like his own voice. He climbed the stairs and peeked under the upstairs door. Inside, roped to a dining chair, sat an upright cat. In my protagonist's voice it pleaded for its life. The upstairs neighbors held the cat at gunpoint. When my protagonist gasped the man rushed to the door and cracked it. "Nothing to see here," he said through the opening. "You better go. I've got a phone call with my mom." Not knowing what else to do my protagonist descended as he was told.

At my desk I tried to turn my protagonist around, send him to rescue his cat-self, but for some reason I couldn't make myself believe in his delusion. The writing felt false, ridiculous, like the ending of a film in which a character awakes from his dream—except in reverse. His reality awoke to my imagination.

I reclimbed my own staircase instead. As if my novel had gotten out of the computer, a sheet of white printer paper hung on my neighbors' door. Scrawled across it was DO NOT DISTURB. Was a sign enough to protect their lives from disturbance? I knocked for six minutes and thirty-two seconds, then pounded with the flats of my hands. No one came. They had noise-canceling headphones or something. They had developed the power to ignore. I wrung my hands out, palms stinging. If no one heard my anger, did it even exist? If I didn't see my doppelgänger, how could I be sure I wasn't him? I knocked again.

At last something made a sound. But it was only whining and pawing. I listened to the ghost of my cat and imagined its purring warmth in my arms. It occurred to me that I hadn't heard the woman's Volkswagen for a long time, just the man's. Was my imagination so poor that it had replaced her presence with that of my cat? Why her and not him? My adoptive parents had often accused me of hearing only what I wished to hear. For a while I stood there wondering whether I was the one who was disappearing people. Maybe I was the villain of my story.

THE CRACK

I woke in the middle of the night, back sore, fogged with sleep. I was on the floor. It took a second to figure out why I was there. I had passed out drunk. I tried to remember the dream I'd emerged from: I was standing in line with my daughter for a pony ride (she was six or seven) and other kids kept cutting in front of us. I said nothing, I watched a girl pull her hood over her head, and when I turned back Charlotte was twelve and I was in the butcher shop again. "Choose," she whispered as she passed me in line. "Your beef shank or mine?"

But in my dream my daughter wasn't in a camo T-shirt and leggings and purple lipstick with spiky hair. We were wearing matching tracksuits.

I rolled over and my shoulder bumped something. It was the empty box with which I had blocked the door. I was in the living room then. I was still groggy, the toys were still gone. I was still a dull version of me who nevertheless was still here.

When I sat up the first thing I saw was the photo of my ex-family. It lay beside my hand. I must have passed out holding it. My phone was nowhere in sight. I wiped the thumbprints off the photo. I missed my family so much I still rolled the toilet paper over, not under, in case they were on their way somewhere and suddenly needed to pee. I had the bidet set to "woman," and I kept the bowl sparkling clean.

Blood ran hot in my cheeks. Bile soured the back of my tongue. My head hurt. In this condition standing was out of the question. I crawled. I pictured that poster of apes evolving into humans: In hundreds of thousands of years I would evolve into Matt. Pain shimmered around my head like a bald man's sunburn. My eyes kept trying to shut. I had the feeling that something or someone was yanking me back into dream.

I counted to five, slowly, as I had seen white heroes do on TV to let their terror take five seconds of their life and no more. But I was still afraid. I counted to ten, twenty, thirty, a hundred. I opened my eyes anyway.

Something new was on the floor. Beneath me stretched a long yellow yarn I was fairly certain hadn't been there before. It seemed to generate its own faint light. It was the same yellow yarn I had seen outside The Cave.

What was going on? "Try making sense this time," my neighbor had said. How to explain.

The yarn trailed from, or actually *through*, the spot where I had slept, under my body, and on toward the kitchen. I didn't want to touch it—it looked solid, but for some reason I felt sure that it wasn't, that I saw only an image. Maybe that image of yarn was what my cat had followed when it slammed its head into the wall . . . I had to get it together. I clenched the photo of my ex-family between my teeth and crawled along the yellow yarn into the kitchen, where I found a half-empty glass of wine (I drank it), then back into the hallway, then into the bathroom and out again, then into my office where I had written the first six thousand words or so of a new novel. For the second time in twenty-four hours I placed the photo back on my desk. All around me the air pulsed with a kind of womb-like pressure. I felt sure something had started here. I was returning, like in the Minotaur story, having unspooled yarn to mark my way back.

I flipped on the lights and leaned on the doorframe while my eyes adjusted to the brightness. The other me was not lying in wait. I had half expected to come to blows with myself. Nausea choked me, but I held it down. The yarn continued to unspool across the floor. It looped around the desk, to the opposite wall, and there . . . it went straight inside. Somehow the yarn went *into* the wall.

I sat on the chair, which as usual dug into my back. That was real. As usual I saw the note to buy a new chair. I had written it. The fluorescent lights washed the wall a bright purple. I had painted them. The yarn was as real as that note and the paint. It wasn't like my cat—I knew it wasn't ghostly or imaginary. Even though I couldn't touch it, it was made of the same reality as the wall it went into. I rubbed my temples, and searched for the exact point on the wall at which the yarn entered. Had it found a hole? A defect in the construction? Once I had discovered a line of ants squeezing through a gap in the molding to get to a single drop of honey on the pantry floor. I had ignored them until they finished the honey, but when they moved into the rest of the kitchen I couldn't let them take my place.

Because you can always get a closer look I lay flat on my stomach. The hardwood was cool and solid. The yarn was insubstantial, yet "there." I tried to see along its route into the wall, I tried to tell whether it was like wool yarn, woven from strands, and what those strands were, I tried to tell myself I was just losing my mind. I moved my face as close as it could get, and the yarn never became any clearer or more physically defined. It didn't become any less believable either, not like the hostage cat in my novel. I wanted to disregard my beliefs—this was typical. I moved my face closer until my nose touched the floor—only the floor—I raised my face, I lowered my face—I moved up and down with no difference. The distance between the yarn and my skin wasn't material.

I concentrated on the spot where the yarn met the wall. The plaster was as blank and smooth as ever. Zero holes or defects. I concentrated on my concentration, trying to see as thoroughly as a glowing version of me would. I steadied my breaths. My breaths went in, my breaths went out. How did I know the yarn was going in and not going out? I wanted to see something the other me would see. As if the seeing made it appear, something slowly took shape.

The word that came to me was *crack*. The more I thought that word the more it became a crack. Like the yarn, I couldn't touch it, there was no visible difference in the wall, no real evidence. But I could feel that something had come apart there, the earthquake or another force had caused some kind of split. I could feel the crack in the wall, and then I could feel the crack in the air too, and then I could feel it in myself.

What was wrong with me?

I told myself to stop feeling and lie there and go back to sleep. What was the point of feeling a crack? Technically not even a thing but a lack of something. Doppelgängers, the yarn, the toys, the quake—all of that was beyond me. You should seek only what you're prepared to find. I thought about Lincoln's two reflections, about Emilie Sagée trying to recover her energy, about the Jumano converted by a ghost. Of course if you saw a ghost, you would believe in its religion. I flattened my cheek to the cold floor, attempting to return to the sleep I had left. I shut my eyes and thought, *Sleep.* I listened to my breaths and thought, *Sleep.* I felt the crack and the tugging from inside the wall and thought, *Sleep.* My body grew heavier. Little by little my muscles let go of fight or flight. Still sleep seemed far away, a word at the end of the yarn. What if each of us were unwinding a spool of yarn everywhere we went—like the red thread of fate, but in reverse? Where would it start? Birth? Conception? God? Upstairs my cat had ceased meowing. Outside no cars passed. The buzz from the fluorescent lights was gone. I could barely hear myself breathe. It was as quiet as it ever got in this house. And yet it didn't seem quiet, it seemed like the room had emptied of sound.

Then I was either dreaming or I got up from my body and stepped inside the wall.

BETWEEN

Inside the wall all I could think was *disappear doppelgänger disappear.*
It was hard to move, because it was hard to tell where I ended and the
air began. In order to move through the air there must be a difference
between it and you, I had never realized this before. This air was thick as
flesh—only squishier, more gelatinous. What it was like was clear jello.
I felt the urge to bite and swallow. The air wobbled at my lips, tried to
get into my mouth. I knew I shouldn't let it inside. It didn't belong in
me. The air welled in my ears, it muffled my hearing, I huffed it out of
my nose only to suck it back in with the next breath. All around the
jello refracted a faint white light of unidentifiable source, artificial and
menacing.

I stood there trying to see and smell and hear through the jello air,
and after a moment a faint scream seemed to make its way to me as if
from underwater, someone sinking to the bottom of a pool. The scream
came from . . . outside. From beyond the jello. But strangely not from
my office, where my body lay. The scream wasn't behind me. It was
ahead of me, as if through a second wall.

That was it, I thought: There were two walls, and I was in the space
between. A single wall had divided like a cell, and in the middle was
jello? Maybe it wasn't the most genius theory. I swept my arms little by
little through the air, and it oozed back in behind them.

I pushed/swam forward toward the second wall, and my chest hurt. A fissure where the two sides of my rib cage met seemed to split apart. The crack inside me tore. My rib cage separated, and my organs shifted aside. With each step the pain grew stronger. Soon any movement felt like ripping a stitch in a wound I hadn't been aware of until that moment. It had almost healed without me even knowing I was hurt. I hugged my arms around my chest, I tried to keep going. But it was too much. The crack pried me open from inside. My mother would have said *the air got into my bones.* I had never understood that saying before. Soon I was screaming, trying to scream the jello out of me. I couldn't go any farther. I sensed the other wall nearby, yet if I took one more step, I wasn't sure who would come out of that wall. It wouldn't be me.

Slowly I turned in place. Very slowly my ribs eased together again. After several steps the pain quieted—it was still there, but no longer demanded attention. At my feet lay the yellow yarn. I followed it back out into my office, pushing through the jello and the faint light and the uncertain time and the wall to where my body lay, as I had left it, stomach flat on the floor.

Everything was dark. My eyes were shut and I couldn't open them. It became clear I couldn't move at all. This time it wasn't the air stopping me. I was back in my apartment. I could taste my bad breath, I could hear the humming fluorescent lights, I could smell traces of the lavender incense I sometimes burned to keep mosquitos away. In other words most of my senses had returned. A motorcycle revved outside and the dog across the street barked loudly. The world was normal again. I was the exception: My body no longer responded to me. I tried to thrash around, and I lay completely still. I tried to shout for help, and my words got stuck in my head. I tried to twitch one finger like a soap opera coma patient, but if it twitched, I couldn't tell.

Time passed unresponsively, so that I couldn't tell how long. Time, it turned out, was a sequence of responses. The only way to guess how many minutes passed now was by the rate of my thoughts, which was inconsistent. Every ten thoughts or so I tried to move as I used to move. What I realized was that I used to *feel* my body—that was how I had known I was there without thinking about it. I realized this because all I could feel now was the breath going in and out of me, quick with frustration. Frustration was the last feeling connecting me to myself.

Inside my head I prayed to Saint Anthony, the saint of lost things, to find my feeling. My adoptive parents had taught me about Saint Anthony: When people wouldn't listen to him he talked to fish. And sometime in the middle of these thoughts the doorbell rang.

Yumi's voice called out, a miracle: "Time to love better. Move it. Tell me why the hell I'm with you when I could have married a doctor."

She called again, then once more. Then I remembered she didn't have a key. She'd never asked for one, and the subject had never come up on its own. I lay on the office floor helpless to turn a miracle into action. Miracles were use it or lose it. Yumi called again and again. I remembered what the church had taught me about my body. The body was a prison, and death was the only escape. I prayed to Saint Anthony to find my freedom. I wondered whether I was ever really free—it was my body that determined where I could go, how people would treat me, what pleasures I enjoyed. And as I prayed, my body stood on its own and stumbled into the living room as if it had given up waiting for an answer.

All I could do was encourage it to keep going. *You can do it,* I yelled inside me. *Good body. Turn the knob. Pull open. Step back. Say hello.*

YOU ME

Sweat matted Yumi's bangs and her mascara was smudged beneath one eye. She swayed and sucked her teeth and sneered appraisingly. She didn't like what she saw. I guessed she had come from a club—she had long, braided pigtails that made her look both approachable and intimidating, and she wore a sparkly silver babydoll with black tights. It was a look I had never seen on her, one I didn't know how to place.

My throat garbled my greeting. She pushed past me and kicked off her shoes. They banged against my wall. She gave me a second appraisal and shook her head. I started to feel bad. She stumbled to the couch, and my body followed in accordance with its own intentions. It sat beside her, a little too close.

"I saw a movie about doppelgängers once," Yumi slurred, not looking at me. "A woman died, and another woman took over her life. She pretended to be the dead woman. She pretended the woman was still alive. She moved into the woman's house, wore the woman's clothes, worked the woman's job. The woman's ex came by, and she slept with him. Then she wanted to leave the other woman's life, but it was too late. She was stuck. No one would believe she was someone else. It was a horror film."

I waited for her to say she was really Sandra.

"This doppelgänger thing?" she started. She gave me a third appraisal and took my face in her hands—not tenderly, like squeezing a lemon to test its ripeness. "Oh, what am I thinking . . . you won't get it anyway."

I didn't know what she meant, but she was crushing my cheeks.

"Do what you came for, Yumi," she said.

My body looked down and saw it was hard.

Yumi followed my eyes. She let go and stepped away from the couch and crossed her arms in an X across her chest. "God, Matt."

My body stood and the front of its pants stuck out.

Yumi went into the kitchen and poured herself out some Syrah. Her hand shook, and the bottle clicked the glass, making it sing. She sipped, and narrowed her eyes over the lip of the glass. The wine lowered in gulps.

When she finished she said, "Okay, I'll give you one chance. Why are we together? A person like me will always fuck a person like you? Tell me how that makes sense."

Well. I was slightly offended. What bothered her about having a doppelgänger was actually that both of them had ended up with me?

Her s's thickened.

I tried to say I had a theory, but it came out all jumbled.

The theory was: Yumi wasn't angry at me, she was angry at fate. Fate was one of her three pet peeves (the others were Dole, which overthrew a sovereign government for pineapples, and white people who coo over Asian babies). Once, after I said biological algorithms, not consciousness, determine our actions, Yumi nearly threw a plate at me. "That belief is immoral," she said. "That belief is what gives us serial killers. If you eat someone's face, your biological algorithms didn't eat someone, you did. Take responsibility." She got so upset we broke up for a week. I hadn't eaten her face though, I had tasted her cookie while she was in the bathroom.

Take responsibility, I thought. It was a popular line on Korean TV. Sometimes an entire romance would hinge on that one sentence, on one lover owning his desire.

"You're not going to crop yourself out of our photos and leave me," she said. "I'm the one who should leave. See, you can't even say anything."

I wanted my body to take responsibility, but for being me or for being two mes? It just stood there dumbly titillated.

I gurgled and gurgled.

Yumi pushed me back, her hand in the center of my chest. I must have gotten closer. She crossed her arms into an *X* again and said she had come to end things. I hadn't given her any reason not to. "It's not you, it's the other you," she said.

As usual the universe had its punch line ready.

There was another knock at the door.

SANDRA

Again my body acted on its own authority. Again the door opened on Yumi. The difference was this Yumi was Sandra. It was an important difference, most ways you looked at it.

Sandra jerked her head back almost imperceptibly, as if surprised but practiced at hiding it. Maybe every time they saw each other they would surprise themselves. For an instant Sandra seemed afraid. Then she tilted her chin to a new angle, and once again she was confident, hopeful, dressed to do business, her navy pantsuit shining with money, her hair in a power bun, her makeup retouched, some kind of designer bag in hand. It unnerved me how such a small shift altered her. They had both changed clothes, changed the contexts of their same body. I was still in the purple tracksuit, only questionably still in my body.

"You," Yumi said behind me.

"Me," Sandra said in front of me.

This wasn't going to be good for our relationships.

"What are you doing here?" Yumi asked. "How'd you even find this place?"

Sandra opened her bag, the leather parting like a mouth, and took out my wallet. She held it out to me as if extending a contract. I had left it in the fancy hotel room. Unintentionally I had given her the information to get here.

"So now you've returned it," Yumi said. "I guess we've both finished what we came for. Time to get going."

Sandra slipped off her white leather heels and arranged them side by side with the toes pointing toward the door. She slipped out of her jacket, draped it over her arm, and drifted into the living room. She wore a white blouse underneath with a black collar ribbon that tied in a bow. She seemed fastidiously coordinated, as if it was something she had gone to class for. Her hair bun arced elegantly as she had a look around.

Yumi said again that she was ready to go, a little more forcefully this time. She took out her phone and using it as a mirror, wiped the mascara smudge from her eye. I felt aware that I had a body even though I wasn't aware *of* it.

"Your apartment is so empty," Sandra said, then repeated herself, louder. She cupped her ears. "Hello?" She was talking to her echo. This made me like her, this comfort with her own voice coming back to her from the walls, but not with her voice coming back to her from Yumi.

"Maybe this isn't the time for a tour?" Yumi said.

Sandra turned and set her jacket on the arm of the couch. "There's something really weird about this place," she said without looking at me. "Not just the emptiness."

"It's him," Yumi muttered under her breath, but I heard her.

It's not me, I wanted to say. *It's the wall.*

Sandra did another quick check of her surroundings, like a surveyor, then walked straight into the kitchen as if she owned the place. Literally.

First she opened a cupboard and took down wineglasses. Then she opened a drawer to get a bottle opener. Finally she pulled the wine out from under the sink where I stored it for the humidity. She never once hesitated. I didn't know what to make of her familiarity.

Yumi cleared her throat. "Have you been here before?" She glared at me suspiciously.

Sandra poured the wine into three glasses, almost exactly equal. She handed one to each of us, then downed hers in one gulp and refilled it with the last of the bottle. When she shut her eyes to us, I couldn't tell whether she was crying. She lay her arms on the countertop. "Matt," she whispered. She didn't seem to mean me.

My body did nothing to comfort her or offer any understanding. I understood it was the other me she wanted.

Yumi sighed and touched Sandra's shoulder. "I'm sure you miss him. It must seem cruel to see him like this, as someone else."

"No," Sandra said. "It's all just so exhausting."

They were interrupted by strains of digital music. Coming from my phone.

Yumi hissed at me.

My body must have put it on. I placed the phone in a mug to amplify the sound. My fingers weren't my fingers—this was something my dad had said when he was dying. Was I having an out-of-body experience? I felt buried deep *inside* my body, like a college student playing a mascot. Bob Dylan's broken-down voice kept trying to put itself back together. Sandra started to hum. Was this the kind of art people bought, a shameless display of shamefulness?

"Who is this?" Sandra asked.

"You got to be kidding," Yumi said, her hand still on her doppelgänger's shoulder.

Yumi loved these ruined voices. Music was the one arena in which she sought out mooning white men.

She took a long sip of wine and clinked the glass against the countertop. "Let's talk," she said. "You could drop me off in that fancy car of yours on the way home?"

Sandra smiled at her, but shook her head.

When the song ended Sandra returned to her tour, checking the bedroom, the bathroom, the office, the closets. She seemed to have a list in her head. With each task she completed she gave a curt nod.

By then Yumi was getting sick of something. She kept pulling at the hem of her dress, first on one side, then the other. I found it fascinating how my body followed Sandra around, though I knew what I would find. Something about this could have satisfied me forever. I would never get bored or annoyed by it.

Maybe I was happy someone took my life so seriously.

"We're not the same," Yumi muttered to herself several times. After another ten or fifteen minutes she made a decision. The door opened, and I knew she was gone. I tried to tell my body to stop following Sandra and go after my girlfriend, but it wouldn't even shut the door. A sense of security my body didn't have.

Sandra stood at the threshold to the bedroom. She had already checked this room, she had already checked everything in the house, but she was still looking for something. Finally she climbed onto the bed and touched every centimeter of it. She lay on the left side and shut her eyes again. Her arm reached out to the right side. When she found nothing she tapped her forehead fifteen times at the midpoint between her eyebrows. She breathed deeply. Then tears came.

I had seen the tapping before but never the tears. Yumi had used that same pressure point to clear her nose. She had never cried in front of me.

Sandra was an ugly crier, loud and inappropriate to her business clothes, not caring now how much she exposed herself. I pictured the other me pulling her into his arms. I always slept on the right side of the bed, avoiding the left side where my ex-wife used to sleep. Which meant that Yumi slept on the left side whenever she slept over.

I didn't know what to do for her, for Sandra. I wouldn't even have known what to do for Yumi, if she let herself cry. I didn't know what to do for myself. Maybe the other me would have known, but I didn't.

My body had already chosen its course of action though. I wondered how it made a choice at all. What was the reasoning behind a choice without reasoning? My intentions contributed nothing. Was I acting on instinct? Instinct didn't tell humans to invent computers and hack into them for money in order to afford the bottom floor of a house. What was it then that made me do what I did?

53

Slowly my body closed the gap between the spot where I would stand and the spot where Matt would stand, beside her, close enough for our skin to meet.

"Can you understand, Matt?" Sandra asked. "I used to stay up all night thinking, *Is this really my life? How is it I ended up here? How is it I ended up like this?*" She swept her hand through the air. "And now? What if I was never supposed to be that person, what if I was supposed to live here, like this?"

I saw what she was getting at.

"Do you know what I mean?"

I did.

I tried to tell my body to stop going where it didn't belong. It continued creeping toward the bed and the doppelgänger of my just-ex-girlfriend. My body crept. My body was a creep. Where had it learned this? *STOP,* I yelled inside myself. *TAKE RESPONSIBILITY.*

I thought, *No. Bad dog. Stay. Lie down.*

"And here I am now," Sandra said, "with you, Matt." She shook her head. "Another Matt."

DON'T EVEN THINK ABOUT IT, I thought to myself in vain.

A breeze swept up my legs, the wind snaking through the house from the open front door. I realized my pants were down. I wasn't supposed to feel the wind. I couldn't.

My body kept creeping.

Maybe we were dreaming. But I knew this was real, I felt the direction of the air shift against my skin, I could feel the difference between the air and me. Sandra wasn't crying anymore. She didn't even turn away. Yet if she welcomed me, it was because my body wasn't mine. I shuffled toward her in my boxers with my pants around my ankles. What was wrong with me? "Here I am now with you, Matt," she had said. That sentence in my just-ex-girlfriend's voice hurt me somehow, and I wanted the pain to go on. I remembered the first time my daughter had said she hated me (maybe she was four or five?) how the pain of those words reminded us of what we meant to each other. Later it seemed like that reminder was what *made* her hate me.

Sandra's hand reached around my waist, and stayed for a moment, as if measuring.

YOU ARE NOT THIS PERSON, I reminded myself half-heartedly. But it was a comfort to be someone else for a while.

Only an act of God, a banana peel or something, would have stopped me.

Our skin touched. We removed our clothes. We moved not like it was the first time but like we were remembering how we moved. Our angles fit together. There was nothing between us but our skin. Our skin was nothing between us. The air was hot. The heat was ours. We seemed to make or remake the room around us. We found a reset button. A way to restart from an earlier save point. And in the middle of hitting that reset button, she raised her knees between us and pushed me away.

I fell back on the bed beside her.

"Not the same," she whispered.

There was a moment when I wanted to say, "Of course it isn't," when I wanted to say that was the point. I wanted to take responsibility, but I couldn't figure out how to choose to be someone who had creeped on her. Before I could think of anything, something solid slammed into my shoulder. Almost at the same time, Sandra screamed and pulled the covers over her head. Glass hit the wall and scattered over the sheets and floor. It was a wine bottle.

Yumi. She must have been standing behind me. Maybe she forgot something, her keys or her phone, and came back for it. How long had she been watching us? Warm liquid wet my neck. I raised my hand to it. It was blood. I could feel every bit of pain now, I could feel the blood and the difference between it and wine. I could move my hands wherever I wanted. I was in charge of my body again, and it was terrible. I was full of regret. I was in charge of my body again, but only as much in charge as I'd ever been, which now I knew had never been much.

CHAPTER 2:
THE LOOKING GLASS

IT'S TIME TO THINK ABOUT WHAT I WANT

I woke in the afternoon, startled awake by a ghost-whine. I was still tired. I was still me. This was typical. I wished I had someone else to blame for my disappearance, but like all humans I could only see time linearly, as a chain of cause and effect, so the person I blamed for everything was the only person there for everything: myself. I hadn't disappeared yet, which meant I was still disappearing, which meant my appearance depended on doing nothing to change my appearance.

As soon as I lowered my feet off the bed, something went terribly wrong.

The first problem was that it wasn't the bed, it was the sofa. Though that was easily explained: I had blacked out again. Less explainable was the rest of the room. For example: the rug beneath my feet. I didn't own a rug.

My toes wiggled in a stranger's lush white shag.

I pulled my legs back onto the sofa, and my shin banged a stranger's oak coffee table. On the walls hung a stranger's modern art prints, not my taste. Mounted on the wall across from me was a TV as wide and thin as a chalkboard. The room was clean and carefully arranged. The only thing out of place was the couch. The only thing familiar was the couch.

I rubbed my shin and hyperventilated.

What made me so anxious was my desire. I wanted the couch to save me. I was a person who wanted a couch to save him. The couch was the same reddish-pink color I remembered, the same pillow-type cushions, even a pattern of milk stains seemed recognizable. I wanted to recognize a pattern of milk stains. My wants had become absurd to me—yet the more absurd they became the more I recalled them. I recalled the exact moment Charlotte had made those stains, how her tiny body had thrashed before she vomited, how desperately she had screamed when I tried to put her down to clean up the mess, how the milk soured while I rocked her and waited for her to sleep. By the time she went down, the stains were permanent.

I was on my own couch. I was in my own home. I had nothing to fear but fear myself. The missing toys had simply transformed into furniture. That was all.

I stumbled into the kitchen and put my mouth around the faucet, trying to get rid of the cotton in my throat. In the cabinet I found a stranger's crystal glasses, a stranger's china dishes. I poured water into a glass and drank more. I opened everything—only the refrigerator held any sign of me. In it were eggs, soy milk, margarine, bread, ranch dressing, kimchi, bacon, mandarin oranges, sweet chili sauce, and syrup. It might be someone else's furniture, but it was my consumption. I toasted two slices of bread and fried the last three eggs with olive oil and black pepper and thyme. I would eat my way back to recognition.

Logic was off the table. There was only one logical conclusion: Logic was illogical. What was left was the experience of something beyond experience. Or—as my adoptive parents' priest used to say—what we couldn't understand we could understand to be God.

After I ate I was still ravenous. My hunger was not responsive. I followed my nose back to the dining room. There on the table, stacked neatly on a yellow-rimmed serving dish, a pile of pork buns let off steam. I must have noticed them before, but at the time I was trying not to notice the new wood dining table (with matching chairs) and the new antique chandelier and the giant painting of red squiggles that now dominated an entire wall. It was typical to not know what you know. I sat directly in front of the pork buns and denied myself. What could I do? Everything stood in perfect balance. Eating a single bun would be like photobombing a wedding portrait.

Beside the dish lay several pieces of paper. I flipped through them: It was one long letter. The ink even changed from one section to another. The last page was signed *Sandra*.

Suddenly the various cracks came back to me—the wall and the air and the juncture of my rib cage. And the second wall. And my body being not my body. And Yumi and Sandra and Emilie Sagée and Emilie Sagée and what Sandra had said: "Not the same." Then the shattered bottle. And blood.

I scanned Sandra's letter for some mention of us having sex. I scanned it for some mention of the furniture. Nothing stood out. It was clear I needed to consult it more carefully. I consulted my schedule: It was clear. I had lost my parents, my adoptive parents, my wife and daughter, and my girlfriend. What I had left was plenty of time.

Do you know that feeling when you realize someone is watching you? Self-awareness? Why are we most aware of ourselves when we are aware of someone else's awareness of us?

Well. It was going to be one of those letters . . . I spread the pages out one by one.

Do you know that feeling when you realize someone is watching you? Self-awareness? Why are we most aware of ourselves when we are aware of someone else's awareness of us? I used to think I was living a normal life before all this. I used to think I understood what people thought of me. I knew who I was supposed to be. I knew how to get people to like me.

I guess that's how I got into advertising.

And now what?

Actually — I wanted to write something else here. I wanted to tell you something. God, how long has it been since I've written a letter? Did it used to be so awkward or did the internet make it this way?

A normal life — did I really write that? I guess it was more of a feeling like I was supposedly living a normal life. Like normal was what other people thought of me. Secretly, though — like I said, something always felt off. Something always felt off. It's a relief to admit that, even in a letter. The thing that always felt off with my normal life? It was me.

Sometimes telemarketers would call — is what I was trying to write, is why I am writing this, I mean. Sometimes telemarketers would call and they would have my name down as Yumi. Can you believe that? I thought someone must have made a mistake on some marketing database, some list, the kind companies buy and sell. Occasionally I got upset, especially when the person on the other phone would insist he had my name right and I didn't. It really happened. "It says right here that you're Yumi Kang, at so-and-so address." Sometimes they would say, "I mean your real name, not your English name." When I corrected them, most of them apologized. But occasionally they would keep arguing with me, like I was just being stubborn. Some people will trust a computer over the person they're talking to.

I guess that's also why I got into advertising.

Maybe I'm really writing this note to myself. I've always left myself little reminders. Though I never kept a formal diary before — a journal — whatever. I always thought it was inefficient, like talking for the sake of talking, for people weak with heart. That's what I am now probably, weak with heart. Maybe I always was. Because you know what the funny thing is about those calls? That name would follow me around for days. "You Me," I would say at the mirror. "Don't you know who you are, You Me?" This is what I was trying to write — that in those moments it felt like I was watching myself, like I had made my reflection self-aware.

Am I crazy? Maybe you wouldn't think so.

One time I came home from a business trip, and Matt had parted his hair on the other side, and I realized it was the only change he had made the entire time we were together. It really freaked me out. He laughed at me, but it seriously seemed like I had caught him at some secret activity. Like whenever I was away, he became a different person. He said he parted it that way so when he looked in the mirror, he could see what other people saw.

I have to keep reminding myself I don't know you — Matt. You're actually a stranger.

After that, the color changed:

You're still asleep. What will you say when you wake up? Will you say, "I'm sorry! I'm back!" Should I throw this whole letter out? It's so upsetting to see your body there. Like it could be either of you now, but when you wake up, there can only be one. I used to have this dream after my dad died that he wasn't dead, just asleep, that Mom had buried him alive without knowing it. I would wake up afraid that she had done the same to me, convinced that my room was a coffin. I would scream that I was alive – I was still alive – until she came and turned on the light.

It's enough to make me afraid (and hopeful) for who your body will choose, which Matt. Though the nightmares that really scare me now are the ones in which I turn into someone else. I hate that feeling when I realize I'm not me anymore. How it feels more like the world has changed than like I've changed. It felt like that when I first saw Yumi outside The Cave. Like I had to make sure I was still me.

You know what's really wild? I've never even heard of a city called Boston.

P.S. If you wake, I've got your keys. I'll be back at 3 ~~5:30~~ ~~10~~ 3 ~~7~~ 3:30.

Finally, in a last color:

The worst part is Yumi and I have the same voice. She reminds me I hate my voice. How it sounds on a recording. How it sounds to other people, all the time. Too – labored. Why does she seem so comfortable in it? She wears it like a skirt. It makes me feel like the other woman, like I'm having an affair with myself. I keep feeling drawn to her. Which is like feeling drawn to myself, I guess. Except I hate my voice when I use it.

I wonder what Matt would think of you. My Matt. Could you be friends? Yumi is so much less petty than I am. I would never want to see myself again if I were her. How is she able to separate her relationship with me from her relationship with you? You should have treated her better.

Is it weird for me to like her?

I'm going to buy some groceries. Your fridge is empty.

P.P.S. My mom taught me about cryptic biodiversity, by the way. I saw the posty on your desk. I think I mentioned I leave notes for myself too? My mom — the Biologist — believed evolution was the one great idea a man ever came up with. One day she showed me these two photos of a red snake with black and yellow rings. They were actually two snakes, she said. One was poisonous and one wasn't. She told me to take my time, study the differences. Then she took the photos into the other room. When she came back, she had one red snake with black and yellow rings.

"Hands out," she said.

I was a kid, maybe 10? But I knew what she meant to do. That's how she was, I mean. I tried to get away, and she forced my arms in front of me. She wrapped the snake around my wrist. This is what she said: "You've studied the flash cards, right? Poisonous or safe?"

Or something like that. Poisonous or safe?

I'd been trained (by her) to register the tiniest differences, the things that identified a species — so I could have figured it out if it wasn't for that cold, slick skin.

Everything went out of my head except that skin.

What's safe, I remember thinking. What's safe if there's even the possibility that your own mom would make you hold a poisonous snake?

And you? Matt? Whoever you are? Are you poisonous or safe?

I read the letter through three times. She didn't leave a phone number. She left all those words and no way to contact her. Instead of providing any answers, she had asked more questions.

Maybe I was being punished for something. My mom would have blamed it on a past life.

The pork buns had cooled, and it was a relief to find them less appetizing. I ate four of them now, then half, then all but two, in case Sandra expected leftovers. They were delicious, the meat tender and still juicy, the bun like an edible cloud.

I thought about the last question in Sandra's letter: Was I poisonous or safe? It depended on who asked. In a toy shop I was a generous father. At a *Star Trek* convention I was a Sulu cosplayer. Maybe to be myself I needed to find people who already knew what I was.

I was out of wine. I needed to find a liquor store.

In my bedroom, where my wallet and keys were, the same transformation had taken place. Instead of my old bed there was a new king-sized bed with a new tufted headboard, a new white duvet, new blue-gray throw pillows. On the window hung new smoke-colored curtains. In front of the window stood a new white bamboo desk with my old computer on top of it. Despite all that new stuff the room seemed mysteriously more spacious. Perspective was a strange way to see the world. It made no sense that all this furniture had appeared in one morning and without waking me, and yet on the other hand: doppelgängers.

I sat at the bamboo desk far beyond my means and tried to think better, as good as a me who could afford it. I googled "Matt Chung" to many results. A violinist, a businessman, an optician, even a forgotten soccer player who never lived up to his talent. None of these Matts, however, had coined city slogans or looked like me. Had Matt disappeared so thoroughly he had disappeared from the internet? I googled "Matt Kim" and waded through pages of results about people named Matt and people named Kim until I came to my old business profile, my wedding registry, my college honors, finally my parents' obituaries.

I switched to Word, and three thousand words came out like a scream. My protagonist paced and thought, paced and thought. Then I forced him upstairs, and he kicked down the door with one blow. His upstairs neighbors were having bad sex on their couch. They looked up at him, sexually frustrated. All my protagonist could do was apologize. The problem wasn't with him, it was with my imagination.

I took my empty wineglass into my daughter's old bedroom and tried to prepare myself. Inside was another new king-size bed with tufted headboard and pastel throw pillows, more new sheers and light-gray curtains, with a new vanity instead of a new desk. On the wall hung a photo of Yumi and me I didn't recognize—because it wasn't us. In the closet hung women's clothes arranged so neatly you could have measured the uniformity of the gaps. The clothing was not in a style I was used to, it was all patterned dresses or monochrome tailored business suits. Below each outfit sat a pair of matching heels. In the corner two leather suitcases stood with their backs together as if comparing heights.

I breathed out into my wineglass, I breathed in from my wineglass. I put down the wineglass because my breath stank. I touched my neck where the shard had nicked me, and found a hardened scab. My body had powers my mind did not. Case in point: Sandra had said we were "not the same," the glowing Matt and me, and yet here in my apartment was her stuff. Probably. It seemed like she had moved in.

The only thing that was still the same was the color of the walls. Still purple. Over the years I had bought multiple buckets of different-colored paint, but could never bring myself to use them. Those walls would always belong to Charlotte. I tried to see the crack in the wall again, I tried to feel the air split apart, I tried to quiet everything down like before; and the roar of cars, the whine of my ghost cat, continued.

I stepped forward anyway.

The pain surprised me somehow. My forehead slammed into the plaster, and an ache spread across the globe of my skull. It colonized the entire surface.

I shut my eyes, ground my teeth, and tried again.

This time I had to sit down and hold my head in my arms. I laced my fingers behind my neck and touched my elbows together in front of my swollen eyes. I held myself together that way until Sandra's fancy car hummed in the drive.

———

It was 3:28 p.m., she was right on time. From the edge of the dining room I watched her put down two brown bags of groceries and undo the clasps on her heels (tan stilettos that matched her tan dress with white polka dots). She placed her shoes side by side with the toes facing the door. Then she took a photo of them, I didn't know why. She took a photo of the street through the open doorway. She definitely was not Yumi. She picked the bags up, and when she saw me she nearly dropped them again.

She whistled slowly. "You scared the fuck out of me."

I moved for the case of Cabernet Sauvignon.

"So, you finally woke up," she said. "We have a lot to talk about, Matt."

"I'm not Matt," I said.

I felt disappointed by her disappointment in me.

"Aren't you?"

"I mean I'm not the Matt you are looking for," I clarified.

She rolled her eyes, wrinkled her nose. It was Yumi's eye roll, Yumi's nose wrinkle.

"Sandra?" I clarified.

"God, you're not always like this," Sandra said, "are you?"

This was typical of me. But I took the bags and tried to be better.

In the kitchen I corkscrewed a bottle of Cabernet while Sandra filled the fridge with her and Matt's food. Everything looked organic, healthy; there were greens I didn't know by name. The only things of mine that remained in the apartment were the keyboard my mom had wanted me to play and the couch my child had stained as a baby. Maybe the only part of the house that was totally mine anymore was the space between the walls. I poured two overfull glasses of Cab. Something strange was about to happen, I was starting to be able to tell. Evolution was the process of getting used to casualties, our greatest strength was our greatest etc.

We sat at the table, and I told Sandra to let me have it.

"Have what?" she asked.

"It's just an expression."

She said she had never heard that expression before. Maybe it was regional.

"You slept an unnaturally long time," she said. She checked her watch. "God, just over eighty-four hours."

"Twenty-four hours?" I clarified.

"Just over eighty-four hours."

Maybe this was an expression I didn't know. I waited what I hoped was an appropriate length of time. Then I asked, "Twenty-four hours?" again.

"Eighty-four."

I wanted to acknowledge her perspective, but eighty-four hours? That would make the furniture and the note make more sense (in the sense that we could no longer trust our senses), but on the poisonous hand . . .

I missed how Yumi could clear up what was normal and what was not. How gently she had cradled my head after my cat died, for example, and told me my wants were not absurd, and even offered a eulogy at the funeral. Guilt tied my tongue.

"Twenty-four hours?" I croaked.

Sandra sighed Yumi's sigh.

My computer showed the date Sandra said it was. So did the internet. So did my phone when it was charged. My last status update was four days ago. ("gggggggh.") Everyone else had spent four more days awake than I had. In that time I had missed three calls from Yumi, her maximum as a matter of principle, 146 emails, and no likes on Facebook.

"I'm sorry I ever doubted you," I said. "The universe is truly master of the universe. Did you move into my house?"

Sandra's face reddened. She downed the second half of her glass as if to make her face red retroactively.

"Wait a second," I said. "If I slept that long, why didn't you try to wake me?"

"I did," Sandra said, touching her cheeks.

"But you didn't try that hard?"

"But I'm not your girlfriend," she said.

"But you moved in?"

Sandra leaned toward the window. She used the reflection to fix her hair—nervously, I thought. She took down a perfect ponytail and put up another perfect ponytail. While she did this she said, "You were unconscious for eighty-four hours, and I was the only one who checked on you. A thank you would be nice."

"Thank you," I said. "You didn't take me to the hospital?"

She said there was no treatment for being a doppelgänger.

She had me. Even if I kept saying, *It's strange,* over and over, she could always answer, *Everything's strange.* The trump card to exceptions was exceptionalism. I wanted a reaction from her that would match my own, that would confirm that this was not typical—but if everything was strange, then everything was typical. I knew this as well as anyone did.

I asked Sandra again about moving in, and she said again that there was something weird about my apartment. She opened a window, stomped the floorboards, kicked the molding. For a moment I worried she would put her arm through a wall.

"I have a little hypothesis about what," she said, not looking at me. She stuck her head out the window. The weather seemed to get inside, a stuffy heat. When she pulled her head back in she said, "I just need to stay for a while to verify things. I did try to make it more comfortable."

Her eyes were wet.

I had to remind myself. It was heartless to forget that in the past week her boyfriend had left her, she had run away and met her doppelgänger, and she had kind of had sex with her boyfriend's doppelgänger. In her shoes the line between strange and typical was pain.

Outside a squirrel chased another squirrel up a tree, a bird flew out complaining, the fleeing squirrel slowed and got caught, maybe on purpose. Sandra watched all that desire with tears in her eyes.

"Thank you," I said. "I really mean it."

But she wasn't done.

She came away from the window and made her way to a chair in front of the pork buns. There were two sad-looking buns left all alone. I took one.

"The first thing I saw after the earthquake," Sandra said, taking the other, "was the skyline with this building all made of glass. I looked it up. They call it the 'Looking Glass,' ever heard of it?"

Sweat dampened my tracksuit and I kept the muscles of my face absolutely still.

"While you were sleeping, I drove over there to check it out—"

"I don't know it," I said too quickly.

"Don't play dumb."

She had spit some bun at me. She wiped her mouth.

"What did you find there?" I asked.

She said she had felt in the lobby an instant intimacy, that (among other companies) the building housed an international ad agency, and before she knew what was happening some ad person took her arm. The ad person chatted her all the way through the turnstile, even *into* the elevator, and only noticed that she had made a mistake when they got off. She had thought Sandra was someone else.

Probably the one other Asian woman.

"I told her I understood her completely," Sandra said. "Once I thought so hard about a campaign that I tripped over a dog and then, minutes later, tripped over the exact same dog again. We started talking as colleagues, I described some of the ads I had done, and fifteen, twenty minutes later I was interviewing for a job."

"Congratulations?" I said, feeling sorry for the dog.

She frowned.

"Don't you already have a job?" I tried again. "Anyway it's cool that you got a job offer here. Maybe it will make you more comfortable?"

We sat in silence for six seconds. She seemed to be telling me something by not telling me anything. It wasn't a restful silence at all. Then she said, "You know, you really need to change those manners of yours. Learn to be a *Homo sapien*."

Maybe she was right and the thing that was wrong with me was my humanity.

My ex-wife worked in the Looking Glass—that was the building she had written to me about when she moved. She made enough money there to afford a mortgage we would have never been able to afford together. In other words why was this happening to me?

Also I was pretty sure it was *sapiens*, not *sapien*, a name not a plural.

"The Looking Glass," Sandra said. "Don't you see? It's more fate, like The Cave, like your apartment. Another thing from my dream."

We shared her hallucination then, not mine. That was a relief.

As if I had challenged her to prove her story Sandra said that she would get me a job there too if I didn't blow an interview. "You'll see," she said. "I'll—" Suddenly she ducked.

This time I ducked too, but nothing flew at our heads. It wasn't Yumi.

A white male face shone in the window. It was my upstairs neighbor.

My upstairs neighbor searched the dining room, looking straight past us as if we weren't even there. I tried to muster an effective level of anger to turn him away, but I wasn't sure whether to be angry at him for looking or for not seeing us.

I made a fist. He didn't see that either. I waved.

Whether because of the wave or not, he drew back.

"The fuck," Sandra said.

"You saw him too then? He's really that horrifying? He's real and that horrifying?"

I was still waving. Sandra pulled down my arm. She pursed her lips as if she had to reevaluate something.

My hand opened and closed on the table.

The anger I had tried to muster before seemed to realize itself now—to become real, that is, and to grow. Somehow I hadn't gotten upset about the toys turning into furniture or Sandra moving in without asking or the wine bottle thrown at my head or even losing control of my body. But now I grew furious. I couldn't get rid of the anger, even though I had always gotten rid of my anger before.

A NEW SYSTEM

Sandra was different than I expected. For someone so successful she was surprisingly insecure about the rest of the world. She didn't seem to believe that anything would last, not even her own experiences. She kept taking photos of ordinary things, for example—I found her photographing a corner of the ceiling, one without even a spider. All she would say was that she was "recording data." She wrote notes to herself everywhere (on the fridge a list of what was in the fridge, on the front door: *Doesn't close all the way*). She tracked every meal she ate. Each breakfast she had a different fruit, pastry, and coffee from shops farther and farther from the house. Unlike Yumi, who flew by the seat of her intelligence, Sandra overprepared. She had even brought with her only outfits that could double for work, though she hadn't expected a new job. In other ways (not only physically) she and Yumi might have been the same—like how they sized people up or hummed while they ate or were afraid of small dogs but not large—but in the way they approached the world they couldn't have been more dissimilar. The only exception was Sandra's notes-to-self, which might have come from the same place as Yumi's extensive class notes.

It hardly came as a surprise then that in a week Sandra accomplished everything she claimed she would do, and somehow I had a job. The whole situation was so beyond my understanding that all I could do was accept her understanding of it. Sandra said the job was a miniature version of the other Matt's (she must have pretended his qualifications were mine). She seemed increasingly anxious for me to start. Each day until then we had the same basic exchange: Sandra said the Looking Glass gave her a bad feeling, but when I asked her how, she said she couldn't put it into words, I had to find out for myself. I felt like she was sending me out, disguised as her missing boyfriend, on a mission to find those missing words.

On the other hand I had nothing better to do. My concern was not with what came between but with what would happen in the end. Would Matt and I both disappear? Or had I drained the energy from him like the second Emily Sagée? Which of us was Emily Sagée and which was Emily Sagée?

———

My first day in the Looking Glass I got so nervous that I woke early and left while Sandra was still eating. On the bus I realized she might have wanted to go together. When I texted an apology she texted back, Kind of fucked up since I was the one who got you the job. I wrote back that I was still learning to be a *Homo sapien*. She texted a photo of me doctored to have Neanderthal brows.

Outside the Looking Glass I admired the mirror effect, I had never taken the time to look at the building up close. The slight ripple of the glass made the church across the square and the street full of traffic and the pedestrians in their personal-space bubbles seem full of unused magic. They should have put up a sign: "Objects in Mirror Less Enchanting Than They Appear." With a clear sky the reflection higher up the building blended with the air. It was all the same blue. The result was a strong sense of vertigo.

I went into the lobby and waited to feel the intimacy Sandra said she had felt. I waited ten minutes, still feeling nauseous. It was possible that I was supposed to shut my eyes. I shut my eyes for ten minutes, feeling even more nauseous. With each moment that passed, the odds that my ex-wife would arrive and slip past without me noticing grew. I opened my eyes and waited a final ten minutes, the nausea unrelenting, until I had to admit to myself that I was waiting for Jennifer. Hers was the intimacy I wanted. Whatever Sandra had felt was unavailable to me.

If I waited much longer, I would be late on my first day as boss. I waited ten final final minutes. Then I took the elevator up to the twenty-second floor.

Just in case I tried one last time to feel something other than nausea. But that high up I felt even worse.

Officially my job wasn't to feel intimate. It wasn't even to investigate my disappearance. I was supposed to manage a team of writers. The team wrote American slogans for new imports from Korea (UV sterilizers, premium massage chairs, skin care products, weight loss pills, etc.). They couldn't use the Korean slogans because the context didn't translate. Profit wasn't in translation, it was in appropriation. But most of the team were ethnically Korean anyway. It helped to understand what each product's original purpose was, to transform that purpose into making money.

Our office space was set up like a long dance hall, an open-floor design with the entrance at one end and my office, a giant fish tank, at the other. In between were the cubes, plus a dedicated tea station, but to use the bathroom you had to go out near the elevators. Theoretically, from where I sat, I could keep an eye on my team without moving. The wall that separated us was glass, frosted to waist height but transparent on top. If I wanted privacy, I could lower blackout blinds that were down now.

Of my other three walls two were also glass—they were the outside of the building that made the mirror effect. Inside the glass wasn't reflective: The long wall that my office shared with the cubicle area looked down on the square with the pointy church famous for being photographed, and the short wall at the back of my office looked down on the public library where people liked to drink coffee.

The fourth wall, which separated our team from the other that shared the floor, was the only wall that was not see-through. Our side of it was tiled. In the middle stood a long bar with stools and cabinets full of loose-leaf teas and teacups and brewing equipment.

I had never been a boss before. I had never worked with another Korean. As a boss my main goal was to escape my employees' resentment. I had never worked for anyone I didn't resent. My bosses had always evaluated their employees' needs against the needs of a thing that didn't technically exist in the world—the company. It wasn't easy for a corporation to achieve personhood. To do so actual humans needed to trade their humanity in for the feeling of belonging to a group. I didn't want to encourage my team's disappearance. So I had to come up with a new system, one that would get me off the hook.

The idea was simple: *Everyone do you.* I would make no rules and set no limits, only that we complete our projects on time and to the relative satisfaction of our clients. However each of them liked to work was how they should work. Each week I would distribute assignments randomly, to myself included. We were all equal, etc.

I was arranging the chairs in the conference room when my team shuffled in one by one. The clock on the wall read exactly nine. My employees eyed the potato shape I had managed and muttered to each other. When all five of them were seated I stood and tried to explain myself.

I got flustered before I could finish introducing my system. One of them wouldn't stop staring at me. They were all watching me, of course, but the way this one woman was watching me was different. It was a little like how Sandra had stared at me, at first, like ants bit me all over. Maybe the look had to do with recognition. My employee seemed to be trying to remember me from somewhere. Finally her face made a series of transformations. First her memory seemed to come back to her, then

Matthew Salesses

that memory sparked some kind of horror, then the horror turned into shock and curiosity.

I had never seen her before in my life.

"Boss?" someone asked.

I had stopped speaking.

Everyone looked between us now, as an imaginary tennis ball bounced back and forth.

"You see," I said, "this way our lives in here won't be so separate from our lives outside of here."

Finally the woman organized her head, clearing her thoughts, and spoke. "Aren't you going to introduce yourself?" she asked. "You didn't mention a single thing about you."

"What do you want to know?"

"No offense," she said, "but it sounded like you were making up that speech as you went."

I couldn't help thinking she must be good at her job.

She crossed her legs and took a snack from her bag, chewing loudly. The others waited on my answer. I imagined quitting on the spot and going back to working freelance from my home, in my pajamas, scrutinizing faceless lines of code.

"I think what Tokki means is, how will we be evaluated?" said the other woman, Yoonha. "What's good or bad work? You know, what's appropriate or inappropriate office behavior? Is it just up to your interpretation?"

I saw their point—who was I to judge? But that was also my point, I thought.

They looked so beautifully normal, four Koreans and one white dude with their tablets and casual business, that it scared me to think I was in charge of them. I couldn't remember my bosses ever admitting any flaws in their systems. Even hacking made a company more secure against other hacking.

"I'm just like you?"

78

The one white guy on the team raised his hand. Not to worry, he said, the women are just playing devil's advocate.

I felt nauseous again. "Don't try to undermine them," I said.

He shrugged like he had only spoken for my sake.

"Okay," I said. "Let's all get to know each other then. Let's do an icebreaker."

"We know each other," the first woman, Tokki, said.

"What does this building make you feel?" I asked.

We all searched each other's faces for a traitor willing to follow me.

"Look," I said, "in the rest of the world there are unspoken norms that determine what is appropriate. At work think of your cubicle as your home. In your cubicle you do what you want, but if you meet someone in the common area, you figure out the shared norms or go back inside. Let's start by figuring out each other's norms."

I indicated Tokki with an upturned palm. She was a tall woman with a long torso and short legs, short hair and bangs that framed a soft hexagonal face, slightly chubby cheeks, a protruding mouth. Her bright lipstick made her rabbit teeth stick out. A harmless flaw that, when emphasized, made the rest of her seem knowingly flawless.

"Everyone calls you Tokki, for example," I said. "Is it because you remind them of a rabbit?"

Tokki frowned.

"What animals do we remind each other of?" I said, closing my arms over my armpits. "That's the new icebreaker."

One of them cracked their knuckles. No one mentioned an animal. Then someone said, softly enough that I couldn't identify who, "She's always eating chestnuts is why we call her that. You know that children's song, '산토끼'? It's her nervous habit."

Tokki was eating chestnuts right then. She hid the bag.

"You already remind me of someone," she said, "not an animal." Then she added my name uncertainly. "Matt—what are we even supposed to call you?"

I hadn't thought about it, unused to the question of whether to go by American or Korean modes of address.

———

After my failed meeting I called Tokki into my office, feeling a little like a school principal and a little like a pervert. Somehow I hadn't anticipated the problem of power plus attraction. As an employee my power had never exceeded the power I had at birth: as male, cis, straight, able, financially never desperate. As a hetero Asian American male, employment had always made me feel sexless and shenanigan-less. Now I was the one responsible for monitoring irresponsible office dynamics. For example: the privilege to not anticipate my own sexuality being a problem. It is easy to think you're not part of the problem when you are part of the problem.

Tokki shut the door behind her, and I opened it. I reassured myself that most people were not attracted to me. We would be fine as long as we minded the boundaries of our work roles. I had noted each of their roles right away, for management purposes. I was the object of my team's complaints, Tokki their delegate. The others were: career woman passed over for her less deserving male colleagues (Yoonha), nonbinary former model with a fashion sense beyond our paychecks (Woobin, called Woo Woo), PhD dropout with precariously perched glasses and equally precarious temper (Sung), and token white dude looking to advance but unsure even of how he got here (Phil Collins, unfortunately named).

My main goal was to establish a relationship—if I got my biggest critic on my side, the others would follow—but my secret mission was to start my investigation of them. That was why I asked what she meant in the meeting, what nonanimal I reminded her of.

"솔직히?" Tokki asked, testing me.

"Honestly. Otherwise why would I ask?"

One side of her mouth rose, as if being understood half pleased but also half disappointed her.

"I got the feeling you know something about me," I said.

"It's kind of strange."

Well.

She hesitated, but I stared at her as she had stared at me during the meeting—I had learned that looking at someone made them aware of themselves only because it made them aware of you.

"You remind me of this guy I used to know," Tokki said finally. "Matt Chung. But not because you're both Koreans named Matt. Because—" She stopped.

I tried to make my stare less frightened, less frightening. The air in my lungs thickened as if the jello inside the walls had been inside me this entire time waiting to be called.

"Matt Chung," she had said. Though there could be thousands of Matt Chungs.

I cleared my throat, tried to hack the jello out of me.

"Gross," she said.

"Go back to *Matt Chung*," I almost shouted.

Spittle flew onto the desk. I slammed my hand over it, too hard.

Tokki startled and mumbled, "Matt Chung," as if compelled.

This gave me what was probably a bad idea.

"I'm Matt Chung," I said in my boss voice. "Don't you recognize me?" Her face pinked.

"You don't recognize me? Look at me."

Tokki's head turned left and right, maybe looking for a hidden camera. It was like this show where K-pop stars pop into karaoke rooms and sing their own songs—often the people already inside will cover their faces as if to confirm what is happening by once again disconnecting the voice from the singer.

"The name on your door says Matt Kim?" Tokki tried. She smiled, biting her bottom lip with her rabbit teeth. She probably got enough sympathy from that overbite to trick most predators. "I shouldn't have said anything."

"Only humans regret. Only humans think they shouldn't have done something they did do. Only humans imagine their lives different from the lives they live," I said. At last I felt the air thin again and go back to something unremarkable.

My understanding of myself shamed back to me.

Tokki stood and poked her chin with one pinky. "I'll just get back to work?"

"It's not like your salary depends on your answering," I said, though I could see how saying this could imply the opposite.

She grimaced.

"솔직히," I said. "How do I remind you of Matt Chung? How long do I have before I disappear?"

Instead of answering Tokki bolted.

———

Alone again I screamed into my hands until I coughed. Then I googled "how to investigate when a boss suspects an employee he is attracted to of hiding important information about who he is." The results that came back were for dealing with a perverted boss. I added "doppel-gänger" to the search and oddly the results turned political. It seemed the Russians used doppelgängers to infiltrate the US government. The president of North Korea had sent a doppelgänger—of himself—to tour the country while he recovered from surgery. I googled "how to search for something without knowing what it is," and the results were about anonymity. The message of the internet was that investigation is appropriate, but vulnerability is circumstantial. You could use the internet to disappear even from the internet. I felt like I was supposed to know something here that I did not.

I tried to recall the junior detective kit I had bought for Charlotte, which had disappeared with the rest of the toys. She had wanted it when she was eight—too young, I had thought. I should have given it to her then and taken the time to explain what she should and should not use handcuffs for. What else was in that kit? A magnifying glass, a microscope, a fingerprinting kit? On my browser a news video popped up and played automatically: record temperatures, fires breaking out, heat stroke, with no mention of global warming. The KKK-candidate kept referring to black people as Chicago, and a guest pundit claimed the election would come down to missteps. What matters most is always what you do wrong, he claimed—a cis white man—rather than your qualifications. I searched my tabs until I closed the right one to stop the video. Elections, like everything, were about attention. The pundits had already forgotten the last race with no incumbent, when the story on both sides was about being ready for a black president. If a woman's accomplishments were less of a story than a man's missteps, it was because only one of those stories made men feel better about themselves. Eight years earlier, when we were ready for a black president, I had cried and Jennifer had cried, and we had said to each other, "It's a different world now." Yet that same week a white boy called Charlotte the N-word, and her school insisted they were post-racial.

With my blinds shut I poked through my desk and every corner of my office, looking for a clue to tell me what I was supposed to be looking for. I had been under the faulty impression that an investigation started with a crime—now I realized that the investigation determined the crime. The reason I needed to investigate was because I didn't know what was wrong.

Online I found entire message boards dedicated to finding crimes where no crime seemed to be. It seemed the goal of a crime was to disappear itself. The goal of an investigation was to stop that disappearance. My investigation wasn't business, it was personal. My body had disappeared once already, and I needed to stop it from disappearing again. On the other hand my body was not the crime.

I switched to positive comments. One blogger wrote that the best thing about private investigation was that you could do it on the cheap. Flour and invisible tape could reveal fingerprints, most clues required only sight. I didn't have any flour, but I had sight. I spent a while inspecting my team's cubes. I started with Tokki's, of course, then went on to the others. They all evacuated to the common area. Maybe the best part of the office was the tea station, with Korean pottery sets and loose-leaf tea all provided by the company. Tokki prepared tea, and the others joked about her technique as I eavesdropped. She had some kind of experience serving tea in the traditional way. They didn't reveal much though. Soon they went silent. The longer they stayed silent the more they seemed to be starting their own investigation—in which I was the suspect. Their silence was their way of talking about me. Finally I remembered that I was their boss and could go out in the middle of the morning to buy flour and tape.

When I got back from the convenience store they had returned to their cubes. I sprinkled the flour all over, all the way from the entrance to our office to Tokki's cubicle. She pretended to ignore me.

"Lift your keyboard," I said.

She went on typing.

I lifted her keyboard and sprinkled flour all over her desk. She backed her chair out of the cube and rolled it around to Yoonha's cube. I thoroughly dusted everything.

Then I went on to Phil Collins's cubicle. He was very compliant, lifting his keyboard for me without my asking.

I could feel them gathering around us. It was just as Sandra had written—I felt very aware of myself and also of my differences from Phil Collins (his whiteness versus my bossness, our shared maleness, my understanding of what I was doing versus his).

At last Yoonha spoke up. "Is that salt? Is it some kind of good luck thing? Are we supposed to know? Culturally, I mean?"

I explained that I was dusting for fingerprints. I lifted up some of the flour with the tape—it didn't seem to work.

"What product is that?" Sung asked.

Woo Woo turned away and put their headphones on.

Over the top of Yoonha's cubicle wall Tokki's head popped up like she was taking her nickname too far.

A voice chimed at my elbow, and Phil Collins sang, against all odds. But that was just my imagination.

"Boss?" Phil Collins asked in reality.

"Yes, Phil Collins," I said.

He frowned. "Do you need our fingerprints? Is this a product test?"

"You told us our cubes are like our homes," Tokki muttered. "Doesn't that mean you're trespassing?"

"This is bullshit," Sung said. "That's what it is. I heard he knows someone higher up. That's how he got this job."

I asked Phil Collins why I would need their fingerprints, and he said who else's prints did I expect to find?

Good point: the only suspects were us.

"I could collect them for you after lunch?" Phil Collins offered.

"That's just Scotch tape," Tokki said more confidently. "And Gold Medal flour. He came in with a CVS bag."

I didn't know why this comment bothered me. I should have been reassured by the return of Tokki's mojo. Things went away and came back all the time. For some organisms it was a natural part of life. Wood frogs stop their hearts during winter, caterpillars dissolve and reorganize their genes into moths, extinct viruses frozen in ice will become unextinct with a major thaw.

I told my team to clear their schedules for that night, we were having a team dinner. "The company will pay," I clarified. "Alcohol included. Don't drive."

———

Woo Woo, the youngest, made our reservation at what they claimed was the only decent BBQ spot in Boston. It was the one Korean restaurant that used charcoal, not gas or electric. I had never gone to a company dinner Korean-style before. My parents, the only Korean business owners in town growing up, ran a Chinese restaurant and never had a Korean employee or customer. To visit other Koreans we always went *into* the city—no one came out. But I had seen on TV, in K-dramas, how company dinners bring people together through compulsory alcohol. I ordered ten portions of meat and ten bottles of soju, and I encouraged my five-member team to consume double their usual.

Woo Woo cooked for us, Tokki talked for us, Phil Collins sang for us (in my imagination). Tokki made no mention of Matt Chung or the meeting in my office. She got the team to talk about their last manager so smoothly I barely noticed that they were telling me to change. Every sentence was a variation of *he didn't care enough* or *he cared too much*. It was like all relationships—no one wanted to care most or least. Sung, an old-fashioned Korean transplanted at age fifteen and still stuck in the nineties, was the only one who had liked the old boss, which he said in my direction with a pointed frown.

In the end Yoonha got some drinking games going, and we had a proper time of it. We were light with consumption. I realized I was enjoying myself. I wondered when I had last enjoyed myself outside the house. I had never been at the top of a Korean hierarchy before, and I hadn't realized how good it was. Whenever anyone lost a game, I made them chug. Woo Woo got affectionate. Sung kept turning his head to burp. I felt like the boss of bonding. As we got drunker some of them bowed and drank with their faces angled away from me, as if they were turning more Korean.

When we had finished every piece of pork we squeezed into a single ride share to go singing. On the way Woo Woo threw up out the window. We tried to distract the driver, but he noticed. He stopped the car and yelled at us to go back to our country. He was a black guy from the South. Phil Collins patiently described why this was racist. Sung ripped a hole in the leather seat with a safety pin and then jabbed it in Phil Collins's thigh. There was nothing else to say until we got there.

At karaoke we begged Phil Collins to sing Phil Collins, maybe being a little mean. We were still on edge. To lighten the mood I flipped through the song booklet to find something about tea. I must have been thinking about Tokki's professional etiquette for a while, because now it bothered me that she could do something that relied on politeness and delicacy, and play such a different role in the office. I found a song called "Tea Bag Me," and entered the number in the queue. Yoonha was singing something in Spanish, a hidden skill. She had a beautiful low singing voice, lower than she spoke, as if it came from a different part of her. Afterward Sung got up and sang about a white room with black curtains, kneeling in front of her. We were happy again. Yoonha sat down and hid her face. She must have been embarrassed.

When the tea song came on I gestured to Tokki and said, "Ah, a song about tea."

They all looked at Tokki like she had chosen it. The song picked up, and Tokki looked back as if she hadn't chosen it, which she hadn't. She had the mic in front of her though. No one else took it. I didn't either. Something was going weird. The song seemed to be about sex. Tokki glared at me, and I could see that something about me made her think I had chosen it and framed her. She jerked her head at the remote control.

I could stop the song, as the boss, but that would level some kind of judgment against her, since everyone thought she had chosen it. Or I could imply that I had chosen it, which would be even weirder since that would seem like I had made them think on purpose that Tokki had chosen a sex song. Plus it would confirm that it was definitely me. The best thing to do seemed to be to keep up appearances.

As if the sex song in the background was totally typical I asked Tokki about her job pouring tea, how she got it and what she did. She didn't answer at first. I tried to make an expression that told her I was sympathetic to her. The others were still staring at her drunkenly or nearly passed out. Finally, with her face darkening from pink to red, Tokki said her parents owned a traditional hotel outside of Seoul and they had taught her the proper way to serve tea as a little girl. It had been a big hit with guests.

I put a beer bottle and a glass in front of her. "Say I came to your parents' hotel. How would you serve me?"

"Tea bag me," the song kept saying in the background, as if those were the only lyrics.

"First I would greet you," Tokki said, her hands trembling.

"Hello," I said, "I'm Matt Chung. I'm here for some tea."

I checked the others, but no one seemed to register the name. Maybe they forgot what my last name even was. Maybe I *was* Matt Chung.

"Get out of here, Matt Chung," Tokki said. "You're not welcome."

The song stopped.

Sung held the controller. "The hell—"

But Phil Collins snatched it away from him. "It was my song," he said. "I made a mistake." He punched some buttons and a Phil Collins song came on.

"Isn't this fun?" I asked them all.

Yoonha said she had to get home to her kids.

Against all odds, Phil Collins sang in reality.

A VISIT FROM THE PAST

It wasn't until Friday that I found out what Tokki knew about Matt Chung. I had told Sandra that despite feeling zero intimacy I had found someone in the Looking Glass who knew my doppelgänger. I had thought this news would cheer Sandra up—she was in some kind of sulk all week—but she said this was useless information on its own. She knew my doppelgänger—just knowing a person meant nothing. I had to use my power, put some pressure on Tokki to give up her secrets. Yet for some reason every time I tried to use my power I heard Phil Collins singing Phil Collins, performing someone else's performance. Each day, after I got to work and felt no intimacy and called Yumi three times from my office, I left a sign for Tokki that I hadn't given up. I crossed out the *Kim* on my door and wrote in *Chung* with a silver Sharpie, I sent Tokki emails with the stories of white people who saw their doppelgängers before they died; I arranged the teacups at the tea station to spell *M-A-T-T*. The only sign the others caught onto was the name on my door. They started calling me Matt Chung, as if the company was making a mistake, not them.

Finally on Friday I had an email from Tokki just above an email from the company that it was bring-your-child-to-work day and an email from Yumi that said only cease and desist eom in all lowercase. When I read Tokki's email it seemed to say almost the same thing:

Cease to exist. Eom.

It was a forwarded email, with a message from her at the top. The email beneath was from the sender: Matt Chung. She had deleted his email address. But it appeared to be real. It appeared to be some kind of mass email. I sat in my office reading with my fingers shaking the keyboard, occasionally typing a letter I then had to go back and delete.

The message from Tokki read:

Matt (if I may):

I'm sending you this email because wtf, the flour, the song at the noraebang, the teacups. Everyone thinks you have some kind of crush on me. I would report you for harassment, but the last time Yoonha reported Sung, nothing happened to him at all. Why do Korean men think they own Korean women?

Whatever your thing is with Matt Chung, I don't want to know. But I searched him up, finally, because of you. And holy shit. And then this email from him really really scared the shit out of me. When I first got it, I barely read it. I thought maybe someone had just hacked his account or something.

Anyway. We need a good boss for once. I'm forwarding you this because I think you said something about disappearing? I don't know. Leave me out of it. But this is really all I can say about him.

Matt's message was much shorter. It said only:

I know this will sound crazy. But don't delete this. Please. You have to believe me.

I had a kind of vision or experience or something. I don't know what to call it. I know this doesn't help. I just had to warn you.

I don't know how, I don't know who, but one of us is going to disappear. Please trust me. I'm trying to help.

I read this email ten times. I could see how it might look like somebody hacked him. But I knew better. I crawled under my desk to hide. Matt had thought someone he knew would disappear, and then he had disappeared. My whole body stress-ached. It was a flaw in evolution that pain developed to tell us we were hurt. The survivors should have been humans who knew they were in pain without being in pain. I couldn't make my muscles let go of their tension—it seemed dear to them. I wanted to call Sandra and tell her what I had found out. But I needed a moment. I needed a year. I heard my door open, and Yoonha's kids came rushing in. I reached up and grabbed whatever I could off my desk. I held something plush: the product I was working on. It was a half-dog, half-cat stuffed animal with one head on either end of a shared body. It had a whole ecosystem: a redubbed TV show on ten DVDs plus coloring books and action figures and an album of nursery rhymes sung only in barks and meows. The cat was a typical Persian, but the dog was a breed I'd never seen before. Yoonha's kids knocked something over and ran back out to the cubes. I petted the cat head, then the dog head, then I ripped the toy down the middle.

———

I woke to someone knocking and knocking. The knocks dragged me out of my dream. I had been hosting some show about disappearances, pointing at people like Oprah and saying, "*You* disappear, and *you* disappear, and *you* disappear," but then I was the only one who did.

By the angle of light I guessed the day was almost over. It didn't seem possible, yet my body felt even worse. My joints were all twisted, having conformed to the space. My body felt as if it hadn't slept at all, as if the hours had simply ceased to exist. Time felt different in the Looking Glass. Each day was like a month—when I got home each day I could actually tell I had aged.

I crawled out to stop the knocking, and my neck cracked, somehow with both pain and relief. It must have bent in the wrong direction under the desk. I dropped the halves of the dog-cat on my desk. My physical world was falling apart. My only hope was that the nonphysical would follow—the email, disappearance, my employees' resentment, etc. Maybe Tokki had made up the entire email, as revenge. I must have done something that required reparations.

At the door was Tokki, which made me clutch my chest and hiccup. Speak of the etc. Though I was the devil in this scenario, waiting to be called to appearance.

"Fix yourself up," Tokki said, not unkindly but also not kindly.

"I was wrong," I said. "I take full responsibility. I will figure out how to take it."

She jerked her head over her shoulder. She meant fix my appearance. Someone was behind her.

How to be a *Homo sapien*? I smoothed down my hair and clenched my teeth in a smile.

Jennifer's hair was up the way she used to tie it for important meetings, a combo of braids and knots, very Nordic, showing off her swan-white neck. She used to powder her neck before her face. She was thinner, hollower in the cheeks, making her seem stately and ethereal. She looked like, for her, life didn't stop at life. She looked more supernatural than any doppelgänger. She looked devastating, impossible to forget, as if without me she had become more herself.

Her suit was blue and tidy, and she wore heels, which she hated, though she never wore anything else. "Women sacrifice for fashion," she used to say. Desire for our old sacrifices clogged my veins. Her Aryan eyes shone and the three years between us were as thin as paper.

"How did you know I was here?" I asked.

Tokki muttered something about all kinds of people showing up in their cube city.

I waved her away and explained that it was personal.

"It's personal? With Jenny?"

It took me a second to register. Tokki knew my ex-wife's name. She was getting my ex-wife's name wrong.

While we were married my ex-wife had always gone by Jennifer, she had even said there were two types of Jennifers in this world. ("One goes by Jen or Jennifer, never Jenny. The other goes only by Jenny.") She had changed types.

I shut the door on Tokki. "How do you know my employee?" I asked. "Are you really Jenny? Are you the same person I knew? Or another you?"

Jenny stepped around me and lowered the blinds between us and the cubes. Someone grumbled.

"Jenny?" I said again to make sure.

She didn't correct me. "I do the legal work in HR here, remember? I have files on all of you."

That seemed to make sense, I distrusted it. Making sense didn't fit the life I had lived ever since she and Charlotte left.

I looked her over once again for a glow like Matt Chung's or even a new birthmark or a scar. She let me look for a second, then snapped her fingers in my face. "Eyes up here." She had seen my paperwork, she said, and had come to find out whether a boulder could change without a millennium of erosion. A *boulder*, she said—that was how she used to describe me. I wondered whether switching to "Jenny" had freed her from "Jennifer," whether freedom was so easy after all. You didn't have to walk through two walls. You didn't have to disappear, only change your name. Sandra. Yumi.

"Are you seeing anyone now?" I asked.

"None of your business. And don't just stand there. I like your office."

I didn't know how to be around Jenny since I was still the same Matt.

"Nice weather we're having?"

She didn't move for a good minute.

"I'm not a *boulder* anymore," I said. "I'm learning to be a *Homo sapien*."

She set an Hermès bag on my desk. "*Sapiens*," she said, "not *sapien*." Then she said: "Why does your door have the *Kim* crossed out and *Chung* written in?"

I shrugged like I didn't know, like maybe my team was pulling a prank.

"Anyway I was never actually bothered by your lack of small talk," she said. "It was one of your few endearments."

She slipped around me, not touching, not even a brush from her skirt, and positioned herself an inch from the outside window. I had been too scared to do that, to get so close I would have to trust that the glass was there.

A thud echoed behind the door, someone listening in.

"What was just so obvious," she continued, "after your stupid attempt to liberate me from you, was that you thought of our family as a trap."

I looked down where she was looking, the peaks of people's heads passing below, and started to count how many pedestrians were balding. I remembered Jenny's hair loss during pregnancy—I had saved the strands in a baggie, and when I gave the baggie to her, she freaked out.

"But that's in the past," she finished. "I don't want to rehash it."

I wanted her safe, even from me.

A muscle in her neck popped out. She seemed nervous about what I would say. Beneath her belly button her fingers twisted around each other. She had slept like that on our bad days, with only her fingers moving. She always slept like the hands are the sole part of us that knows we aren't dead, just asleep.

"Maybe you feel like you're disappearing too?" I said. "I've been feeling like that lately . . . It's been 1,122 days, give or take eighty-four hours, since we were together."

She sighed and said that was more like the Matt she knew, assuming other people thought like I did. But I didn't do that, I did its opposite. She reached over and rubbed the stuffing on my desk from the dog-cat I'd pulled apart, then touched the edge of the cat half's wound. A frown whitened the corners of her lips.

"I want to be different," I started. "Like you—" But she cut me off.

"What I want to know is are you stalking us?" she asked. "Again? We saw you in the butcher shop. Now here you are in the same company I work for. I thought you were done stalking us."

You could see it that way if you believed things happened by purpose, not by coincidence.

"I took this job to investigate my disappearance," I said slowly. "Not yours."

Her white neck elongated, shivering.

"I'm not saying you'll disappear."

"You don't make me appear or not," Jenny said.

That wasn't what I meant. I apologized.

Yoonha's kids pushed open the door and ran in again, not caring that it was closed.

This time I saw what they must have knocked over before: another product, a soccer ball in the design of a globe that would say the name of the country you kicked.

"Russia," it said now. "Ocean. Ocean. Ocean."

I made a mental note to suggest that the ball should say which ocean.

"Anyway," Jenny said, "I didn't come here because *I* wanted to see you. Charlotte thinks you're stalking us again because you miss us. She wants to see you. Her therapist says to let her make her own bad choices, but please tell me you can be a normal dad."

"What is she like now?" I asked. "She seemed so different in the butcher shop. She has a therapist?"

Jenny said our kid was just a normal kid, changing constantly. "She's like that," she said, indicating the boys playing in the corner then suddenly fighting to the death. "Even you couldn't stop her from changing, thank God."

"Ocean," the soccer ball said. "Antarctica. The United States of America. Ocean."

I hadn't wanted to stop Charlotte from changing though. I had wanted to teach her to protect herself from a world that only changed slowly, if at all. That couldn't keep up and didn't want to. The problem was I was part of that world. In my wallet was a photo of Charlotte at six, unwrapping the gifts we had gotten wrong, that she never wanted at all. In the moment the photo was taken, she was happy—still hoping we would understand her this time. Minutes later she had retreated to her room to deal with her disappointment on her own.

"Don't tell her anything at all about how to grow up," Jenny said. "She's figuring it out for herself. She has friends now, hobbies, flexibility, interests."

"It's weird to miss you when you're two feet away from me."

"Boys!" Yoonha shouted in Korean. She appeared in the doorway and apologized.

I was going to say it was fine, but she wanted Jenny to say so. Jenny smiled and said she was about to leave anyway. She picked up her bag and dusted off the bottom as if to decontaminate it of me.

"I don't know what's weird and what's normal when I'm around you," she said as a parting shot. "And take it easy on your employees. I'm already hearing things downstairs."

Then she swept her bag over her shoulder like a shield.

I picked up the cat half of the dog-cat and ran after her.

She fake-smiled for the sake of my team, who had come out of their cubes to give her a formal goodbye. I caught her at the elevators.

"Maybe it's not a purr-fect apology," I said as I handed it to her.

She looked about to curse me when the elevator dinged.

My daughter stood there. It was the same Charlotte I'd seen in the butcher shop, yet instead of her teenage rebellion outfit, she wore a perfect little navy business suit like a twelve-year-old office worker. I barely recognized her, and yet I recognized her completely. She stared at me with almost the same resentful look Jenny had just given me, like which of us was the bad joke: the cat head or me?

"I knew it," Charlotte said.

I stepped toward her. But she pulled her mother inside and the doors closed excruciatingly slowly and awkwardly in my face.

"Hi," I said as the floor numbers changed.

Behind me I heard the ball say "ocean" through the stifling glass, and then something else I couldn't make out.

A VISIT TO THE PAST

Back when my family and I were together I tried hard not to be a burden to them. If someone wanted to get under my skin, I let them have it, I gave the skin away. What good was that skin to me? I had worked so hard to get to that point—to have a job, and a family, and a home and two cars. I had everything I thought I wanted. I tried to teach Charlotte the value of that happiness, of holding on to every little sliver of a chance. But Jenny believed our kid would have endless chances, would learn best from making mistakes. Charlotte's mistakes weren't what I was worried about. I had worried about something I couldn't describe. I had made my mistakes as a kid, of course, but those mistakes hadn't really seemed to be the deciding factors in whether I was praised or picked on.

It wasn't until Sandra showed up and held out the photo of her boyfriend, exactly like me except glowing and perfect—and disappeared—that I knew what it was that worried me. It wasn't my mistakes or my daughter's mistakes—it was the things Charlotte would think were her mistakes but were actually other people's mistakes. Jenny hadn't understood that. She had never had to admit that she was an orphan or fit herself into a second life or been called a Chink or a Jap or a Gook or had to dress up for the school Cultural Day in the traditional clothing of her dead parents.

I hadn't been able to explain this to my ex-family in time to let them know I wasn't rejecting their lives but surviving another.

———

By the end of that Friday Jenny sent me an email detailing all the rules I had to follow to see my daughter again. At the elevators, she wrote, she had needed to get back to work, and Charlotte hadn't been ready to talk. I understood: Three years was too long to resolve in the amount of time other people would tolerate the doors staying open. Jenny said both Charlotte and I needed time to prepare ourselves.

> You need to get some things straight. Don't do what you used to do. Don't try to teach Charlotte to be friendless or to survive on her own. Don't insist you're making her tough. She just turned 12 (if you don't remember). She's very adult for her age (your fault probably) but still sleeps with a night-light. She wants to know that you are okay (even if you are not) so don't let her think otherwise. Clean up. Make her think you are doing well on your own. If you've got your girlfriend there, keep her out of this. Two women who could put up with you could never put up with each other. (I should know.) If you make my daughter cry even once, I will kill you and leave your body somewhere no one will ever find it. (I have a place.) (For real.)

I wondered when Jenny had become so parenthetical. I couldn't exactly tell tone over email, but this seemed serious (even if not as serious as when she had put her hand over mine and moved me through the motions of signing the divorce papers).

What I needed to do, still, was love better. But Yumi still wouldn't answer my calls. Her forgiveness was probably some kind of measuring stick. Maybe I had never known her well enough to know how to respond to her anger. To know another person's anger was to know what world they really lived in—you had to live in their world to respond to it. If I wanted to love my daughter better, maybe I had to do some reconnaissance, observe her in her natural environment. The two times I had seen her recently, she had two totally different styles: one pseudo-Goth and one pseudo-businesswoman. What was she like unguarded, when she first woke up or got the flu or consumed ice cream straight out of the box? That was what I had wanted to know after the divorce, during the period of time that Jenny referred to as *stalking*. If I could figure out how Charlotte appeared only to herself—when she didn't know someone was watching—maybe I could figure out the best way to appear to her.

I followed the address from my child support checks to East Cambridge, a gentrifying neighborhood pushing out its Portuguese community. The street number led to a powder-blue Colonial. I parked down the street and then doubled back, leaving the sidewalk and sneaking along the wall of their house to the backyard. From there I searched the upstairs windows for a purple bedroom. It was a giant house: They still lived as we always had, beyond our means. It was all very typical, a typical white family's property in a typical gentrifying neighborhood of Cambridge.

As I crept around the yard, mud sucked at my loafers, and I moved slowly, careful not to fall. I wanted to be inconspicuous if anyone came downstairs—through the sliding glass doors I could see the dining table we'd bought when Charlotte was a baby, and behind that an open-concept living room and kitchen.

Upstairs the ceilings were interchangeable, the same white popcorned paint and wood-colored fan. Maybe Charlotte had grown out of purple. I gathered pebbles and chose two windows at random. I hit each on the first shot and hid around the corner.

From one window emerged the bare face of my ex-wife, who looked from right to left and then drew back inside. The second window stayed shut.

I waited for a moment, then threw pebbles at two more windows. There didn't seem to be an alarm system. I was concerned for their safety. What if I wasn't me? Suddenly I understood the email Matt Chung had sent, the desire to protect everyone he knew even if it meant being dismissed as strange or deluded.

This time no one stuck out her head. Good, I thought.

A dog barked from another house. In my pocket I petted the dog half of the stuffed toy. I wondered what Jenny had done with the cat half. I had considered a few slogans for the franchise: "A Tail of Two Heads," "Back to Back, Dog to Cat," "Which End Poops?" But I wanted a line that suggested unity in the literal face of differences. I was imagining the cat half sitting by Jenny's bedside, overseeing her sleep, when something squeaked above me. A window opening—not one I had hit, but one sensitive to barks.

A square chin emerged directly overhead.

I threw my back against the wall.

Here is what I thought: My family had replaced me with a white man.

The dog barked and barked, identifying me in its language. I was a foreign smell. I held my breath. A sense of general menace came from the chin, as if anyone outside was his enemy. I was pressed against the wall so that he couldn't see me unless he stretched his head completely out of the window and looked straight down, and then he would see only my hair. Was my hair enough to make him hate me?

The window shut and footsteps pounded down the stairs. Forceful thumps as if he wasn't landing on the ground so much as trying to break through it. My hair was a complete and ordinary peril. I fled.

I remembered, after my adoptive parents took me in at twelve, how the other foster kids began to hate me. I was as confused as they were. Why was I the one adopted, when I didn't seem especially liked? Maybe I was only especially pitied. The more confused we kids got, the more we fought . . . it was an animal instinct, an instinct that survival of the fittest depended on our predators' definition of fitness.

Maybe the chin hated me for something like this, because there was only one opening in the family and it wasn't up to him why or how long it was open.

I raced back along the wall and out onto the street to my car. With each step I felt the possibility that I would never see Charlotte again. Being caught lurking in the backyard was likely to be defined as stalking. I got halfway home before I could consider my own responsibility—I had terrorized my family. I hadn't intended this, I had done it because I hadn't thought about intention. I had involved them in my terror simply because they had once loved me.

IT ISN'T OVER UNTIL YOU FALL IN LOVE

I was supposed to see Charlotte on Sunday. On Saturday I told Sandra about my plan to re-replace the white guy who had replaced me. I explained that in order to see my kid, my image needed to match the image my kid had of me: that I had changed my life without changing whom I loved. In other words I was asking Sandra to pretend for a day that she didn't live with me and that her upgrades to the apartment were mine.

Sandra wasn't paying rent, but I didn't use this line of reasoning. I appealed to her as she wanted me to: as one *Homo sapien* to another. I had lost my parents, my adoptive parents, my family, my girlfriend, myself. She had lost her father, her boyfriend, her city, her individuality. Each of us had lost the context that had made us appear to be ourselves. Context belonged to other people. I was beginning to understand that being a *Homo sapien* was precisely about *appearing* to be a *Homo sapien*.

We were binge-watching a K-drama together, one I had planned to watch alone, little by little, to make it last. She had started it by herself, so I had to guess what had happened in the first four episodes I hadn't seen. Luckily I had consumed dozens of these shows. In a sixteen-episode arc the first four episodes were usually about the process of one main character realizing they were in love with the other. This only became conscious love in the fourth episode. The first three episodes were always about unconscious love, because they were about taking actions before taking responsibility. In the fourth episode love became conscious to one half of a couple; in the eighth episode love became conscious to both. Then the show became about taking responsibility for what they knew was there.

The lesson was that people act freely on their love until they know they are loved back.

Sandra pounded her fist against her chest, frustrated somehow by my understanding of things.

"I just want to know where the show stands—at this point in time—in the episode arc."

She hit pause, pushed her glasses up her nose, and glared at me. This was another difference between her and Yumi: Yumi never wore glasses, only contacts. The glasses flustered me.

"Did I get it wrong?" I asked. "Do neither of them know they love each other? Do both of them know? Have they already kissed?"

It was rare to get the main couple together early, since what seduced viewers was seduction, not contentment.

"Is it fun for you," Sandra asked, "to watch TV like that? Like it's math?"

I didn't see what she was getting at.

She described the two main characters: a powerful male politician in a tight election race and a woman who grew up fishing in a struggling industry with her father and three brothers, who together cheated rich tourists out of thousands of dollars. But I already knew all this from the parts I had seen. They were the same main characters as always. Opposites whose love at first threatened each other but eventually would teach them how to be happy in the middle.

"What do you watch for?" I asked. "The acting?"

Sandra said she was talking about *characters*, not *actors*.

We were looking at a real person though, a person whose emotions we attributed to a character in our imaginations. I didn't say this for the sake of our species.

I asked Sandra what else she liked about the show.

What she said made our differences clearer. The one thing she liked other than the characters was a clever use of product placement. We watched the show differently because we wanted differently. We looked for what we thought would bring order to our lives.

For me K-dramas were about potential: the life you might live if you could escape the only life you knew, the love you might give if you could escape the only love you knew. That was why I was drawn to the structure: because I too could love better if I had sixteen episodes to improve and met in the first episode the person who would surely love me.

That was when I asked her to pretend she didn't live with me.

For a long time Sandra didn't answer. We continued watching actors perform love. Then she said that the night before (while I was out stalking) she had searched the apartment. She had looked every-where, even down to the cracks between the floorboards and the seams where the molding met the wall. She still knew there was something wrong with the place, she said, but she couldn't find its cause. Maybe the cause was me.

In other words the apartment was a sustainable ecosystem.

"I must be the weird one for staying here," Sandra said.

"Does that mean you'll leave tomorrow?"

She went back to her silence, which was one way to communicate. I missed the echo off the walls.

On-screen it began to rain. The female lead walked away from the male lead, opening her umbrella. The male lead's secretary opened an umbrella for him. The male lead took the expensive umbrella from his assistant and snapped it over his knee, then ran after the female lead and asked to share her cheap umbrella.

"These shows are all just one long advertisement for love," Sandra said with longing.

Which confused me again about the difference between attraction and creepiness.

"He wasted a perfectly good umbrella," I said.

She punched me in the arm.

"He should have given her his nice umbrella," I said, "and thrown away her crappy one."

Sandra punched me in the arm again and said the woman would never have accepted it. "You know even in this country Asian women make only three-quarters of what Asian men make," she said. "That's the biggest pay gap between genders of any single race. It's bigger in Asia."

She surprised me with this fact attack. This difference meant that the woman would feel condescended to, to be asked to switch umbrellas with the man.

I did know about this pay gap—somewhere in my memory with how Asians have been in America for five hundred years and which wave of immigrants from which Asian country was forced into indentured labor in which century and how banning women from immigrating and men from miscegenating was a way to sustain white supremacy and thus miscegenation became a way to attain sexual legitimacy, etc. But what I wondered was: when had Sandra started to talk like Yumi?

"Speaking of work," I said as if I hadn't been thinking of it the entire time.

"Yes?" Sandra said, reenergized. "Did you have some kind of weird experience in the lobby?"

I said I still didn't know anything about that.

"Then what?"

"I found out about the other Matt," I said cautiously.

She paused the TV again and gave me all of her attention. I wanted to take it back, but it was too late.

I asked whether she remembered an email from Matt that said someone he knew was going to disappear, he had sent it to all of his friends. I tried not to imply that I suspected Sandra of keeping this information from me, who was disappearing, even though this didn't seem like an email she would forget after Matt disappeared on her. I gave her the benefit of my self-doubt.

Sandra's eyes narrowed, her nose wrinkled, her lips drew in. She didn't seem surprised or suddenly reminded. She seemed worried, with anger gathering in the distance like a storm.

"Explain," she said.

I hesitated, sensing explanation wasn't what she wanted—she wanted me to snap my umbrella in half and plead to share hers—but what could I do? I forwarded the email.

When she'd read it she said, "This is made up. Obviously it isn't real. I never got anything like this."

She stood in front of me and clenched her fists. The storm rushed in as if she barely restrained a desire to stab me with whatever was on hand.

"I don't think it's made up—" I started.

"Who are you to say?"

Luckily the only object nearby was the remote.

"You don't know him," she said. "He's not like this."

But she knew who I was: I was Matt.

I said at first I too had thought what she thought, but I hadn't been able to figure out what Tokki had to gain.

"She just wanted you to stop talking to her."

"She could have said anything. The email would have taken a lot of effort to make. It would have been easier to—"

"Shut up," Sandra said. "Let me think."

I thought she was really going to sock me in the face. Not a colloquial punch, but a knockout.

It seemed clear now that she had not been on Matt's email list. I wondered why. On some level I could see what was bothering her—though I didn't see why she had to take it out on me. I was just the easiest target, someone who looked exactly like a person who had left her. But the Matt she had dated—I was sure she was thinking now—the glowing Matt in her photo—wasn't paranoid or unstable or depressed—he wasn't typical.

In the same way that a word only has meaning in relation to other words, a person is only an individual in relation to other individuals. Which meant that the Matt who had sent that email could not be the same as the Matt aglow in Sandra's photographs.

On the other hand: I was Matt.

While I was thinking all of this Sandra stormed into Charlotte's old bedroom and clicked the lock on the door.

———

She didn't come out all night. With each moment that passed I got more and more worried and drunk. I finished four bottles of wine, which was a half bottle over my limit, because what would happen if she stayed in there tomorrow too? If she refused to vacate the premises?

I tried to clean up a little, make the house ready to appear to my daughter. But I kept stumbling into things and making a bigger mess. The stumbling reminded me of when my cat would run into the wall, and soon I heard meows upstairs where I should have heard a white male and an Asian female arguing about whether their love would work. I remembered the one time they invited themselves downstairs for dinner. We ate frozen pizzas, and they glanced around at the empty walls, not looking at each other. I felt bad for making them feel worse about their relationship.

The cat was alive then, and it whined from the other room about the presence of strangers. It wouldn't come out. It liked to protest from a safe distance, unseen—it was a cat of the internet age. "Where's the kitty," the woman kept demanding. Then it became a joke to her, like maybe there was no kitty, like maybe I was making it up. She kept making jokes about the emptiness too, saying my apartment was like a serial killer's hideout, like it could be left at any moment. After a while I realized she hadn't wanted to come to dinner, it had been her boyfriend's idea.

He kept insisting the cat was real—he was a stickler for accuracy. He had seen it preening on the driveway. Several times during the meal he corrected my grammar. He made a joke that if someone saw us they might mistake whose girlfriend his girlfriend was. No one laughed, so he kept going. He said the truth was a monogamous relationship. He too was anxious, just not about my empty apartment, but about being compared to me in any way.

I wondered whether the white dude who'd replaced me with my family felt anxious at all about the person he had replaced.

———

In the morning I woke with a splitting stomachache, a rumbling head. I ate a couple of bananas for potassium, then took a hangover pill imported from Korea, but nothing worked. I had taken my liver too far.

I had to figure out how to get Sandra back on my side or at least to neutral where she might take pity on me. I made toast and eggs for her, the best I could do. As they sizzled I worried that Jenny would text that she was already on the way. I would try to push Sandra out, and just as she stepped out the door they would pull into the driveway—and then I would lose everyone. (I had seen a lot of dramas.) I plated the eggs and a text did come through . . . from Sandra. Since a child is involved, she texted, she would stay out until I let her know it was safe to return.

Probably I had benefited not from her doubt but from her own fatherless childhood. She knew what it was like—she had told me she'd envied her two-parent friends and especially the ones with divorced parents, because they would get four parents sometimes. Her mother's sole control over her meant practicality always came before fun. "Evolution before devolution," her mother would say. Sandra was expected to become the biologist her mother had wanted to be, since her mother had stopped publishing and traveling after her husband died.

When Sandra was fourteen she went away to boarding school, and that was when she really missed her dad. Her mother drove four hours each weekend to check up on her, which meant Sandra spent the weekend as a daughter and the weekdays as someone else. Whom, she wasn't sure. For the first time the pressures from other children seemed even greater than those from her mother. Sandra was expected to be a certain type of young woman, especially as one of a handful of Asian girls there. She watched the other Asians react either by accepting or rejecting this type wholesale. On the weekends, when her mother came, the only parent who visited so often, Sandra became another "type" entirely. So she knew how to switch and how to use a performance to get what she wanted for herself.

The only problem was that she had no one she could tell this to. It became a secret life, hidden away from her friends. Before her father died he had been the one who talked about pack animals, animals that simply wanted to find their rank and animals that challenged the rankings. The fittest didn't always survive, he had said. Sometimes it was the survivors that determined what survival was. That was what Sandra missed, those times when her father had appeared to be talking about science but was really talking about life. No snakes on her arm (it wasn't until later that she realized her mother had been trying in her own way). More and more Sandra felt that in the process of figuring out how to fit in she was forgetting to figure out how to survive fitting in.

When Sandra told me this it was the most connected I'd felt to her since the night we almost had sex. I had tried to be exactly her type of father for Charlotte. It had backfired because the world Charlotte wanted to join didn't need me for either fit or survival.

I stood in the kitchen reading Sandra's text as the eggs crusted. They were divided among two plates, since I hadn't realized she'd left the house. Now I dumped everything on one plate. The distended pupil of food stared up at me. The second plate, which was supposed to be an offering, lay bare.

Sandra came out of her room and looked at the two plates and sighed.

I tried to move one portion over, but she shook her head. "I thought you had left," I said. "I even garnished it?"

Her fingers clattered over her phone.

A minute or so later my phone dinged with another text from her. It seemed she wasn't talking to me. When her fingers moved again I counted. Eighty-four seconds later another message came. Though I could have been rushing or slowing the count.

I still didn't know why she was so angry at me about the email. I was missing some reason that would help me understand what I personally had done to upset her. I wasn't the one who had written the email. I was simply the evidence that Matt could have written it, that maybe he wasn't who he seemed.

I supposed this could be enough to blame me.

It only seemed fair to shove every last bite of eggs down my throat. I ate until I was ill. Sandra's mouth twitched with disgust, and I remembered what Yumi had said about disgust, that it existed to teach us what was bad for us. We knew not to eat garbage even before we knew what garbage was.

After I had eaten, a deliveryman showed up. Sandra went to the door. The man took four covered plates from a little tin box—less like a deliveryman and more like someone doing a personal favor. The food was far too fancy for delivery. Inside Sandra transferred it to china dishes: noodles like gods' hair, thin and dark and not of this world; dumplings with other dumplings inside them; side dishes I hadn't seen since my parents died.

With each bite she shut her eyes and moaned.

Afterward the man returned and took away the used plates in the same tin box.

It was a totally different universe than the one I knew.

When Sandra left I surprised myself by crying. I tried to figure out what the tears were *for*. Not to mourn the other me. They were tears for myself. They indicated my own regret. And then I knew—I was crying because I had done what the other Matt had done to her, again. He had cut himself out of her life, I had asked her to cut herself out of mine—we were complete and ordinary assholes. I had asked her to disappear instead of me.

THE NATURE OF A TEXT

When I was alone I shouted at the walls. No sound returned except the ghost of my cat. Despite all the fancy decor I missed my echo. I was aware that this meant choosing an illusion over presence. But one of Jenny's rules was hiding reality from our daughter. Parenting was a magic trick, of course—it just always confused me who was supposed to see through tricks and who was not. I remembered when Charlotte was six and she asked why some people got more money from the Tooth Fairy than her, were her teeth not as good? I wanted to tell her the Tooth Fairy was a fake, so she wouldn't feel less valuable than anyone else, so that she would know how the world kept stacking belief in certain people's favor. Jenny wanted her to hold on to a sense of magic.

It was like Sandra in her boarding school, I just couldn't tell how. I knew the similarity was there. Once in college I went to a history lecture where the speaker said that in order for people to communicate they must share a belief in imaginary things: nations, limited liability corporations, money, gender, race. The first step to disappearing is to disappear from belief. I could never seem to be myself in other people's imagination.

I sat at my desk and tried to use my imagination to write my novel. I drank one glass of Chardonnay to loosen up. I laid my phone beside me, ready for a text. Memories of Charlotte kept popping up like skylines. Each year her happiness grew further from her wants. As a toddler she would dance over a slice of cheese. Yet by the time she started school she denied herself what she liked to eat. Her first day of first grade she had wanted fried rice for lunch, she had screamed at her mom to pack it for her—and yet when I got out a pan to make it myself Charlotte wept. She said I didn't care about her like her mom did, I didn't care that the other kids would say she stank.

I wanted the memories to stop.

I reread the 28,512 words I had so far, in which I had given my protagonist the other Matt's glowing confidence, his job branding cities, his determination to make the most of life. Nothing like a plot. Ultimately the weirdness of his world didn't touch him. Instead of traveling he researched cities online. He could get his groceries delivered. He fretted about his kidnapped cat, but also looked for a new pet. He didn't worry about what was real or unreal, because he was in a novel and everything unreal was real to him.

I was so tired. The wine had helped my hangover a little, but I was still afloat, bloated and achy. The only way forward was to drink more. I started a second bottle of wine.

I thought about the test Sandra's mother had done on her, with the snake. I could understand that about Sandra, I could feel her fear in that moment and how the question was really about her mother. Poisonous or safe? But then I realized the answer was obvious. Why had Sandra ever considered poison? Her fear must have been about something else. I tried to remember what more she had told me—how had her father died? Maybe he had been bitten by a snake on one of her parents' trips? Maybe her mother wanted to prove she had nothing to do with it?

Charlotte had loved stories about snakes, which she imagined not deceitful and dangerous but misunderstood and jealous of legs.

I started a third bottle of wine and thought about dumping it all over the keyboard, getting rid of my bad writing, my email, social media, online bill pay, the rejections from publishers, all the remnants of my previous lives, every single lie. I set my glass beside me. A good Christian believes death is also rebirth—my adoptive parents had told me this to help me grieve my parents. I had told Charlotte this when a baby bird fell out of its nest behind the house. Even at twelve I had pictured rebirth like a tiny alien baby inside my stomach that would grow and consume until it took my life. I knew that my parents' cancer was somehow my cancer. I knew that Charlotte's rejection of me was somehow my rejection of myself. Somewhere in the depths of my hard drive were my parents' medical charts and photos of my daughter in her mom's makeup and scanned love letters signed *Jennifer* and dirty texts from Yumi and Google alerts for my adoptive parents' names and technical reports on the academic impossibility of completely securing the internet.

I leaned back in my uncomfortable chair, and it tipped over. As I stretched out my legs for balance my big toe slammed the bottom of my desk. The pain webbed across the surface of my foot. I could almost hear the lullaby Jenny used to sing to heal a booboo. Memories lashed. Charlotte, Charlotte, Charlotte. A famous doctor had once paused surgery to record the time gap between his patient's decision to move and the signals sent down the nerves. The results had surprised him—movement started before decision.

I was pretty sure that as a good Christian he had explained this as God.

My pants were wet. Liquid dripped from the edge of the desk, and I caught it in the cup of my palm. It made a small translucent pond. Soon the pond overflowed. I wiped my eyes with my dry hand. I didn't feel any tears this time.

My wine had spilled all over my computer, as if to fulfill my earlier impulse.

———

As I cleaned I felt the tug of the yellow yarn from the second bedroom. I tried to ignore it, but I knew what the yarn was saying: What if Charlotte wanted to see her old room, check that the walls were still purple? How could I keep her out of our past? I remembered the sign on my upstairs neighbors' door: "DO NOT DISTURB."

When I went into the bedroom right there on Sandra's nightstand lay a pen and notebook, as if a sign to write a sign. She must have been recording a dream or a phone call or writing another letter. I noticed on her walls that she had stuck little photos and reminders to herself. I didn't have time to read them all, but I made a note to self to read her notes. A few days earlier I had found one inside my shoe. It said: *These stink!*

Stuck in the notebook was a sheet of paper. I unfolded it, and on the side that was still blank I wrote, *DO NOT DISTURB*. It didn't seem as impressive in my handwriting, so on second thought I added, *DIRTY BOXERS EVERYWHERE.*

I held the note up to the door. I could see the shadow of the words on the other side, double underlined. *BEWARE*, it said. No. *BEWEAR*. Sandra didn't seem like the kind of person to misspell *beware*.

I turned the paper over. *Sandra,* the message said, *your boyfriend = toy fetishist, kiddie abuser, maybe Muslim terrorist. BEWEAR.* It was the same handwriting I had seen on the paper upstairs. I wondered how my neighbor even knew her name. He must have thought he was writing to Yumi, whom he called Sandra.

The rest of the note said he had snuck into my apartment and found a box full of children's toys, so probably I was luring kids home.

There were white dudebros everywhere trying to ruin my life, I didn't know why. Unless maybe they had been planted there . . . I imagined my upstairs neighbor observing me for years, reporting back to some Head Disappearer or to another spy watching the other Matt.

Maybe the two of us broke some rule of appearance. I remembered the photos strewn all over my upstairs neighbors' floor. They were up there doing something. Maybe my cat was telling me something. My head hurt. I couldn't tell whether this was a drunk thought or what a private investigator would call a *hunch*. What I knew was that there must be some connection between the chin in my ex-family's house, where they lived because they had left me, and my upstairs neighbor who had tried to get Sandra/Yumi to leave me. If there was someone behind these abandonments, someone who had even gone so far as to inject my nonsmoking parents with lung cancer cells and convince my adoptive parents to stop talking to me and infiltrate all of my relationships, then it would all make sense.

This was the hunch that made me go through Sandra's notebook. It was full of tear-off pages, half of which were already gone. And the very first remaining page read *Dear Yumi,* like an echo of my neighbor's letter.

My stomach felt queasy. I knew I had found something.

I skimmed down the page—down, down—until I reached the word *murder.*

Murder, I thought. *Murder doppelgänger murder.*

Everyone was writing messages to each other. I had written DIRTY BOXERS EVERYWHERE for my daughter. My neighbor would be validated. I rested my head on the wall and half expected to slip into another dimension, a parallel universe in which my daughter split weekends or in which I hadn't been a coward who made his nine-year-old kid decide whether she wanted to see him or not or in which *I* had disappeared and the other Matt had a family or in which any doppelgängers had to fight to the death until only one remained.

Matt had been murdered—that was information Sandra had withheld. Maybe that was why she had gotten so angry about the email. Maybe that was what I had felt this entire time: murder, not disappearance.

My cat whined and whined overhead. It was about time for my neighbor's pasty face to appear outside my window. *Bewear.* Disappearance was not like murder—was it? A murder was a type of disappearance, but a disappearance was not a type of murder.

In movies the murderer was always hiding in the open, someone nearby whom you weren't supposed to suspect. Which was why it was always a white man or Morgan Freeman.

But I wasn't sure about this.

My head hurt. I had gone too long without a drink.

The next thing I knew, I rang my upstairs neighbor's doorbell. It was becoming a habit.

BRINGING THE
CHARGE

I panicked, my watch said I might be having a heart attack. I was a
regular guy stepping into a villain's lair, as if simply by acting a hero he
might become one. This was not a plot, it was poor impulse control.

No one answered the door. *Okay,* I thought. *That's it. Turn around.
You're off the hook.* But another thought, as if not mine, said: *Take
responsibility.* I pictured my protagonist's cat tied up inside, calling out
for someone to love it. Which made me realize the cat in my novel was
a stand-in for Charlotte. Which made me realize the cat I had bought
was a stand-in for Charlotte. As I understood psychology everything
was a stand-in for something—even reality, for humans, was a stand-in
for reality unfiltered by human perspective. For the couple who hal-
lucinated bugs, loving someone else's delusions could be a stand-in for
loving them.

I felt that this was a very beautiful thought, and I wanted my neighbor to know I had very beautiful thoughts before his next attempt to
make Sandra leave me—or worse, to murder me in my sleep. So despite
knowing I should just leave a note I knocked again. With each knock I
felt more afraid, yet I also felt more beautiful to myself. How to explain?
I wished to face my neighbor/murderer/stand-in for the chin that had

taken my place in my family, and dazzle him with my beauty. I kept my phone in my free hand in case my daughter ever started on her way.

Finally the man opened the door, this time in a white polo with the collar up and tan slacks and boat shoes. He had brushed his curls, which hung stylishly over his big brown eyes. He looked as if he was always prepared to stand trial and get off without a sentence. His teeth literally glinted.

"Why are you clapping?" he asked.

"For my imagination. I made all of this up, right? You're not real?"

He tried to shut the door, but I pushed inside. Scattered over the floor were the same photos as last time, with more pasted on the walls. More spread out on the sofa and armchairs. A stack of milk crates lined one side, each stuffed with records or books or clothing. A few bookcases huddled together, busy with inscrutable objects—a few snow globes and seashells and glass figurines and old bottles and abalone jewelry, etc. "I made all of this up," I said again, but now it was less comforting. "Where's my cat?"

"Get out."

"It's a trap, isn't it? This is how the hero puts himself in danger? This is the death drive?"

"Get out," he said again. "What are you even talking about?"

"In my imagination," I clarified, "did *you* kill Matt? Are you the final boss battle?"

"Are you crazy?"

"I don't want to die," I said. "Also, using *crazy* like that is kind of offensive."

He made a sound somewhere between a scoff and a laugh.

For a moment I wondered whether I had made up his face outside my windows too, but then I remembered that Yumi and Sandra had both seen him. There was a part of him that really was out to get me, I had to remember that. My head hurt and I looked for a drink.

Luckily he had a flask out, which seemed to be in use.

120

I took a drink and gazed down at the photos the flask had sat on. My neighbor made a small teeth-sucking noise of frustrated surrender. He didn't make any move to hide them.

"Pass it over," he said with a sigh. "Asshole."

I recognized the woman in the photos: They were all, every single one, his girlfriend.

I backed away with the flask in one hand and my unringing phone in the other.

"Hey," he said. "You can't take that. If you want to drink with me, whatever. But give it."

"I made all of this up—right? You're just a version of my problems?"

"Why do you keep saying that?" he asked. "It's a pretty fucked-up thing to say." His hand went out to me. "Whoa, dude."

I was falling. My elbow banged the floor. He had attacked me. Or I had slipped on a photo.

"It doesn't make sense, this shrine you built to her."

He leaned in and I flinched. He took the flask from me.

"How much did you drink before you came up here?"

"I don't know, a couple of bottles."

He picked up a Kleenex box and wiped his eyes, which now I noticed were tear-streaked. He blew his nose and tossed the used tissue into a trash can full of tissues. He had a whole setup.

"I thought your girlfriend maybe left you too," he said. "But now she's moved in or something?"

"You loved her to death?" I said, indicating the photos. "You killed her?"

"What?"

"Bewear," I said. "Was that letter real?"

His eyes burned into my eyes.

"This *shrine*," he said, drawing out the word as if that made it not what it was, "is all the stuff from our relationship. She broke up with me after I loved her this much."

He took a swig of the flask. My throat dried.

"I was just about to go to her," he said. He picked his car keys up off a table.

"Okay," I said. "I've had enough. When I go down this will all be gone. You're a figment of my imagination."

"I'm a real fucking person," he said.

"It would be hard to kill me with those car keys."

"God, what is wrong with you?"

The Catholic inside me didn't like the way he said *God*.

He spoke in something between a sneer and a whine: "She took a box of her stuff and broke up over text message."

"Dear Lord," I tried, "bless this broken heart."

He cried so hard his shirt darkened.

I started to feel sympathy. His crying sounded like my cat.

Bewear, I thought. He tossed more and more tissues onto the pile of tissues. I blew my nose so he wouldn't be the only one. If I wasn't careful, his reality would take the place of mine.

What was it about me that wanted to give his reality a chance? He had gone to Harvard, he had a good job at an NGO, he was raised in a loving family. If that guy couldn't get an in-person breakup, what hope was there for the rest of us?

"You aren't a killer then," I said, though it sounded like pleading. "You won't murder me?"

I pulled the flask and keys away from him. His tears continued to confuse my sympathies.

Swigging from the flask I drove to the address he'd given me. I had challenged him, and a dudebro never turns down a challenge from someone he thinks is weaker than him. It was like a code for them. I regretted everything. One more time I couldn't make my intentions into actions. My phone never vibrated, Charlotte probably changed her mind—she had every reason and right to do so. My upstairs neighbor and I passed his flask back and forth until he lowered his window and vomited.

I pulled halfway over the curb in front of a concrete apartment complex, a fair-sized disturbance in a world of disturbances. I stepped onto the sidewalk, and it quicksanded beneath me. My neighbor got out in his yachting outfit, slapping his chest, stomping his boat shoes to pump himself up. He pointed out her top-floor window.

"Let's do it," he shouted. "Anything's possible!" Then he ran across the street and up the steps to the entrance so fast his hair swept out of place, as if he was in a Polo ad. He pressed a buzzer at the door, and another buzzer, and another, until someone let him into the lobby. That was when he looked back and saw that I was still beside the car. I was still waiting for Charlotte.

He raked a hand through his curls and they bounced back into place. The glass between us made me think of the goldfish I had kept alive just short of a year, how long a year had seemed until the kid at the pet store said goldfish could live decades and grow a foot long while mine had died the length of my pinky. The kid said goldfish made hormones that inhibited growth, and the hormones collected in still water, hence why they lived in rivers and lakes. The verdict: it was my fault. I rarely changed the water.

My neighbor sat right where he was, on the lobby floor, and I calculated the time it would take to get back to my apartment versus the time it would take Jenny to get there from East Cambridge.

"If this is real," I mouthed to my neighbor, "try and win her back." He folded his arms.

"You just need to make yourself real," I mouthed. But I was talking to myself.

He lowered the rest of his body to the floor and lay there halfway to where he wanted to be.

"I'm driving home," I said aloud, in what sounded like my voice but drunk.

When I got back to the car the setting sun reflected against the side of the apartment complex. As a last test I tried to see a crack in the concrete, a seam in the glow. I pictured Charlotte in her blue house, saying to her mother, *On second thought.* Second thoughts were wise. Second thoughts were humans correcting their animal instincts. Why hadn't I gone to Charlotte, for example, before the custody ruling, to kneel at her feet and beg? I had stood outside their house dozens of times, and never once rung the bell. I dug into my pocket for my neighbor's car keys, and out popped the dog half of the stuffed toy. How had it gotten in there? My neighbor would probably count it as more evidence of my corruption of children.

He must have his keys with him. I must have handed them back after accepting reality. The lobby was empty now, maybe he had gone up after all. I laid the dog half on my lap and held my phone and tried to feel a crack in the building and looked for the yellow yarn against the ground and swigged from the flask.

The phone rang.

I fumbled the little green symbol.

"We're on our way," Jenny said without greeting. "You didn't respond to my text."

"I just stepped out for a second," I said. "I'll be back in a few minutes. It won't take long."

There was a pause. Then she said my name full of its old accusation.

"Fifteen minutes," I said.

"Have you been drinking?"

"Can't you wait thirty minutes? I'll be there."

I heard her say into the air, "It's okay, Charlotte." Alcohol clogged my throat. "Listen," she murmured into the receiver, "we'll run a few errands and you call me when you get back. I want to know for sure that you're there before we head over."

Seconds later I got a text in all-caps: DO NOT FUCK THIS UP OR YOU ARE DEAD.

The reality was that I knew someone with a motive to kill me. Still it didn't seem a sensitive text to send someone whose parents had died.

I leaned back in my seat. The wall would not open a shortcut to my daughter. It was never going to. I wanted another drink, but the flask wasn't going to produce more alcohol. I had to wait for my neighbor and his keys. Maybe he was making up with his ex right now.

As if in answer I heard a crash.

On the top floor a shoe stuck out of a broken window. The shoe retreated, and after a moment a body followed. It flew through the hole in the glass, dropped all seven stories, and landed with a thud on the grass.

A single boat shoe tumbled afterward.

One, I counted. *Two. Three. Four. Five.* I couldn't seem to get rid of my fear. At *ten*, a woman screamed, probably his ex, my former neighbor. Other people opened doors and windows. I approached the body, wondering about that delay. There wasn't much blood. But something was missing from the flesh. In the body there was no sign that my neighbor had gotten any satisfaction before the fall. What was my responsibility to the body's failure? I texted Jenny, A little longer, it's a matter of life and death. For real. Sirens turned the corner and joined the continued screaming. I stood there holding my phone. Maybe it looked like a gun. A pair of white cops strolled up, and I put the phone away. A black couple stepped back into their building. I bent to dig the keys from my neighbor's pocket—and a familiar woman burst out of the building. She pointed at me, and everyone turned to me as if they had found the killer, and I wondered why I felt so recognized.

CHAPTER 3:
THE AIRING OF
GRIEVANCES

IN THE EYES OF THE LAW

The cops took my phone and wallet and keys, plus the keys I had taken from my neighbor's pocket, plus the dog head. In exchange I got my own room and interrogation. No one had paid me such attention since my parents died. Though justice was conditional. When I answered as myself the cops got frustrated. When I said it was my fault my neighbor died they nodded and sympathized.

Without my phone I couldn't be sure how much time passed, how big Jenny's anger had grown, how small Charlotte's opinion of me. I asked them for my phone call, plus the dog half, which couldn't hurt anyone. I knew my rights.

"Well, hold on," said the first cop. "Slow down. Go back to where you said it was your fault."

"Have some water," said the second cop. "Clear your throat, start over."

"It was my fault," I said, "but I didn't kill him."

"Calm down," said the first cop. "Calm down. It's not a good idea to make things worse. We saw what you did to that stuffed animal."

"If you don't calm down," said the second cop, "we'll just talk to each other."

As far as I could tell I was calm.

"Say," said the first cop, "what kind of Oriental would mutilate a poor stuffed animal?"

Oriental made it sound bad.

"They're supposed to be smarter than that."

"I bet he didn't even memorize a number to call."

The second cop said it was a common mistake. "He probably doesn't know he's got to call collect from the station phone. And they don't call them Oriental anymore, now that they make a lot of money. Now they call them Asian."

I asked who *they* and *them* referred to, wanting more pronoun clarity.

"See," said the second cop, "he's as smart as all of them. Just angrier."

"Doesn't he know we got the girlfriend saying it was him?"

Someone must have seen me in the car, I said. "There must be plenty of witnesses."

"If you don't calm down," said the first cop, slowly, "we'll have to neuter you. Then you'll be real calm. Wouldn't want you to try to mutilate us like that dog."

Neuter, didn't they mean *neutralize*?

I asked them to give me my calmness back.

"What I want to know," said the second cop, "is why'd he take his neighbor's keys? What was he planning next? I get the toy, typical kill souvenir. But you think this was his first murder?"

"Look," I said. "Go to his apartment. He made an entire shrine to her. It was depression, open and shut."

Two solid slabs hit the table, and I jumped. They were hands. The hands belonged to the cop who'd said *kill souvenir* like it was something you won at an amusement park. He said: "You do your job. And we'll do ours. And you're not being accused of anything. Yet."

"If I'm not calm," I tried to say calmly, "it's probably because I just saw a dead body and now I'm being falsely accused and my daughter is waiting to see me for the first time in years. I've been trying to love better."

"Enough," said the second cop.

"In here," said the first cop, "there are two types of people, get it? Criminals who confess, and criminals who eventually confess. You can think about which one you are while we keep you for public drunkenness. Spend a little time in the holding cell. The other guy in there's a murderer too, by the way. Maybe mercury's in retrograde."

"You said you weren't accusing me."

"The law's the law," said the second cop, cryptically.

I really did want to confess—I was willing and able—I just wanted to confess my own sins. If confessors were the only two types of people, I wondered, what were they trying to say to me? How could people so in need of absolution absolve someone else's sins? I was supposed to accept the sins that they wanted to forgive.

———

The holding cell looked like a holding cell on TV. Sometimes reality was the same as you imagined. This didn't comfort me. I sat on the bench and wished, absurdly, that I could send my yarn forth to bring someone to me. No one who knew me knew where I was. Without possessions I was a ghost. I couldn't stop seeing my neighbor's boat shoe falling after him. I couldn't stop seeing the words in Sandra's notebook. *Murder.* I was a wreck. Could you be a wreck if you knew you were a wreck?

Murder.

Chopped.

Burned.

Dumpster.

Dear Yumi, Sandra had written but hadn't mailed, *I didn't tell Matt everything.* But why did they even write each other? Why letters? Maybe it was the draft of an email.

Sandra had written about a protest they went to together, some rally against legislating bodies. She said she didn't understand the laws in this city, as if they were different in hers. Her mom had always treated her like they were one body—climbing into her bed and wrapping around her until they became a cephalopod, all limbs. Sandra was tired of that borderless love. It was hard for her to look at me, she wrote, because each time, she thought maybe I was the other Matt playing a trick on her. This was what she hadn't told me:

The day she left she didn't just wake from a dream, she saw Matt's face glowing like a burning bush. It was on the news: a photo in the top corner of the screen. The reporter was giving the crime report.

A body had been found, the reporter said,

chopped up

burned beyond recognition,

and left in a *dumpster*

and the police were looking for leads.

The guy in the cell with me was supposedly a murderer: what did a murderer look like? I was in jail for (not) murdering my neighbor. My neighbor in jail *was* a murderer. I couldn't tell what made us different—he looked no more murderous than anyone would look in jail.

Likely the cops were trying to scare me. Likely he was a complete and ordinary thirtysomething able black guy. I wanted to put my trust in his innocence, because it was both of ours. On the other hand I worried that if the other Matt had been brutally murdered, I was next.

As my kid used to say, it was a dilemma!

My ex-neighbor had pointed at me—she must have had her reasons for doing so. I had angered her too somehow. It wasn't just the things you knew you did wrong that you had to take responsibility for.

Outside the moon rose. Time passed. There was something cruel about its linearity, that I could not open my eyes in my apartment only three hours earlier, to wait for a text that I knew in my cell would come. At some point an officer checked on me, asked whether I was ready to confess. I asked whether he was ready to understand my confession. He rolled his eyes. If I hadn't murdered my neighbor, then I was nobody.

I sat on the opposite end of the bench from my cellmate now. He had his head in his hands. Maybe it was simple: Without freedom you appreciate your freedom. You want what you don't have. I wanted the other Matt's life. My cellmate turned to me with large, kind eyes, not like a predator, like fellow prey. He smiled wryly as if he knew how I felt, that no matter how hard we tried to live our own lives, no matter how much we believed in our own free will, there was always a predator around to remind us we were somebody's dinner.

By the time I got my phone call, I could barely remember which me I was supposed to be in which context. I hadn't exerted any physical effort, yet my body could barely support itself. Maybe it was the alcohol.

A cop led me to the station phone at the end of a short hall and waited to escort me back. I asked him with my eyes: *Since when has anyone memorized phone numbers?* I asked: *Do I really need help to call for help?*

"If you don't have anyone to phone," he said, "that's fine. I got things to do."

I ran my fingers up and down the three columns of numbers. I had never been good at divination. I thought to myself, 5-5-5. Some pattern started to come to me. Memory knocked. Charlotte at a table in The Cave, ordering a hamburger from Yumi. My poor kid begging me not to make things difficult for myself.

Whom should I beg to save me?

Some people faced that question over and over, until it became a life.

Before I knew what numbers I had pressed I was prompted to give my name. I waited to see whether the other person would accept my call. A recorded voice said the number was invalid. Of course. My overseer wouldn't give me another chance. When I asked why not, he said he didn't want it to go to my head.

———

It had happened like this: My biggest fear was that because of me my family wouldn't get to do the things they wanted to do. I never wanted to hold them back.

It could have been any unavailable desire that broke us, but what did was this—my wife had liked a guy in her office.

He was a big white intern with a goofy grin who didn't mean me any harm, whose role in the office was to start the dancing at their office parties. Every month to celebrate some success they threw one of these parties, and I would watch her watch him with hunger, her mouth slightly open, as he danced. Once, at some coworker's wedding reception, we were dancing across the room from him and Jenny tugged us through the entire crowd until their backs touched. Because of our marriage she denied herself. Everywhere her desire stuck like cobwebs. She pushed through those cobwebs as she walked through the house. I pushed through those cobwebs. Our daughter pushed through those cobwebs, brushing them from her little face.

When I told Jenny to go for it, she thought it was a joke. When I kept telling her, she said it wasn't funny anymore. But she only wanted him because she didn't have him. What was so different about sending Charlotte to an all-white Catholic school or asking for a knife and fork at a Korean restaurant or wanting flesh-colored Band-Aids to match my skin? During my lunch hour at The Cave I would give Yumi the latest update. She was the only one in my life who seemed to get what I meant. One day Yumi said to ask for a date or to stop monopolizing her time. I hadn't thought I wanted a date, but she sat at the table and folded her arms. "Hey," the perv said behind the bar. Yumi called back that Hey wasn't a name. She poured sriracha on my Mac and Grilled Cheese and said it was a tasteless clump of carbs, why else had I been eating it every day if not to talk to her?

To Jenny I proposed to get rid of her guilt. If I went on a date with Yumi, Jenny could feel better about sleeping with her crush. She threw my phone at the wall. This was about my desires, she said, my inferiority complex, my weird racial hang-ups, not hers. She was so certain that I started to wonder. Had I made it all up? I had thought we believed in each other so much we didn't need to hide what we wanted. But now I wasn't sure. It was the middle of winter, and she pushed me outside and shoved my face into the snow. She explained that my face would dry, but it wouldn't mean she hadn't humiliated me.

For about a week, brushing away the cobwebs, I considered humiliation. I considered the possibility that I was humiliating myself. But if there was one thing humiliation could tell you, it was whose rules you were playing by, what was or was not considered taboo.

I didn't know how to tell Jenny that I was trying to take responsibility, not shirk it. The problem was her belief in her own power. She thought it was a choice whether or not to act on her desire, just like she thought she could choose to desire her coworker or not. But it was really circumstances that determined that choice—she didn't sleep with him not because she didn't want to, but because she didn't think she should. (In the end she didn't sleep with him because the circumstances changed. She didn't want to prove me right.) What I could do was free the circumstances of her desire. I took Charlotte to The Cave and asked her to give Yumi and me her blessing. I knew involving our kid would convince my wife I was serious about humiliating myself for her.

The sound of bars rattling woke me. I had cried my fears to sleep. I opened my eyes in the holding cell, which was typical. What in life wasn't a holding cell? A white face grinned down through the bars as if I should know whose it was. Behind me my cellmate snored peacefully, unaware of our visitor. From the floor, looking up at the man's square chin, I did have a strange sense of familiarity. I wondered where it was from. He had pointy earlobes and yellow hair, double eyelids and a long, bent nose. I rubbed blood into my cheeks. He said he was a detective offering help. "You're in the clear," he said. "Witnesses turned up after all."

I understood the change was in other people's opinions, not mine.

"Anyway I don't consider my relationship with Jenny to have anything to do with you, so there's no reason I shouldn't help you."

For a moment this confused me more. But then I remembered where I had seen him. I had looked up at that chin, those earlobes and nostrils, from the backyard of my ex-family's house.

I choked and coughed. I couldn't see how this helped me.

"You okay? Don't want anyone to say we 'mistreated' you here." His giant hands shrank into air quotes. "You even got a visit from a detective."

"Your relationship with Jenny may have nothing to do with me," I said. "But my relationship with her has something to do with you."

"Your relationship with Jenny doesn't exist," he said with a smile.

Another thing that had disappeared. Weren't detectives supposed to find missing things?

"How did you know I was here?" I asked.

"You want the good news? Or the bad?"

"In my eyes," I said, "you're the one behind bars."

He laughed and rubbed his nose.

"Tell me," I said, "in a murder case, wouldn't it be suspicious if the victim had just broken up? Wouldn't the first person questioned be the ex-girlfriend?" I had thought about it all night, and I couldn't get rid of the idea that if Sandra had seen Matt's body on the news, the police would have already questioned her.

The sound of the gun handle on the bars woke my cellmate, who stared up at my ex-wife's boyfriend with fear and hatred. I liked the murderer more than ever. A cell was a mutual habitat.

"Listen," the detective said, getting angry now. "We questioned the woman too. Don't think you can do my job."

He was the second cop in that station to say that to me. It must be a sore point—they felt attacked when people pointed out their attacks. I never wanted to do their job though. If anything I wanted them to do their job.

My cellmate bit his fingers and spat out the bits of skin at me.

"On TV," I said, "whenever someone gets murdered it's always the partner who did it."

"It's always the partner in real life," the detective said.

Well.

I asked what the good news was.

Finally a genuine emotion crossed his face. It was a kind of amused wish to do me harm. "Charlotte is here, in the station," he said, licking his bottom lip.

"That's the good news?"

"And the bad news," he said with pleasure, "is that I didn't know you were here. I found out because she asked me to get you out."

HONG GILDONG

How to be a *Homo sapien*, father of a *Homo sapien*, member of *Homo sapiens*? I was in a police station where I had been arrested for possibly killing my neighbor, and in my apartment lived a doppelgänger who had possibly killed my doppelgänger, and my daughter waited for me. I asked to use the restroom. While the detective supervised me I washed my hands up to my elbows, then washed my hair with pink hand soap and dried it with paper towels, then washed my hands again. I told the detective that my cellmate had been racially profiled. He said his rule was never trust a man he saw pee. I got my possessions back. The dog half was leaking cotton. Near the station entrance stood my daughter, with her hands on her hips and a purple backpack slung over one shoulder, her face longer, eyes smaller, cheeks higher, taller, etc., than I remembered. She wore a space-themed T-shirt and a plaid miniskirt, the tips of her hair dyed purple—only the tips—and waxed at odd angles. I remembered the baby fat that used to make her frown cute, now a ghost in her cheeks. We were the only one-and-a-half Asian people in the entire station, a ratio I became more aware of the more everyone else tried to figure it out.

I extended the dog half through the light years between us.

"What's that?" Charlotte asked.

"Half of a stuffed animal."

"Half?"

"Your mom has the other half."

She wiped her eyes with her fists and shook her head. "You're giving me a broken toy?"

"Not broken," I said. "Individuated." I offered her the paper towel in my pocket, which I had saved in case I cried, but she pushed it away. "You're a sight to make someone's eyes sore," she said, her eyes red. She still had her old way with words.

"I had other gifts too," I said. "They disappeared."

"I feel like I should chaperone this," said the detective. "But I don't want to. Let's just say I did."

I put my hand out for Charlotte to take. She put the dog half back in my palm.

What could I do? I petted it, since I could use the support.

———

During the cab ride Charlotte spoke only to direct the driver through the streets of Somerville, not answering when I asked how she had known I was in jail. She still wasn't ready to talk to me. The driver let us off with obvious relief. We got out at the top of a hill—I didn't see what was so special about it unless it was the view, which made it clear that Boston had been built with zero planning. The streets were old horse paths, colonial forays. A city built on the infrastructure of who knew whom. On the platform beside us reared a bronze cavalryman, dumbly patriotic, growing further and further from the history in which he was a freedom fighter, not a terrorist. Someone had fit one of the red anti-America hats over his oversized head.

I waited for my daughter to talk. I wanted to recognize her right of way. I wanted to love better, evolve, make up for lost etc. In other words I wanted to be present. In order to do so I couldn't think about how Jenny probably didn't know our kid had freed me from jail on a school day or what my team would do without me in the Looking Glass or how Sandra had hidden Matt's murder from me or the email my God the email. Being present with Charlotte, I realized, meant erasing the presence of other people . . . this didn't seem right. I needed Yumi to explain it to me again. How could I understand the difference between murder and disappearance if I couldn't understand the difference between being present and being presence?

Charlotte held the dog head by the ear and shook the loose stuffing out of the hole. I must have given the half back to her. Then she dug the rest of the stuffing free with her finger. She left the head on that finger so that the body drooped past over her knuckles onto the back of her hand, a puppet. She pointed its sagging jowls at me and bared her teeth, which had come in late at almost nine. I had the baby ones in a resealable bag.

She was a twelve-year-old teenager now, full of mis-attitude.

With the dog half leading the way she climbed onto the platform, and I followed. As I stood before that open vista the air felt somehow clearer and more expansive. I tried to breathe in the vista and breathe out jail. Charlotte frowned over the city as if disgusted with everyone in it living their small, no-vista lives.

"That driver acted like we had super B.O. or something," she said at last. "What an asshat. I bet his kids hate him." She unzipped the side of her bag. In the pocket was a pack of menthols. She exchanged the dog half for the cigarettes and tapped the box on her bare thigh.

Was this who she was? I wondered whether she remembered how my parents had died. She had never known them, so maybe they didn't seem connected to her.

I wanted either to open the pack for her or to absorb its slow death in her place.

"Aren't you going to tell me not to smoke these?" she asked, adding "Dad" late enough to show it was an afterthought.

"It's your decision?" I said. "There are more constructive rebellions. Probably. Remember when you beat up those two white boys who called you names at school?"

She weighed the pack in her hand and smelled the wrapper.

"But who am I to say?" I added.

"That's right," she said. "There's the truth. You don't care either way."

This seemed like an intentional misunderstanding. I listened anyway.

She said she hadn't forgotten for an instant how I had left it up to her, when she was nine and her parents were divorcing and she was bullied every day at school, whether or not I should continue parenting her. This was not a misunderstanding: It was a progression of circumstances that confused both of us.

"I still remember that like gangbusters," she said. "I still remember that better than Disney World."

I hadn't taken her to Disney World, that must have been her mom.

She drew back her arm, and I flinched. But she was too far away to hit me, I just wished to be hit.

Right before she tossed the pack down the hillside, I noticed it was still in its wrapper.

"Why wouldn't you see me yesterday?" she asked softly.

I chewed my lip, swallowed the rising jello. *Disappear doppelgänger murder.* I didn't want to worry her too much. If I could have, I would have taken her away a long time ago from this place in which you could be murdered for your looks—or, just as easily, for someone else's.

She got the dog half back out of her backpack.

I tried to explain. But how could I explain my internment without explaining all of the historical context as to why race might complicate my upstairs neighbors' relationship and why Charlotte could pass for white but only when she wasn't with me and why I could be locked up and also released so easily, unlike my cellmate, and even why her grandparents and therefore I and therefore she were in this country in the first place and the sad fact that the most accurate predictor of your future was not you or your intentions but the actions done to your family in the past?

"Race isn't the point," she said. "The point is you weren't in jail when Mom called. The point is you didn't want to see me again. The point is you didn't want to see me so badly that you went to jail."

I tried to translate what she meant by *point*. "You're saying I went to jail," I clarified, "just so I wouldn't have to see you. I *wanted* to disappear?"

"Are you asking a question?"

Maybe it wasn't language that betrayed me, but tone and expression. "How did you know I was there?" I tried again.

"Gosh, I don't know, ever heard of *Find my iPhone*?"

I got out my cell. I had missed plenty of calls and several inappropriate texts, some from Jenny and some from Sandra. None from Yumi. Was one of them tracking me? My phone was only a year old. A ghost breathed down the back of my neck. I shrugged, trying to shake it off. Then I pictured myself, an estranged dad, shrugging at his daughter. "That dog isn't a finger puppet," I said. "Its other half is a cat." My battery was almost dead.

"You're pathetic."

I was pathetic. But that was typical. In her presence my presents failed me. I didn't know a normal way to express exceptional love.

Charlotte stalked the platform in a sort of faux catwalk. She was a miracle of survival. Her mother was right—even I couldn't fuck her up. A breeze rose, and I shifted position to keep my jail smell from blowing into her nose.

"I'm deeply, paternally sorry," I said. "I should have been there yesterday and in general. I didn't know how to raise you. I wished for you a beautiful life." I pointed down the hill to where the cigarette pack had disappeared. "Those menthols were a test?"

"Don't cry," she warned, adjusting her purple hair.

Liquid was coming out of me now, maybe that was why I felt so empty.

I remembered, in second grade, Charlotte had gotten a riddle from school: what is both rigid and flexible at the same time? I had said water, which was 33 percent wrong. All of the other parents got it 100 percent right. The answer was people.

"The point is," she said, "you never cared about me enough to stop me from doing anything. You were supposed to protect me."

I nodded.

"Instead you pushed me like some kind of Energizer Bunny—on and on."

She swiped something from her face, a cobweb, and her hair wobbled. She shuffled her feet, stuck out her arms for balance, then went back to being a woman. My heart never stood a chance.

"I hear you," I said. "I see you."

"No." She came up beside me. It took everything I had not to try and lift her onto my shoulders. "Be who you are. Like okay, you grew up a little. But also I just asked Mom's boyfriend to get you out of the slammer and you gave me half a stuffed animal. Freak you."

"I really was going to meet you yesterday—" I started.

She made a smoking motion with her empty hand. The design on her T-shirt appeared to be a glow-in-the-dark star. When she held her fingers to her lips, they were in the shape of a pistol. She aimed at me.

"You were going to meet me," she finished, "but you were too chicken."

"I was scary," I said, trying to get her to remember how she used to mistake the word *scared*. During a thunderstorm she would shout, "I'm scary. I'm scary." Sometimes, I realized now, I would pretend to run away from her when she needed me for comfort.

"You don't get a get-out-of-jail-free card," she said, holstering her fingers. "If you were scared, how scared do you think I was?"

"Every day," I said, "the last 792 days, I have wanted to see you. But every day I have also been scary. I didn't want to ruin your chances of becoming someone else's daughter."

She seemed to move in slow motion. She scrambled away from me, clapped her hands.

"Someone else's daughter?" she said. Clap. "What the literal freak?"

I was an orphan, estranged adoptee, divorcé, deadbeat dad, one half of two Matts. I had meant to give Charlotte what I didn't have. I had meant to give her a sign that I loved her. Why couldn't I make my words mean what I said?

Clap. "Don't you even know why we came here?"

She opened her palms as if to indicate the entire hilltop. The statue seemed familiar, proud and bloodthirsty, but a hundred others like it occupied Boston. You could even follow a trail of bloodshed around the city from one slaughter to another. In other words: dude was your typical war hero and it didn't comfort me. The rest of the hill was grass and two trees.

I shook my head no.

Then Charlotte did a strange thing. She lifted the dog head to her ear, seemed to listen to it, and finally screamed as if to translate what the dog told her.

Here is what I thought: She was transferring her pain to the toy.

When she finished screaming for the dog she said, "You really don't remember? Really? Really? You told me if I ever had to run away that I should come up here and you would find me." She stomped; her shoes lit up, little lighthouses she ignored with each wreck of her feet. "I've been coming here for years and you never showed."

I tried to push aside my excitement that she still wore light-up shoes, that they still fit her body size and personality, in order to remember . . . When had I told her to meet here? I still saw nothing special about this hill. Giving her the option did sound like something I would do—I could imagine imagining the rest of her difficult life and offering her a way out—but why here? Until now I had never even known this hill existed. I never went to Somerville at all. There was nothing here that I couldn't do equally poorly at lower altitudes.

"Well?" she asked.

I really tried not to think what I was thinking.

She squatted and dug furiously with one bare hand and one dog. Dirt piled up behind her.

I was thinking maybe the other Matt had told her.

"What are you doing?" I asked anxiously.

"Duh, I'm digging."

In her hole something brown and flat appeared. Soon I saw it was cardboard. Then it was the lid of a box. It must have been buried pretty deep. Charlotte cleared dirt until there was a big enough opening to see the entire size of it—a regular Amazon shipping box about big enough to hold an instrument.

A burp came out of me and she wrinkled her nose.

"A couple of weeks ago I was up here and I found this."

She opened the top. Inside were the toys I had bought over the past three years. Right on top was the dog-cat, fully assembled/not broken. I couldn't explain this. It was not something that had an explanation in cause and effect. I really wanted to feel surprised.

"You buried this," Charlotte said, "right?"

I did not bring a box here and bury it, I did not know a thing about this, yet she waved the dog half in my face. And she had a point. Existence was futile. Intention meant nothing if effects had no direct cause. You watched where you were going and yet you fell in a manhole. Did you black out for a moment or did the manhole move itself? Did you do something wrong to the kid who called you a Chink or did the attack belong to someone else? It was possible *I* had been murdered and the other Matt was still alive. All impossibilities were equally and

145

oppositely possible. If I disappeared without ever having appeared, who would take responsibility for that?

"I'm pretty sure it wasn't me," I said.

"You've wanted to see me for eight hundred days and it wasn't you—do you want me to believe that? Why? Just because I told you I never wanted to see you again or because I wouldn't give my blessing to your side-chick? Ew."

"I didn't know how to be a parent," I said.

"No. You didn't."

"I don't remember telling you to run away though."

"You send a couple of cards a year," she said, shivering with nerves. "*You* ran away."

She lifted her dirt-stained hands to her face and painted her cheeks brown. "Why are you so dumb?" she said.

I rushed forward and threw my arms around her.

Or I tried to. She squirmed away. My skin remembered how tiny she had once been. Now she was tall and wiry and mud-streaked and furious and hurt. Child and adult. I tried to save on the surface of my skin that instant of touch. But it was the same thing I had done with the toys: held on to my own disappointing. She stomped again, lighting up her feet, and her little fists shook at her sides.

"I freaked up," I said. "No excuses. I didn't show up. Sorry Daddy was dumb."

She sneered. She didn't like this claim on her lexicon. I wasn't cool. I was ew. I was scary.

I remembered how my adoptive parents used to say they adopted me because I spoke English so well. And they didn't mean compared to the other foster kids—we were all native speakers—they meant compared to the me they wouldn't have adopted.

I had been trapped by language ever since I'd thought it could save me. The hardest thing in this world was to really say something. I had replaced myself with language—first English and then zeros and ones.

I had grown up watching my parents try to speak a language that wasn't theirs. To compete with the other Chinese restaurant in town, which was Japanese, they encouraged smoking, even making a cigar room. They died one after the other of lung cancer. Who killed them? The easiest thing in this world was to get yourself killed without knowing who killed you. After the second funeral I mixed their ashes together and threw them off the top of a hill, over as much earth and as many people as I could, so that their ashes could go places they had never gone in life, so they could ride in the folds of other people's coats to Peru, Algeria, back to Korea again. They had been so sure that we would return to Korea triumphantly—not to resume life, but to start it. They believed to their deaths that to be an American was to eat bad Chinese food and smoke cigars and tell unfunny jokes to strangers. I stood at the top of that hill, and I threw their ashes into the wind willy-nilly, and only after they were gone did I realize they wouldn't have wanted that. I wanted it. I wanted us to get free of what we wanted.

"Freaking dumb," Charlotte said. We were as restless as regret. "Did you really think a box full of toys would make me forgive you?"

I must have thought so once, but I hadn't for a long time.

"Do you want to be my friend, Dad?"

"I want to try being your dad again," I said, "for as long as I'm able to stay alive."

Her eyes softened. "My friends are all freaks anyway," she conceded. She wiped her nose on her sleeve, then chewed her lip, as I do. Small progress.

A roar came around the corner, and two SUVs sped by. First one and then the other swerved slightly into the middle of the road as they went around her.

I didn't rescue her, and she survived.

She scratched the palm of one hand with the fingernails of the other. I rubbed my knuckles as she scratched. But this time there *was* an ant. I brushed it off. She sniffled and wiped her hands on her glow-in-the-dark star, then took out a cell phone. Jennifer and I had agreed not to give her one until she was a teenager. I kicked dirt back into the hole, and asked her to move onto the sidewalk so she wouldn't get hit. She was all hard angles, underfed, all fugitive time.

She rolled her eyes. "I can't stand this anymore. You're making such an obvious *effort*. Is it that hard to be with me?"

I shook my head. I held my arms open.

Then she screamed again.

Before I knew it she was halfway down the hill. Her footsteps thudded farther and farther away from me. She was so fast. I had to remember again that she was older, stronger, bitterer. Her purple schoolbag flopped up and down. Her skirt flapped. I followed the lighthouses of her feet.

I was alone again—*marooned* was the word for it. Though I must have taught her to do exactly what she had done. To keep moving until she wasn't leaving one person but approaching someone better.

On the ground where she had started running, a workbook lay fallen or dropped. It was the kind of workbook students use while learning to write Korean, a grid with a box for each syllable. Was Charlotte learning Korean now? Even counting me she had no one to speak it with. I opened to the first page, it was only half-full. Over and over again she had written: 홍길동. The rest of the workbook was blank.

I went back to the box and closed it up, taking only the dog-cat. Then I filled the hole back in with dirt and smoothed out the top so only Charlotte and I would know it was there.

BREAKING UP

I found an empty bench and lay down to cry, pretending to be a sleeping homeless person. I envied the power the homeless had over sheltered people. Wherever a homeless person appeared, making their invisibility visible, sheltered people tried to disappear.

In my dreams Charlotte and I sat in a theater watching a black-and-white noir. I knew this was some kind of daddy-daughter day; I was supposed to apologize. She kept her eyes glued to the screen. In the film the private eye was me. I locked the door and hung a "Closed" sign. I flipped through a thick case file. I narrated that I had to be alone to get my work done—my clients always screwed things up, since they didn't really want answers, they wanted the mystery prolonged. The mystery shined a faint light in their dull lives. I sympathized, but it was my job to give them the information they had hired me to give them. It was the information I satisfied, never the client. Suddenly the door rattled. The dream shifted. With a start I remembered that I was in the audience with Charlotte. I realized the office didn't belong to the on-screen me. Outside stood the real private eye, trying to get in. Who was the on-screen me? A client? A suspect? In the theater Charlotte pinched my arm. "Dad," she said, "you're mixing everything up. It's not a murder mystery, it's a love story. And stop talking to yourself. Everyone's looking at us. Ew. It's bad enough you aren't wearing any pants."

A homeless man shook me awake. He said he'd never seen me before, but I should know this was his bench, he'd taken the money someone had dropped, as it was rightfully his, the most he could leave me with was half of my stuffed animal. In his hand was the dog-cat—in two parts, just like the last one. I must have taken it from the box. I wondered whether the toy naturally made people want to rip it apart. He inspected both heads and handed the dog to me. "Now stop crying and find your own bench. It's going to be okay." I felt oddly accepted. I got up, and he lay where I had lain.

I went the long way around to Mount Auburn Street and walked back to The Cave to clear my head. The perv rushed out and blocked the door. He said it was bad for business, breaking up, and I should leave if I knew what was good for me, he'd always wanted to kick my Chinese ass.

In the past I would have pretended to leave and later would have either snuck in or waited until Yumi's shift ended. But something was different now. I wiped my eyes. Maybe because my daughter had freed me from jail or because she had run away again after three years or because she had waited for me on that hill before or because the toys had reappeared in a box in the ground—I didn't know exactly why—I felt that what I would have done in the past had never worked. It had taken me that long, probably, to realize that I hadn't individuated myself, I had ripped myself in half and dumped out my insides to fit my head on another person's idea of my body.

Anyway the perv no longer intimidated me. He had never intimidated Yumi, and now I knew why. He was a cliché. Not that he wasn't real—he *was* real, his reality just depended on there being only one accepted view of reality, and no more. The pervy owner, the dudebro Harvard kids, the police were exactly whom they were expected to be—because they hadn't realized they were expected to be anyone at all. The really scary thing was trying to love and be loved against expectations.

My thoughts went something like this. In the moment all I felt was anger toward the perv.

"My ass is Korean," I said, "and it has a second-degree black belt in taekwondo." Upon further consideration I added: "It has nothing to fear, but fears myself."

The perv disappeared inside, and one minute and twenty-four seconds later Yumi came out.

She was still Yumi, she still had the same purposeful aura, as if what confused other people clarified something for her. She must have figured out how to live as a doppelgänger, I thought. Her hair looked a little glossier, her cheeks a little fuller, she was taking care of herself. Before she could say anything, I said I took full responsibility, I couldn't love better enough.

"What are you doing here?" she asked as if I hadn't just answered that question.

I repeated myself. I was the one to blame for driving my neighbor to his ex's apartment, for taking the keys from his cold body, for sending texts instead of coming in person sooner—

"All of your sentences start with *I*," she said, brushing her hair from her face.

Well. The first rule was to know your audience.

"Matt was murdered," I said. "The other Matt, I mean. I haven't— no one has murdered me. Yet."

She shook her head. "That's basically still *I*."

But how else to explain? I was scary. The fact that *Matt was murdered* also meant *I was murdered* was exactly why I needed to tell her about it. As doppelgängers, as lovers, we had a shared base of knowledge that almost no one else in the world could claim.

"If you're done," Yumi said, "why don't you get out of here?"

For the first time I could remember, I felt frustrated with her, I felt that her self-clarity left no room for conversation. Conversation was about doubt. Even when she quit medical school it wasn't because she didn't know herself, but because she did.

"Look at your face," she said. "I knew you weren't really going to love better. You're just a customer, not anyone special. You have nothing to offer a relationship."

I couldn't help myself. "Then I guess you wasted three years of your life," I said.

She shrugged. She turned to the window and her reflection rested a hand on its head.

"Won't you just hear one thing," I said, "about Matt's murder? I need your advice." If only I could stay alive until I saw Charlotte again.

As if she had read my mind Yumi said, "You're always asking women to get you out of trouble. You know that? I'm not doing your feeling for you anymore."

I was pretty sure I hadn't known that until then.

"I have to get back to lunch."

She walked back. As she went I noticed her reflection wore a regular blouse and skirt, not her uniform. "Are you not working today?" I asked.

She didn't even answer. When the door shut her reflection seemed to remain in place, one hand on its forehead, meeting my gaze. For as long as I stared at it, I mean, it stared back at me. It was as if her reflection was now mine—maybe we had swapped, why not? Stranger things etc. I tried to think of anything I might have said to her that could have helped her as much as she had helped me. I must have said some stuff if she had stayed with me for so long.

Then Yumi came into the frame. She glided over to her reflection, gesticulated and laughed. Her reflection nodded. They both sat down.

One of them was Sandra.

I tore a page out of Charlotte's workbook and upon further consideration went inside to borrow a pen. The perv lent it to me aggressively, jabbing it into my palm.

"You're null of surprises," I said.

On the loose sheet I wrote: *Dear Yumi, You're right. And I'm sorry you had to teach me that. Plus I'm sorry I interrupted your lunch. Thanks.*

For some reason my sincerity came out sarcastic.

I balled up the letter. Instead I copied 홍길동 into the grid squares beneath Charlotte's handwriting. It was hard to tell our letters apart. On the other hand I had copied her. I tried to write in my own hand, but it had been decades since I had written in Korean. I remembered writing 홍길동 in a similar workbook of my own. He had meant a lot to me as a boy, Hong Gildong—a hero like Robin Hood, except Korean and magical. Because he hadn't been allowed to call his father Father and his brother Brother, he became an outlaw. The circumstances of his language became the circumstances of his resistance. But what I remembered best was that to protect himself, he had created seven doppelgängers out of straw, who could be killed while he stayed alive.

I called the operator and got the number for Charlotte's school. When someone answered they said she had already given them my note, not to worry. They knew she was late because I took her to the dentist that morning, so her tardiness was excused.

Not to worry, I said to myself. *Just a little forgery.*

After leaving me on that hill, Charlotte had gone straight to school as if it was a complete and ordinary day. She had used my handwriting to excuse herself. Maybe she often did so. Maybe that was why my writing looked the same as hers. Not to worry.

I set a timer on my watch for one hour of crying and no more.

THE AIRING OF GRIEVANCES

America is a hall of mirrors that makes you a taller or shorter you, a wider or slimmer you, a curvier or straighter you, a longer-legged or no-legged you, any other appearance besides race. Why was I not the other Matt? Why was he not me? The one story Sandra had told me about Matt was about his brother's death. He had died on an unusually warm day near the end of winter. Their childhood house bordered a hill that sloped down to a skating pond, and a sledding run far enough to hit the ice meant neighborhood bragging rights. Matt's brother had built a jump to give him extra distance. He died still pumping his fist. Someone must have already cracked the ice before them and left no warning. Matt raced down after his brother but couldn't save his brother without falling in himself.

That was what had made the other me so determined—a promise to live for two lives. He worked twice as hard, cared twice as much, and still didn't live to medium age. I too had made a vow like Matt's, after my parents died, but I hadn't stuck to it. I had learned to hack into the system: another family, a "better" school, an acceptable career. But in the end I came up against defenses I couldn't hack into, because I was inside them. It was like that science joke based on the *Matrix* movie, that if at some point in time we ever *could* create a simulated world, then of course we would make many, as many as video games or ice cream flavors, and with infinite possible simulations and only one reality, the odds that ours was the real world were laughable—we were almost certainly simulations of a more advanced us. A system within a system within a system.

I too had made my vow in the woods. I had made mine in the middle of the night. I had snuck out of my adoptive parents' house— they still fostered me then and I was trying hard to be good enough to adopt even if what was *good* wasn't up to me—and I crept into the woods in the moonlight toward the small pond that was back there. Soon I found myself kneeling on the mossy banks. My future adoptive parents had taught me to kneel. But I wasn't praying. I had gone to my knees out of the strong feeling that if I walked any farther, I would keep going until I vanished, and that I wanted this. I was terrified with want. In that moment I had vowed to give up my desires in order to be considered in other people's desires.

The moon was one of those orange moons on a clear night, and the pond glowed almost yellow. Somewhere nearby a stream or a brook trickled in from the woods. I looked for its source, and instead a human figure appeared . . . or maybe I was rewriting memory now . . . at first I thought it was a reflection. It knelt on the opposite bank in the same pose as me.

———

When I got to work, at two, the first thing I saw was an oversized sign on a metal stand. At first I thought I had the wrong floor. The sign stood about two feet high and three-and-a-half feet long, the font simple and nonserif, attention catching though not attention keeping. It looked like the signs outside of concert halls. It read: "The Airing of Grievances." What that meant I had no idea—but I planned to do something about it.

In a square on the floor sat Tokki, Yoonha, Sung, and Phil Collins. They sat on the floor because they didn't have chairs. They didn't have chairs because they didn't have cubicles. Other than the sign up front and the tea station in the middle and my office at the back, everything else was gone. It was as if someone had moved my team out and was moving a new team in, without telling us. Woo Woo came over to greet me, and the others eyed each other with career panic. I didn't know how to comfort them, because it wasn't comfort they needed, it was careers.

A box, a building, was meant to contain. Life was an attempt to avoid being dispossessed of life. Consumption was lightness. The universe was a consumer, a predator, a thief. It was stepping up its thefts. We needed to step up our defenses.

Woo Woo tapped the sign with his knuckles and it sounded like starting a toast. Phil Collins gestured to me and then to the emptiness. One side of his face grimaced, the other stuck in his usual careerist smile.

"You're finally here," Sung said loudly. "We only sent a million texts. Where were you?"

"Please tell us you know what's going on?" Yoonha asked.

"What happened?"

"Are we going to be okay?"

Woo Woo threw an arm around me for the others' benefits. "Were we supposed to dress down today?" they whispered. "You smell like you haven't taken a shower."

"I've been in jail," I whispered back.

"Not funny. Ha. Ha."

"They don't need slogans anymore?" Phil Collins asked. "Are we fired?"

"Not needing slogans is unlikely."

"What does it even mean—the Airing of Grievances?"

"Why are they doing this to us?"

Their questions were not unreasonable. Most disappearances weren't realized suddenly but little by little over time.

Tokki hadn't said a word so far, which was unlike her. I pulled her aside and asked her to join me for lunch, since I hadn't gotten to eat at The Cave. I reassured her that it would be strictly business, not Matt, related, and I would let her choose where.

We ended up at the bad Thai buffet across the street, likely because it was fastest.

"Hurry up," she said. "Everyone is freaking out that we left together. What's up with the sign?"

I indicated that we should get our food first. I was starving. As soon as we filled our plates I told her that I would resign. I would file a harassment report against myself and recommend a successor. Not to run away but to reinstate their norms.

Tokki looked like she was going to throw up. "Is that what the Airing of Grievances means?"

"I don't know anything about that," I said. "But I can ask."

"What happened to our cubes? Where were you all day? Why are you dressed like that?"

I said I wanted her opinion on my replacement.

"Matt?" she said. "The whole floor is empty except for your office. Due respect, you think I care who replaces you? Are we being replaced?"

That was when I saw how she saw things. I had gotten so used to nothing making sense.

A shout came from outside. Then a crowd appeared, waving signs. As they drew closer to the restaurant Tokki scarfed down her plate. I said I would ask the company about the cubes and the sign, but they shouldn't worry about their jobs. I didn't tell her the disappearing was probably because of me. I told her I had personal business with my daughter that morning. That was why I looked like this.

"Fine," Tokki said. "Let's just go back."

I had eaten two spoonfuls of tom yum goong and one long, dry noodle.

"Am I doing the right thing?" I asked.

The rally passed by the window. Their signs referred to police shooting black men. *You Don't Get to Choose Who Is Human*, one said. Another said: *Respect Existence or Expect Resistance.*

If You Believe All Lives Matter, a little girl's sign read, *Why Don't You Believe My Life Matters?*

"Why do you want my validation?" Tokki asked me. "I'm leaving."

In the middle of the crowd I seemed to recognize two familiar figures, since they looked the same. Maybe I saw what I wanted to see. Yumi often recruited for demonstrations with a laundry list of reasons Asian Americans should protest. After certain late shifts she would take the last T to Chinatown so she wouldn't have to hear English for a while, then pay the extra fare for a cab back.

"I want your validation," I said to Tokki, "because you know how much better I can be."

But she had already left me there.

———

Back at the office the cubes had not reappeared. No one was airing their grievances. I had to be the boss. What was our grief? I hacked into my team's work accounts. I checked their HR files, past performance reviews—but they were all totally normal. The Looking Glass was totally normal. Etc. Grievance was relative. In my inbox was an email from a superior I had never met, which said I was getting a promotion, because my ideas for the dog-cat had been so good. My ideas had been especially bad, and the dog-cat was destined to fail. But maybe that was what they wanted to know all along. The slogan I submitted was "Which End Poops?" It was possible that if there was an instinct (in America) to tear the toy apart, then that instinct was an attempt to provide relief. Possible, though unlikely. I replied to the email with a formal complaint against myself and the recommendation that Yoonha be named interim manager.

I hacked into Sandra's file, and her CV was a long list of achievements that no one outside the industry would understand. I didn't understand. There was nothing about her personal life. This was typical. All that mattered to the company were company matters. I could have hacked into her email, but I had limits. Instead I hacked into my own file. I wasn't surprised to find the other Matt's qualifications, the other Matt's work experience, the other Matt's sample writing, alongside my personal information. I wanted to live in the other Matt's city of the future, home of the now. His copywriting carried a sense of perpetual motion, constant forward momentum, as if the words were written anew each time in the instant before you read them. Will this guy be content with a simple management position? one of the notes on my application read. I wondered why Jenny hadn't set the truth straight, told them I was misrepresenting myself. Someone in HR had read my file thirty-six times. A response to the first note said: Does it have to be another Korean?

I gathered these grievances and went out to my team to demonstrate. For the first time in my life someone wanted to hear my grievances. My team sat in a pentagon now instead of a square, coming together, as humans always had, out of paranoia. What else made us fitter for survival?

I stepped up to the sign, feeling that if I could air everything that grieved me, the yellow yarn might reappear. The very path I had taken through life was one of grief. "Here is my Airing of Grievances," I said. "We are all straw versions of ourselves, and we have to be for protection. I had wanted us to avoid making straw selves at work, so we could work on ourselves. But maybe without our defenses we would be murdered by our jobs. Each day is more and more straw. Maybe that's where the cubicles have gone, back to the straw they always were. More and more, little by little, we are becoming stuffed animals that cannot poop except from our mouths. We've got to get some relief. We've got to tear ourselves apart. We've got to evolve. If the real self is murdered, the straw selves can't live on. We're all figments of figments' imaginations . . ."

Their eyebrows squirmed. Tokki poked her chin over and over. I waited for someone to take over from me. No one did. I went on, though I had nowhere to go on. My grievance, basically, was that appearing was not the opposite of disappearing.

Finally Yoonha stood. "If we're going to do this," she said, "let's really do it. Let's start with how Tokki and I make less than the rest of you. Let's start with how you look at us." And she began a much longer and better thought-out list.

For the first time the Looking Glass seemed to be the place Sandra had said it would be, like it was revealing something you could see only by looking at yourself.

I sat in Yoonha's place on the carpet.

"People are always erasing me," Woo Woo said beside me. "You think you're so oppressed, boss? You don't know what you're doing, and yet you have this job."

The others joined in and piled on. Who was I to be aggrieved? In some ways I was better off than all of them.

"Are you guys listening to me?" asked Yoonha.

Things could be worse, etc.

"Listen to Yoonha," I said.

"I don't need you to step in," said Yoonha.

"This kind of complaining is the oldest trick in the book," Phil Collins said. "It's how white supremacy has always turned people of color against each other."

They turned on him then, and Yoonha and I were left. "What happens when all of our grievances are aired?" Yoonha asked me. I met her resigned eyes. I accepted their accusations, which were not oppression.

"You'll be the new boss," I said.

When they were done turning on Phil Collins, Sung said to me, "It's quite possible you're the one who got rid of the cubes. You've wanted to air your grievances from the moment you came in and told us our old ways wouldn't work anymore."

I shut my eyes and nodded. The fluorescent lights were oppressive.

"Dude," Sung murmured after a moment, "I wasn't trying to make you cry."

But I was crying for Charlotte and the future she would have if it was anything like the present.

I sent everyone home early. It was while I was leaving that I discovered what Sandra had meant about intimacy. In the lobby people milled and dispersed. I seemed to watch them from afar rather than from among them. It was my last day of work. I felt warm, like I could feel all of their body heat surrounding me. I looked out the glass into the square where the pointy church posed incessantly for photos. It was burning.

Fire poured out from under the archways and through the windows. The church had been built with stone and brick, but it was burning from the inside out. One of the stained-glass windows broke, and glass rained down on the square. If it kept burning, the mortar would loosen and the whole thing would come crashing down. Whoever was still inside would not survive. Yet in front of the church, no one seemed to care.

People went on photographing the whole thing as if it were part of a show. Other people walked past without a glance. No one in the lobby seemed to notice either. No one stopped to look except for me. I threaded my way through the crowd and out the revolving door.

When I got outside, the church stood as it always had, no fire.

I went back inside and the church burned and burned.

Even the end of the world wasn't the end of the world. I went back outside and walked past the complete and ordinary church to the cab pickup at the fish restaurant nearby.

I paid the cab extra to wait outside Charlotte's school. It was the same school I had met the principal of two years earlier, K-6. Afterschool activities were just letting out. Charlotte used to do soccer and music and take private lessons in self-defense. When she finally came out she was in running clothes, drenched with sweat. I had the cab driver pull into the car lane. I didn't want to mess up Charlotte's thing, and I didn't want her to emergency-exit me again, so I waited for her to come to me. I could hear her conversation with her two white buddies. They were talking about some video game where they made real money via a virtual store, which sold virtual things, to real people playing virtual lives. They didn't make any move to leave, they just stood around in a group and then sat in the grass in a group. When I asked the driver to pull up, I heard one of the white girls say to my daughter, "There's some Asian guy checking out me and Julie." She said it loudly enough to make sure I heard. A few white moms walked in to get their kids, chatting together, and stopped when the girl said that. They looked at the taxi, with me in it.

"Whoa, man," said the driver, "this isn't what I signed up for. I thought you were picking up your kid or something? Maybe your car's in the garage? I don't do any pedo stuff."

"No pedo stuff," I said softly.

Charlotte didn't look up, but she said, "He's not staring at you, he's staring at me."

The girl who had spoken up sneered. "How do you figure?"

Charlotte waved, and relieved I waved back.

"Do you know him?" the other girl, Julie, asked.

There was no hesitation. "I don't know him," Charlotte said. "It's just obvious he wants to know me. Typical creep." She grabbed their arms, and they marched off.

"I'm getting out of here," said the driver.

"Let's get out of here," I said.

The driver said I shouldn't make it sound like it was my idea when it was his. Money could only get you so far.

I was typical, I was a creep, it was typical for creeps to stare at my daughter. What she was saying was that her appearance mattered to me not because I was her dad, but because she stood out from her peers. It was creepy for me to be typical. If I wanted my particular appearance to matter to her, I had to destroy my apparent typicality.

THE SUSPECT SUBJECT

I waited for Sandra at home. I wondered how to take responsibility for the fact that she must have been the prime suspect in Matt's murder. All of his things had been moved out, all of his photos had been cut out of her albums, they had broken up and she was hurt and angry and scared. Had she escaped the investigation? Had she come here to finish the job? I must have suspected this from the moment I read my name so close to the word *murder*.

On the other hand I had the sneaking suspicion that I only suspected Sandra because I had never been able to trust her. I had never been able to trust her because I had never been able to trust myself around her. I could still look at her and see Yumi—which was surely a failing of mine, not her fault. I could still look at the photo of the other me on her wall, and see who I wished to be.

Sandra had been six when her father died. Her mother had come back from that expedition a different person, cold and unforgiving. She hadn't wanted to forgive herself. Her biology lessons became more and more extreme—e.g., the snake—they always seemed to be getting ready for some dangerous adventure. It felt to Sandra like the day her mother finally deemed her worthy, her mother would go back to her career and give up the whole parenting charade. Like this, Sandra grew up feeling disappointed with each success. She had the urge, she'd told me, drunk one night, to burn her life to the ground. Yet it wasn't until she met Yumi that she could see herself in any other life. I realized now that I had been disappearing for even longer than I had thought. It might even have started that night beside that pond, when I turned back to the house. Where had the *I* gone who on that night had been trying to dismantle my life? *Some I* had returned and continued on, but afterward I had never fully recognized myself. In the mirror I saw someone who every day grew further and further from the boy I had been before my parents died.

On the TV the news said the KKK-candidate had proposed a ban on Muslims, citing as precedent the concentration camps for Japanese Americans. There were no new stories, there was no new history. Every empire was the same empire. What changed was whose lives it took.

I played the electric keyboard for a while, reliving my childhood. I wished I had played for Charlotte. I played my mother's favorite song, about a boy and a girl who fell in love and so were never allowed to see each other again. Then, in a fit of self-hatred, I played "Arirang."

When Sandra got back I brought up everything that had happened in the past few days. I searched myself for fear—but I didn't find any. I calmly related finding her letter, my neighbor's suicide, jail, the toys showing up on the hill, Charlotte running away, what the detective had said about her as a suspect in Matt's death. I calmly asked what she had been doing in The Cave, with Yumi, how long she had been having secret rendezvous with her doppelgänger. What did they do? What did they share? I envied her ability to meet herself halfway.

When I finished Sandra said, "Matt, I need to tell you something."

I had thought this was what we were doing.

"Why do you think you're the only one who wants to disappear?"

Her hair bounced around her neck, newly cut. It made her look a little less like Yumi.

"I don't *want* to disappear," I clarified. "I want to stop my disappearance. I don't want to end up like Matt—sorry."

She held up her hand and sighed. It was a sigh that could blow your hair back.

"I mean I'm sorry your boyfriend was brutally murdered," I said, making things worse. "I acknowledge that's more than just disappearing."

"Stop," she said pleadingly.

I covered my mouth with my hands.

"I've been seeing a therapist," she said. "She's this great black woman with a bad sense of humor and three kids she slips into the conversation from time to time. The other day, when you never texted me to come back, I felt like I had come home again to find Matt gone. Most of the time I walk through this city and feel this weird sense of home. I can't get rid of this feeling, like I'm on some kind of side path, like I'm living a side life. Like hiking trails—I left the main trail. My therapist says this is all grief, the feeling that I'm in another world now."

I had had this feeling when I was adopted, but also when Charlotte was born. It was the feeling of your old circumstances not applying anymore.

"You want to know what Yumi and me do? We give each other comfort. She lets me read her class materials and we talk about what we've read and go to rallies for fair housing policies and wealth redistribution and women's health and so on. It feels like its own kind of therapy, with her."

I remembered when Yumi had shown me an article that said all Asian Americans are melancholics—unable to stop grieving the loss of an equality that had never been theirs to begin with. It was compelling to share ideas even when the sharing caused pain.

"Aren't you going to say anything back?" Sandra asked. "I'm trying to sympathize and get sympathy."

I still had my hands over my mouth.

I lowered my hands into my pockets and slipped my pointer finger into the dog half. Then I lifted it out, and the dog said, "Then can I become a *Homo sapien*?"

I barely saw her hand move before my left ear popped under her fingertips. She'd slapped me. A sharp whine echoed through my head. A little circle of heat spread between my ear and my cheek, then across my face. She gasped, surprised that she had hit me.

I didn't know how she wanted me to respond . . . it was a bad joke . . . the room softened, whitened. As a whine like a mosquito started in my ear I thought again about all of the words I would have liked to take back. In the moment they had all seemed to follow from the words before them. I recalled the ten-second delay after my neighbor's suicide. In those ten seconds his ex had asked me to take responsibility instead of her. You could repeat those ten seconds forever, and live a perfectly typical life.

"I've lived without sympathy for three years," I said. But as I said it I knew it wasn't true. "I have a family though. And I had Yumi. And I had my co-hallucinations."

"I don't know what you're talking about," Sandra said. "But I like you more somehow when you remind me less of Matt. It must be a problem of mine."

This was the first time someone had ever said they were the strange one, not me.

"I'm eating my regrets," I said. "I'm trying my softest."

Sandra shook her head and took another step away from my sex repeal.

"This may be bad timing," she said, "but what I'm trying to say is: I'm moving out. I'm moving on."

"What?"

"It's time for me to leave this house."

Well. I understood this time she could leave Matt first. But I was just beginning to figure out that leaving was no comfort. An old myth said that the Korean people came from a bear and a tiger who were told that to become human they must stay in a cave for one hundred days eating nothing but mugwort and garlic—the bear became a woman, but the tiger gave up partway through. The tiger stayed what it was, except that now it was ashamed of itself. Shame was the first part of it that turned human, and also what made it hunger for humans.

"Put out your hands," Sandra said.

I didn't want to, knowing what I knew about her mother.

She laid a journal in them.

So I was left with two journals—or one journal and one workbook. The one Sandra had given me was the journal from her nightstand, full of letters to Yumi either never sent or, stranger, retrieved for this very purpose.

"My sincerest thanks," I said sincerely. I regretted having nothing to give to her.

"And one more." She placed a sheet of paper on top.

The paper said: *DO NOT DISTURB, DIRTY BOXERS EVERYWHERE.*

In my dream I waited on a train platform for a long time, holding my ticket, for someone to meet me at the last boarding call. (Who was it? I knew in the dream but not afterward.) The train took off, and I took off with it, leaving my body behind until the right body would come along. Our bodies would join us later. The train stopped at my ex-family's house. My daughter chatted on the phone, negotiating the obstacles of a middle school girlhood, half-white, half-mature, pretty and freaky and different and feared. The train stopped at my own middle school, where the best and worst days had been days I wasn't noticed at all. How did you fight something that existed only in the imagination? After my parents died, six months apart, I had *wanted* someone to bring up their deaths, to offer something for my anger to hold on to, to treat me like a regular victim of an irregular tragedy, and no one would. What was it that could never be mentioned? Was it that in order to attract white customers my parents had hung photos of pleasant opium dens and made it seem Asian to smoke through dinner? Was it that they didn't trust white doctors, so their diagnoses came too late, and my dad refused surgery and died, or that my mom got the surgery and died of complications? Who had murdered them? Who had murdered our ability to talk about them? What I knew as a child was that murder was relative. Model was a minority. Love wasn't always used for love.

I jerked myself up from bed and blinked in the darkness. The dots and dashes on the alarm clock rearranged: *SOS*. Time called out for rescue. I crossed the room against an invisible force that threatened to wash out my legs. It was the force of where I shouldn't go, what I shouldn't do. I put on the suit Sandra had bought for me to wear to work in the Looking Glass. *Matt,* I said to myself, meaning someone else.

Matt, I said to myself.

In the suit I walked through the little hallway into the second bedroom, still as purple as the day my family moved out, and pulled a suitcase from Sandra's closet. It was already full, ready. On it a note read: *Pack me.*

All around were other notes Sandra had written to herself. She had pinned them to the back of the closet, to the headboard, to the walls. She had stuck them all around the frame that held the photo of her with the other Matt. There were smaller notes on objects like a pair of shoes I'd never seen her wear (*Goes only with the blue blouse and white jacket*). There were sets of photos all of the same square of sidewalk, the same edge of a puddle, the same doorway.

I read through a dozen or so of the notes—the most interesting ones were above her bed, she must have written them before sleep or arranged them there in some kind of dream logic.

Stop being attracted to injustice

Don't buy so much junk online, you're running out of money

Why do you feel so nervous in the Looking Glass?
I am not a nervous person.

You're idealizing the past. Matt did things to piss you off.
Remember them.

Why do you get turned on when you get angry?

Do something unexpected today. Something not you or Yumi.

If a. You want something and
b. You suddenly find it all around you
Remember that doesn't mean c. it was there all along

Tell Yumi about the time Mom tried to give you better stomach
bacteria.

Don't forget what you know about ads. A pet rock is still just
a rock.
What you own is your relationship to it.

Protest is a way of grieving what is too alive.

"Matt?" Sandra said sleepily. I had leaned over her to see better and my head was just above hers. She must have thought she was in a dream.

How to explain? Maybe it seems strange, but I wanted to explain I was respecting existence, or maybe I was expecting resistance. I wanted to bring up evolution and earthquakes and name changes. I wanted to relate her dead dad to my dead parents to the other Matt's dead brother to the other dead Matt. I wanted to accuse all of the mini-murders we suffered each day and all of their accomplices. Before the existence of *Homo sapiens*, time had been a continuous cycle of species, not a line leading up to one species at the expense of continuity. Human beings had created the concept of the end, because they had created the concept of the beginning. Where had my yellow yarn gone, I wondered. How else would I know where I stood?

I wanted to say all of this—but if I opened my mouth, what would come out was *meow*, what would come out was *my daughter*, what would come out was a cry for help. I was not an exception to humanity. The only cry was a cry to love better.

I took Sandra's hand. I pulled her up from the bed, and she blinked rapidly with sleep. She cupped my cheek, Matt's cheek. Her hand lingered—just short of making me fall in love. Moving in her sleep like that she seemed free and uncensored, which made me realize she usually was not. On the bedpost a Post-it read: *You used to have dreams. Don't forget.* Had she stopped dreaming? When? She dropped her hand from my face, and I lifted it again and held on. I searched once more for the yellow yarn, then regardless I walked us through the crack in the wall.

ONCE MORE TO THE WALL

Inside the two walls Sandra shuffled along still half-asleep. She seemed unable to open her eyes. I led us slowly. The light shone warm and low, like wherever we were it was sunset. The jello pressed against us, as thick and insistent as before. Everything—that is, no-thing—was the color of concrete. Sandra dragged on my left arm, her suitcase on my right. I was tiring, yet bursting with Mattness. Like before, wind swept into the cracks in my bones. If it never let up, a slight breeze could cripple you. I moved forward now into the pain. I felt like a toy coming to life, finding itself in production. I wasn't sure whether Sandra felt this toy thing too. She showed no reaction. With each step the gap at the base of my rib cage opened, until I seemed to walk myself inside out. Skin peeled back. My bones readjusted positions. Instead of my flesh protecting my bones, my bones protected my flesh. I wanted to give up, turn back, restart—the pain made the other wall seem far away—but ahead of me was the present, behind me was another eighty-four-hour blank.

I pushed through the jello, I tried to be the Matt Sandra needed me to be to get home. Again I had the feeling that another me waited on the other side—this time I would face that self and become me. This was my plan: to take responsibility for my twoness. My only regret was

Charlotte. I pictured her ahead of us too, also going to meet herself. I had seen her in three complete and different outfits, in three complete and different contexts. Maybe she too was realizing that we had to leave behind our old ways of loving each other in order to love better. From the second wall another crack tugged at me, as if trying to yank the yarn out of my mouth. And then some store of expired energy, useless before, surged through me and gave me a second burst. The jello quickly filled the vacated space. For a moment I almost became a part of that jello, I and Sandra and her suitcase like little cubes of fruit preserved in its jiggly reality. I had to get out of it before it filled me completely. I lowered my head to the second wall and made one last charge. As my head went through, the surface felt somehow both sticky and slick. My neck and shoulders and chest and finally the other half of me sucked through, and I felt Sandra come through behind me. We passed into whatever was on the other side. An intense loneliness struck me then, as if no one else existed or had ever existed or would ever exist again. With the loneliness came a powerful longing for obliteration. Or was the order the other way around? I clung to Sandra's hand, trying to convince myself she was still there and I couldn't give in to the jello, that we were in this together. I couldn't see or hear or smell. Her hand didn't seem to have any weight. The membrane of the wall stuck to and burned my skin, and for some reason my first thought was for the suit, which might ignite and fuse to me or reveal me naked and ashamed . . .

. . . and then it is an orange sky, the first break of dawn, grass and trees like a tiny park, and no one is waiting for us as we come out in the middle of nowhere.

CHAPTER 4: DEAR ME

THE COLLECTED LETTERS OF SANDRA KANG TO YUMI BAE

Dear Yumi,

I don't know why, but every email I send comes back undeliverable. So a letter must do. I apologize for my bad handwriting, though perhaps yours is the same.

    I've never seen anything like yesterday, never felt anything like the energy of that crowd. Thank you for inviting me. It would be easy for you to hate me, considering the events of the day we met. But maybe you have the same feeling now, that when we are apart, a part of us is missing? Thank you for giving me another chance.

    Anyway — the size of that crowd, the sheer organization it takes to shut down a thoroughfare, I can see what you mean about having something you actually <u>want</u> to put your body on the line for. (Our body?) I'm writing this letter because I didn't want you to think that's why I suddenly left the rally, because I didn't want to put my body on the line. I *didn't leave because of that. I felt like an imposter. An advertising career doesn't give a woman much faith in the discerning public. It doesn't give a woman much faith in discernment. The power of slogans and signs — is power built up over a whole history of dictating what's good and what's bad. I won't bore you if this isn't something you're interested in — but I've seen profits double with a single word change, the perceived deliciousness of "fresh" versus the perceived deliciousness of "delicious." One thing we always said at my old firm was that even a bad rating on a restaurant door is more welcoming than no rating. Another thing we said was that what makes a place welcoming has nothing to do with that place — it has to do with other places.*

Actually — that day made me realize that in my city there are hardly any demonstrations. I wonder why. It's not a sign of acceptance, I don't think. It's more like depreciation or something — like people don't think they can get much back on the investment that goes into protest. Though I know my parents used to do things like that, like picket a company to force it to take a stand. You said something like that yourself — about destroying something before you can love it. Maybe I'm screwing that up? You and Matt are always going on about love. Maybe I just miss my Matt. Ads, pain, love — in the end it all comes down to perceived value, like anything persuasive. The funny thing is — advertising isn't about destroying perceived value but about protecting and serving it. That's a joke I learned in the new firm. Here's another — the problem with advertising jokes is that they'll sell anything for a laugh.

I guess what I'm saying is I'm not the kind of woman who leaves her entire life behind and then believes it was a choice. I guess it depends what you call a choice in the first place. In the evolutionary science my mom studies, everything happens by variation. But I'll be thinking about what you said — that it was brave to leave. Right now, it seems braver to me to accept who you are. I feel like a coward for leaving. But maybe you can convince me it's possible to leave the past behind — or sell the past for the future.

Yours truly (ha ha),
Sandra

———

Dear Other Me,

I've been thinking — I guess I don't define personality like you do. Maybe the differences between us just come down to you growing up in a big family and me having only my mom. Like maybe we would have been the same if we had been sold the same stories? To go back to what I was saying before, my dad is dead (not to be too dramatic about it) and that's a differ- ence that wasn't my free will or even his. Maybe you would say he chose to go on that research trip with my mom or chose to marry my mom or chose to be a scientist in the first place. But I've never once felt like I chose advertising. It's stupid, but ads just felt natural to me. I'm not sure why I'm getting so upset about this. Maybe because after meeting you I feel even less control over who I am? (When we disagree, does it feel to you like you're arguing with yourself? It's like I want to convince myself, but I'm convinced! That's how it feels to me.) Maybe — don't take this the wrong way — it's our disagreements that make me remember we're different people.

If I'm forced to say it, maybe you're right it's kind of a Buddhist thing. I believe we're all too connected for any of us to step away and have a will free of each other's. Or maybe I just think it's wrong. When we were girls my friend Em's mom heard from a fortune-teller once that Em should stay away from ice or she would break her leg. Her mom kept her from skating and ice hockey and even sledding all winter. We all thought it was unfair. Then Em slipped on an ice cube, in her kitchen, and broke both her legs. True story. We couldn't believe it either. The whole class visited her in the hospital, and she was just pleased with herself. She said she didn't have another leg to break and she'd been wanting ice cream for weeks. She said Buddha had answered her prayers. She had felt so alone before her legs broke, the only one trying to avoid her fate.

I think about that every time I wonder why I still go to temple. I never seem to make a decision to go, I just end up there, and when I get there, I realize I needed to be there and that was why I went.

(Other) yours truly

———

Dear Yumi,
I'm worried. I haven't been able to get a hold of anyone from home. Who else can I tell? (Matt will take any single thing I say and fixate on it until it's lost all meaning.) Before I left, actually — the police visited me. They didn't tell me Matt was dead — they let me find that out on the news. Assholes. I thought they were there because I'd reported him missing. They just asked if I knew anyone who had a grudge against

him. They had a look around the apartment like maybe it would help them find him. I told you he had even cut himself out of our photos when he left, right? Maybe that's why they didn't take me in — I've been wondering why they didn't. I've heard murderers always keep objects from the people they murder. That's as creepy as any other fact about murderers, isn't it? They kill a person because she's an object to them, and then they replace her with an object. I dated a guy once who really just wanted a vase with a vagina. I'm lucky I got out alive.

What if the police went to my mom, though — that's what bothers me. When I try to call her — should I tell you this? — it says "the connection cannot be made." This is what I mean. Forget free will — it's not even up to you who you're allowed to talk to. Is there a hand phone shop you'd recommend I go to for help? I tried a couple of places already, and they kept saying I'd have to send my phone in through the mail. One place said it could take a month for the company to get it. If you need your phone to communicate and you have to send it away to get it to work, where's the communication in that?

P.S. I know I said I should just accept things as they are, and I'm not taking my own advice. But I've been thinking about what you said about women's anger — you know, when I apologized for what happened with Matt. Do I have this right? You said something about how anger is a sign of injustice. Letting anger go is letting injustice go, doing anger is doing justice. I was glad for your anger — I'd never thought of anger as something you could _do_ before. Maybe that's why I never knew how angry I was. I'm practicing my anger now — not against *you, against technology! (And the men who treat women like technology.)*

P.P.S. I keep forgetting to ask — did you ever see Matt sleep for a really long time, like 3 days? Remind me to bring this up next time we see each other?

Me

———

Dear doppelgänger,

I've started taking photographs of everything, two of each. Remember how I told you it's hard to trust what I see here? I was inspired by the dolls you collect. I liked what you said about how you collect them for the differences between them, for what the designer did to make the face look just a bit kinder or happier or more alive, the tiniest additions and subtractions; how you showed the difference a millimeter could make for a smile, one edition of the doll with a sincere look and the next playful. It's the most normal things here that seem out of place to me. When I look over the photos I took that day, I find like twenty photos of the sidewalk. But here's the thing I noticed recently — I can't seem to get exactly the same shot twice.

You've got to see for yourself. I'll show you next time. There isn't a huge difference between the shots. Yet even when I take them an instant after each other — like by holding down the button — they don't give me the same image. It doesn't matter how still I keep my hand. I even tried standing my phone on a flat surface. It's almost like when you shut one eye and look through the other, then switch, how the views are just slightly different. What else is a camera supposed to be if not an extension of my eye? I wonder if something is wrong with my vision.

Sorry to write a whole letter about this. It seemed relevant somehow. On ads we do the same thing you do with your dolls — adjust the slightest angle, photoshop the smallest mole. And we say it's not for the details but for the overall feeling you get. Most people don't notice the details, only whatever emotion the ad evokes. The thing about my photos is — I get no feeling from them, only a little spook that I can't get the two to come out exactly alike.

God, I hope this isn't a metaphor.
Doppelgänger

———

Dear Yumi,
I am freaked the fuck out. Remember how I tried using your phone to call my mom and it didn't work either? I tried using Matt's phone too, and same problem. I guess it's not about the phone.

But! I didn't know Matt's passcode, I snuck in. Guess how?

I used my Matt's passcode (!!!) — they have the same one.

I tried some other things first, of course. I only tried my Matt's passcode because I wanted to make sure it <u>didn't</u> work. I guess I shouldn't be so creeped out. It's weird enough that they look exactly the same and we look exactly the same.

But somehow having the same secrets seems over the line. I guess I still believed we had some free will. Now what do you think? Don't tell me what your passcode is — I don't want to know if it's the same as mine.

Actually — later that day I went down to the rally you mentioned to try to find you, to tell you this, and I got swept up in the mob. I was about to text and ask where you were when I thought I saw Matt inside a restaurant. It looked like he was hitting on some Korean woman. This was during work hours, so I was worried the woman was an employee. I was going to go in and stop whatever was happening, but you'd never guess — he actually stopped himself. I saw it on his face, the realization that he was doing something inappropriate. (Not to buy him a drink for being normal, but I almost thought he didn't have it in him.) Anyway — I was so surprised I forgot why I had my phone out.

The reason I'm writing now is that, even so stressed out, that rally gave me energy. There was hope, and fellowship, and I get why you like it. Like maybe it didn't matter if protest made anything happen, as long as it made it seem like something _could_ happen. When I like my job, it's kind of similar — you want a new product to fill a hole, but the hole doesn't yet exist. A vacuum cleaner that works upside down? You've got to show people that a ceiling has never been clean before. A product creates its own possibility.

Or maybe that's when I _don't_ like my job? I'm getting confused. I'm starting to really miss people from home. Sometimes I can't stop crying.

I'm going to stop writing now because I don't know what else to say.

———

Dear Yumi,

I started seeing the therapist you recommended. At first I told her I had nothing to work on, even though I knew that was a lie, and she just let me talk until I was telling her everything I could fit into the last ten minutes. Maybe everyone seems crazy in therapy because it takes a while to get going and then you have to stop?

She asked me what my perfect life would be if it could be anything, and I didn't know what to say. I'd never thought about perfect, only the best way to live the life I had ended up with. But I've had a generous paycheck for years and I own my apartment and I could afford to quit my job without notice and walk into a new job. So why, I thought, have I been living like I have to survive? When I started to describe what I wanted, I couldn't do it by saying I want to advance in my field. And not because I don't want to advance — because it never feels like I'm really advancing. To describe my perfect life, I had to first describe what life would look like — in balance. (There's the Buddhism again.) Then I was talking about my mom once more, because I could hear myself sounding like her, saying a species has to be in equilibrium for it to evolve the ability to be happy.

The moral of the story is that unless we find equilibrium we'll evolve to be our mothers.

————

Dear You,

I don't know the TV show you mentioned, but I've been reading the book you loaned me. Did you ever find the one

I recommended to you? I even bought the e-book so I could secretly read during meetings. There's a lot I didn't know in there. I feel kind of embarrassed about it. The part about different waves of Asian immigrants trying to win rights the others didn't have by claiming to be more acceptable — I hate how much I understand that. At the office today someone made a joke about kimchi being the latest fad and looked right at me, and I did what I always do — I let the silence hang over us — even though when someone says "Ni hao" to me in the street, I say, "I'm not fucking Chinese."

At first I couldn't even feel angry. It's always like that — I guess that means at first I don't admit to myself it's an injustice? I felt panicked, my heart sputtered, I felt like I was protecting something precious. I couldn't tell whether I was unable to speak or choosing not to, but I wanted my silence to make the guy realize he'd said something wrong. The conversation went on as if nothing had happened, of course, and that was when the rage came. Why do I do the same thing every time? Am I _allowing_ it to happen? I keep thinking, like in your book, that by not getting angry I can come out the good guy and embarrass the bad guy. But no one even seems to realize they made a mistake. They don't even notice my silence — they think it's normal — it's never embarrassing to them to be the only one talking.

———

Dear Me,

I used to like the K-dramas where the lovers with the bad fate in their past lives get reincarnated and spend 15 episodes reliving that fate and 1 episode beating it. Those shows seemed

186

more true to my life as I knew it. The truth is, even before I met you — maybe especially before I met you — I felt like I was living someone else's life, not mine. Now I think maybe those shows are about how you can take a whole series and two whole lifetimes to do one thing that is really your own.

But I don't think this letter will get to you. I guess I'm writing it for me. There's a joke in there somewhere about who we are really selling things to. What's not funny is that Matt pulled me through the wall — this really happened, we really went through the wall, just like he said could happen — the fucker. And now I can call my mom and my friends and live in my apartment and resume my fate, but I can't seem to reach you. And I miss us.

With love,
Other You

CHAPTER 5: XXXXXX

WHEN WE COME OUT

When we come out we are in a place I do not recognize. I try to make sense of the dewy grass beneath my dress shoes, the juniper trees all around, the sound of cars nearby. Behind us is typical air, no crack, no wall. Sandra pulls her hand from mine, and I throw up in the grass. The pain from the wall is gone. The pain that remains is complete and ordinary. I seem to move okay, to be in control of my body.

Sandra, on the other hand, screams.

She's in a frock-like button-up with no pants for pajamas, and bare feet. I wait until the scream stops and she wraps her arms around herself.

I want to sleep for eighty-four hours again, but I take responsibility. "I'm Matt Chung," I say, which feels true the moment it comes out.

Sandra shakes her head no.

"Why can't I be Matt?"

She squats in the grass and rubs both cheeks in a circular motion with the heels of her palms. "This is a dream," she says hopefully.

"We went through the wall," I say. "This is where we came out. I'm going to be a better human here. I'm going to be the other Matt, not Matt."

"We went through the wall?"

"We went through the wall," I say again, to normalize it.

Sandra bites her bottom lip, tilts back her head, and glares from the wells of her eyes. My ants return, this time on fire. Then she re-rubs her cheeks and slides her palms up over her eyes. Five seconds later she looks around again.

"Fuck," she says.

"I'm hungry. Are you hungry?"

"Matt was murdered," she says. "You can't be him." Tears spring up. "I've never said that out loud before."

"Matt is dead, all hail Matt," I joke to lighten the mood.

"This isn't funny."

I apologize.

"You don't want your body chopped up," she says. "You look like you've already been to hell anyway—I mean what is up with your fucking face?"

This seems like a low blow. It wouldn't help to remind her she slapped me.

I stand straighter and offer to cover her while she dresses. "The trees will make an okay screen." So we roll the suitcase behind the thickest juniper, about half as wide as I am. Through the trees a blur of colors indicates passing cars. I keep my back to her and listen as the engines burn the remains of millennia-dead organisms. How many years of evolution, I wonder, do we use up to go a mile? I feel more and more certain that I can't return where we came from, forward is the only way forward. Leave what is typical behind, and you leave what is creepy behind.

"I guess you'll have to work harder to become a *Homo sapien*," Sandra says behind me. She shows me an entire suitcase full of shoes.

"Also," she says, "you really do look horrible."

Horrible is as horrible does.

———

We come out on a big street or a tiny highway, my suit jacket over Sandra's shoulders, shiny silver heels on her feet. She squats to hide her legs. I raise my thumb. Cars speed up as they pass. After twelve minutes Sandra sighs and raises her thumb. Right away a furniture truck stops, driven by a big-eared white cliché. "I can't keep up with fashion," he says as he lets us in, his ears unfurling like sails and his eyes big with greed.

The cab of the truck is a mess of things you can buy in a convenience store for luck: a plastic hula dancer, furry dice, scratch-off lotto tickets. Sandra's eyes settle on the driver's pro-hunting shirt. "You really can't keep up with fashion," she says.

This doesn't faze him. "You going into **XXXXXX**?"

It's a city I've never heard of.

I confirm, and the truck rattles or Sandra elbows me.

"This is something my friends won't be-lieve," says the driver. "Like the start of a porno, excuse the language." Since he hasn't sworn, he must mean the language in his imagination.

"What is **XXXXXX** like?" I ask.

Sandra definitely elbows me.

"What?" I mouth.

"A few political scandals, a few murders, occasionally a big lottery payout. Hey, do I know you from somewhere, bro?" But he doesn't wait for an answer. It's Sandra he's interested in.

She scowls and braces her hand on the dash.

"That's a good description of a city," I say, impressed.

"You hitchhike a lot? You got any crazy stories?" he asks her.

Sandra says to drop us at the next exit.

"You know **XXXXXX**? Aren't you just passing through, looking for a good time?"

"I feel like that's crossing a line," I say. Though I can't say how exactly.

"I live here," Sandra says so fast and soft I almost have to re-create the words from memory. "Drop us at the all-night diner."

The guy's lips draw in like he's sucked on a lemon, but he steers into the exit lane.

———

He drops us on the feeder road and makes us walk to the diner, which is called The Diner. What Sandra said ruins my concentration. Sandra lives here? What is leaving worth if you end up where you began? On the other hand: the circle of life. The buildings look like they were all poured out of the same concrete mold in the last ten years. A few skyscrapers cluster in the distance, but nothing marks **XXXXXX** as exceptional. Yet a few months ago Sandra got in her car in **XXXXXX** and drove through the earthquake to Boston—and thirty-six minutes ago we walked through the wall in Boston and came out in **XXXXXX**. Maybe I just have to take over where Matt left off. On the other hand that means death.

Sandra orders two plates of pancakes, a giant waffle, a supreme omelet, hash browns, corned beef, and extra bacon and sausage. With each dish my hunger grows. I shake all over. When the waiter turns to go I stop him and order the same. He side-eyes us and writes the dishes like a prescription, diagnosing. "To go?" he asks. I point to the table. We sit silently, paling with hunger, until the food comes. We devour everything but the last dry sausage.

Afterward Sandra breathes deeply, as if about to vomit. The meal wasn't what she's used to—I can't imagine her in an all-night diner in Boston. She crosses her arms on the table, lowers her chin on her wrists. She blinks at something across the room.

And hyperventilates.

I look where she looks: On the wall is a monthly calendar. It hangs open to November. It's definitely August.

Since time is a matter of perspective, I look again—but it's still November.

"Maybe it's a mistake," I say.

She draws a square with her finger. Drawing one side she breathes in, drawing the next she holds her breath, drawing the next she breathes out, drawing the last she holds her breath.

Maybe it's some kind of stress relief. I copy her.

All around us are those red hats—like we didn't get very far. Like the distance we traveled was not through time and space, but something else. The faces under those hats face us. I tell myself it's just because of Sandra's pajamas or the invisible squares we draw.

The waiter says of course it's November and is he on hidden camera, are we celebrities in Japan?

I don't need math to know eighty-four days are missing.

What happened in that time? I remember thinking, in college, that we shouldn't care so much about the past. Later I realized I just hated history classes. They always made time seem something you could split into segments. My distaste for the past was precisely because it isn't past. As soon as we use a word we participate in its past, present, and future—otherwise it is a sound. Without its past a diaper is a wad of manufactured fabric. To be born as a human is to enter a world that, if you ever could isolate it in time, would be completely without human meaning. Which is why it's so hard to answer, for example, when someone asks whether I can speak English. The question isn't about me—it is about a history of white supremacy and its continuity into the future, without which the question is empty. The only way to change the meaning is to completely change its humanity.

"Are you professional eaters?" the waiter asks.

Sandra reaches for money, but I forgot her wallet, also her phone. I didn't think a trip through a wall would require cash. Though I worry my money won't work, in this other November, it goes through fine. The fact that money is an imaginary construct doesn't stop our real belief in it.

Outside Sandra pulls my jacket tight and says she still owns her apartment. "I never sold it—you know what's funny?—I didn't want to have nowhere to come back to." Her voice trails.

"Are you asking me on a date?" I joke.

"Stop it."

"Time didn't change when you drove through the earthquake?"

She hits her chest with her fist, saying in Korean the words my mother used to say whenever she met the limits of her patience.

I ask whether this is a yes or a no.

"It's a no," Sandra says. "Nos all the way down."

THE FUTURE IS ASIAN AMERICAN

Ever notice how much science fiction is set in a city half futuristic Asia and half typical America? San Fransokyo. Ridleyville. Asia provides alien tech and ancient philosophy, and America provides consumption. Even the imagination is colonized. This is typical.

I used to ask my adoptive parents why the Middle Eastern characters in our Bible looked white. They *were* white, my adoptive parents said, because they were Jewish, and I should say *Caucasian*. It was my first lesson in how faith is an alternate universe. In my adoptive parents' house I used my first computer, which they barely used themselves— they wanted to have what their neighbors had. That digitized world was my second lesson.

In computer engineering there is a method called parallel programming. It is a way of compressing two times into one. To do it you need a multicore processor, which those first computers didn't have. Each core of a computer is like a new consciousness. When you parallel program you program each consciousness to process a different task. Say you have a multipart problem—you assign different parts of the problem to different cores. Each consciousness considers its own part of the problem, and at the end the answers to the various parts come together. In this way multiple times happen at once. (Imagine a trip in which you travel a certain distance faster because you travel multiple parts of that distance simultaneously.) It is similar to multitasking, except that the computer doesn't use one part of its brain to do one thing and another part of its brain to do another. A computer has multiple brains that operate in simultaneous yet separate timelines.

Trouble can occur when those times collide. Say you have two cores, and you program one core to think *Sandra* and one core to think *Yumi*. If the results of those thoughts appear in the same time you might get *YuSandrami* or *SandYurami*. This trouble is called a *race condition*. To get out of a race condition you need to keep each brain pseudo-independent of the others. The solution is: you program only one core at a time to have possession and to give up possession when the other core has it.

When I first learned about parallel universes it was through computers. Even if a multicore processor can do two things at once, it exists in the same universe you do. In this universe possession determines independence; the answer is always singular. You can have a zero or you can have a one, but you can't have both. The next step in processing power is quantum computing. Quantum computing allows you to have both. These computers are still rare—NASA has one—but are sometimes described to be working in parallel universes. The upgrade to multicore is multiverse. Instead of a human experience of time (for example in Schrödinger's experiment, your act of observing his cat splits the universe into one universe in which the cat is dead and another in which the cat is alive—but since you exist in only one universe, you see only one cat in only one state) quantum computers exist in quantum time. A quantum computer can observe the cat in both states and make the corresponding calculations for both possibilities in one answer. In other words: it's only in a colonized multiverse that a person's perspective splits the whole world in two. The future is Asian American, and you can be multiple people at once.

SHOCK

At the door Sandra warns that her apartment might shock me. "It freaked me out to see yours." Then she gets her key from her shoe suitcase, at least one bit of luck. I picture another me and another her inside, who've lived there the entire time. But behind her door is a foyer that looks exactly the same as mine, leading to a living room and dining room that look exactly the same as mine, with an exact same kitchen in the back and an exact same bathroom off an exact same shortened hall with the exact same twin bedrooms at the end.

"Okay," I say once her tour is done. "How does this work? You live in an apartment complex, and I live in a duplex."

"I told you there's something wrong with your place."

She hangs my jacket on her coat tree. I reach into its pockets and take out the dog half to pet it. The cloth is wearing down. I used to ask my adoptive parents for a dog—they would say I was allergic even though I'm not.

"Don't do that," Sandra says. "You look like a bad guy in *Jim Bond*."

"You mean *James Bond*."

She wrinkles her nose.

"In my opinion," I say, trying on a British accent, "it's the nation that has gone evil, not I."

She retreats into her bedroom and shuts the door.

She goes into the same bedroom as in Boston, the one on the right, which I always thought of as the second bedroom. Though technically they're the same size. Her walls are white, not purple. Charlotte has never lived here.

I take a second look around. Except for the few pieces of furniture I had before Sandra moved in (the desk and electric keyboard and couch) everything else is the same. She has the same bad art, the same big-screen TV, the same wood dining table, the same California kings, even the same china dishes and crystal glasses in the cupboards. She must have decorated my place to make it even more like hers, on purpose.

When she comes out in a sweatshirt and jeans, I ask why. Why did she move into a copy of her apartment to live with a copy of her ex-boyfriend?

Not the same, I remember her saying.

"Do you really not know?" she asks.

I guess I do know. She tried to re-create, in Boston, the circumstances under which she last knew who she was, in **XXXXX**.

She sits on her better sofa and sighs.

"What furniture did Matt even take?" I ask. "It doesn't look like anything's missing?"

"I never realized how little he had here until he was gone."

I feel bad for us that I couldn't be what she wanted.

"Why did you bring me here?" she asks, shifting her legs so she's lying down. "You did bring me, didn't you?"

"We're co-hallucinating," I try.

The more I look, the smaller and closer together the furniture seems. We fit our lives into our perspectives.

———

Auto-pay kept Sandra's lights and Wi-Fi on while she was gone. I wonder whether she really planned to come back or simply forgot to turn her payments off. Her calls from Boston never got through. Anyway the first thing we do is go online. She shouts from her desktop about how many new emails she has, going back to the day she left. I have no new emails, which means either that jello stops email or that my eighty-four days aren't so much missing as unloved. My spam folder is full—nothing can stop spam. To take responsibility for the lost months, I search Matt Chung's name online.

This time his murder is the first result.

I remember finding nothing in Boston. I want this gap to mean that Matt Chung has since gotten justice. But the dates on the search results are five months old. The case never progressed. I click the tab for local news: In June the murder made front-page headlines. Now it's forgotten. I spare Sandra these details, since I'm taking responsibility in general.

It was a grisly murder—and yet the burning and chopping is not what most articles focus on. They tell the story of Matt Chung as the model minority, a marketing savant with immigrant parents whose assimilation and top education brought him nearly to the top of his profession—a profession that let him brand America—until he was brought down by death. Praise is as predictable as reproach. The rest I skim for a twist, going so quickly that the first time I nearly miss it. I would have missed it if not for the name.

The last person to see Matt Chung alive was a friend of his, Matthew Salesses. Another person named Matt. The multiverse is one bad joke.

The night before he was murdered, Matt Chung visited this friend in an agitated state. He predicted one of them was going to die, and said they had to protect each other. Article after article starts to make Matt suspicious, like a superstitious foreigner. Matthew Salesses tells reporters he tried to calm Matt down, making tea and ordering takeout. After they ate Matt wanted to stay overnight, to be certain they both survived. Matt said his girlfriend had kicked him out, so he had moved in up the street from his friend to keep watch. In the most positive articles the reporters pause here to offer evidence that Matt was not a stalker type, quoting coworkers and citing his contributions to local charities and shelters. One reporter even goes so far as to dig up the story of Matt's dead brother. He gets in touch with folks from their old hometown who describe Matt as a perfect son who helped the elderly cross streets and mowed lawns for free and served as president of his high school. Some articles get pretty sappy. When we return to reporting on his fateful night we believe either that Matt had some other, secret reason to protect his friend or that he had a psychotic break. Matthew Salesses, creeped out, forced Matt out and locked the door. The next day Matthew Salesses called to apologize, but got no answer. He followed the address Matt had left him to a crummy side street in a "dangerous" part of town. No one was there. The apartment was crammed full of stuff—not furnishings but boxes and boxes of knickknacks and other junk. The reports all confirm this. Three days after Matthew Salesses reported Matt missing, the police discovered a mutilated body, three days old, in a dumpster a block from the apartment. They have no other leads, and the ex-girlfriend—Sandra makes a little gasp behind me—is never available for comment.

"Oh God," Sandra says. "These stories make me the murderer."

I don't know when she snuck up on me, but it's not a good move for a murder suspect. I reconsider my position on her. My heart turns. The truth is the more I read, the sicker I feel. The articles have a strange celebratory tone—it's spectacle, of course, but the spectacle is Matt's life, not his death. The articles aren't so much a description of a great loss as an invitation to behold what could happen to even the greatest version of me. Why did they show his body on TV, for example? Not to mourn, but to show its destruction. To encourage not grief but awe. In other words no responsibility-taking necessary.

Suddenly I hate the people who must have read this story with fascination and spread it far and wide, which maybe now includes me. Which is troubling.

"I've met that guy, Salesses, a couple of times," Sandra says, "and never liked him. I don't get why he would lie that I kicked Matt out. It's like he's trying to frame me."

Little by little I remember who she is to me, and how I haven't loved her well enough. I touch her on the shoulder, and she jumps. I fall off the chair.

"Shit," she says. "I have to get a hold of my mom."

She zooms in on the three headshots atop the article: Matt, her, and Matthew Salesses, a typical white nerd type who doesn't see much sun or company in real life.

"Stop looking at me like that," she says. She means her photo.

"We'll clear it up," I say, brushing myself off. "You must be panicking. I don't know why it sounds like a frame-up."

"You have to be him," she says quietly.

"What?"

"If you're him, if he's alive, there won't be any suspects."

Well. This was my plan first, so why do I suddenly hate it?

THE END OF THE NOVEL

Once Sandra leaves the room I scroll back to the bottom of the article and the links to other news. I cover the links with my hand and slowly reveal them. I'm pretty sure I saw another nightmare there. A candidate endorsed by white supremacist groups has won the presidential election. In this other world—if that is what it is—another KKK-candidate represents the country. Impossible, but likely one of the eighty-four days we missed. I remember the red hats in the diner. The room spins.

The shower splutters on, and I click through more articles about Matt, looking for the body. The internet gives and the internet etc. The corpse is ash-black most of the way over, unrecognizable, though the ankles could be mine. I lift my pants to check. I realize I don't know the first thing about ankles. In one photo the corpse's arms and hands and face all lie separate from the torso. I can barely tell they belong together. The scalp is a red mess. It's hard to look at me without vomiting. But nothing except those ankles seem mine.

Why would Matt Chung be murdered—Matt Chung who glowed and got to the top of his field and had no enemies—why would that Matt disappear? Myself I can understand. But he had everything we would want and still wanted more. Why else would he leave Sandra? He had another life planned.

I remember a documentary I watched in college about a guy named Vincent Chin. On the night before Chin's wedding, a white father and son mistook him for Japanese and beat him to death with a baseball bat. *Who Killed Vincent Chin?* the film was titled. The answer seemed obvious, but the murderers never spent a night in jail. The only real result of the case was outside the courtroom, where it brought Asian Americans together, in anger. They saw what the stakes were now of being mistaken for each other: life and death, existence and nonexistence. Together they fought for justice, together they failed. If they couldn't control how they appeared, they at least took control over how they disappeared.

Why did Matt Chung die and I live? Maybe, like parallel programming, disappearance was assigned to one Matt and appearance was assigned to another, but only one can have possession at a time. If I become Matt, will I become *Homo sapien*? Impossible, and likely.

I have tried to take responsibility. And yet, from a certain point of view, it would be easy to say I did exactly the opposite. You live in the universe you observe.

On Sandra's hard drive I find the photos with Matt Chung photoshopped out of them, and I wonder what they would look like with me. Sandra jumps on the beach beside a blank. She raises a beer beside a blank. She forms half of an arm-heart. Even with Matt cut out, the older photos look happier than the newer ones. In the newer ones Sandra faces the camera, but in the older ones, which are also the most numerous, she always gazes into the blank space where Matt used to be.

Sandra's hard drive holds everything that legally identifies her. All the consumption. Does her social security number and bank account info and credit card history really distinguish her from Yumi? I wonder. What made their personalities different? Did they start out the same as babies? Where did they split off?

I click on the documents folder, looking for documentation, and deep in the archives (helpfully labeled "Archives") I find a grant application Sandra wrote a couple of years out of college. It's a proposal for a kind of community program where women of color mentor girls of color who wish to pursue alternative options to school, girls afraid to let down their parents and selves by following their alternative dreams. The program would pay for the mentor pairs to develop professionalized business plans and pitch them to potential investors. In the application file is a too-long essay about Sandra's relationship with her mother, as if she got going and couldn't stop.

I click through other folders and stop on a subfolder titled "ME," as if she too has wanted to know herself better. The folder has a single file: "My Novel." Everyone is writing a novel. Anyone can become president. The possibilities are relentless.

———

The first chapter is about an earthquake in Boston. I read slowly, saying each sentence in my head. Sandra didn't know about Boston before she left **XXXXXX**. The story is familiar to me, because I am the one who wrote it. I am also the one who destroyed it by spilling wine all over my computer.

I skim down, down. The sentences return to me. My protagonist uses Wikipedia to describe far-off destinations, he wants to visit those destinations yet the knowledge that he doesn't need to traps him at home. He projects his trappedness onto his cat, his neighbors, not seeing that the trap is himself. It's a cliché, the writing is ew.

When I get to the point where the mysterious someone shows up at the door, I remember my desire to write about Sandra and then my kick and the sputter as the wires shorted out. But after that paragraph is another. In the next paragraph the person at the door is my protagonist's daughter. Of course. In this paragraph, in this world, it is clear that her disappointment in him is also some fear of herself. She pushes him out of the house, first on foot, then by bus, then by taxi. Finally they reach an airfield.

His daughter demands they visit someplace he wrote about. He will never have a better reason to go. As a last protest he says, "I'm in the middle of something, I'll have to quit it." His daughter nods. They have already left that something behind. Finally he names a place—a city I've never heard of. Yet as soon as he names that place he loses his desire to go. During the flight his daughter asks why he's so unhappy, and he confesses his change of heart. "Let's get out here then," she says and straps on a parachute. "Here is somewhere else too." When he panics she says what's the worst that can happen, he'll die? She says, "Please, Dad, you need to dismantle your life. This flight will only crash anyway." She jumps before he can stop her. He straps on the second parachute, wondering about what she said, but from the plane the world looks totally different, alien, nothing to which he can return.

———

It's almost what happened to me, figuratively speaking. Maybe that is evidence I wrote it. Most of the things I write are almost what happened to me. But instead of writing it, I spilled alcohol on my keyboard, then I waited for my daughter to come, then I couldn't wait anymore and drove my neighbor to his death, then I went to jail, then my daughter bailed me out with the help of the white man who replaced me.

The scroll bar still shows more. My protagonist rides his flight to its bitter end, but he doesn't crash. Where he lands is someplace impossible. A city in which all of the tourist attractions of the world exist side by side: the Colosseum next to the Great Wall next to Angkor Wat next to the Pyramids next to the Taj Mahal next to the White House. It's a mirage of human achievement, and what is a mirage if not a co-hallucinated oasis? For a long time he walks from sight to sight, it would take months to see all of each of them. He memorizes every detail, inside and out, and yet he can't shake the feeling that he hasn't seen anything. He starts to wonder how the monuments got there, where they came from. He starts to wonder how he got there, where he came from. Finally he remembers what he has forgotten: his daughter, the flight, the parachute. His daughter floats on the thick air—the alien world looming closer and closer, until it is neighborhoods, buildings, people, persons. He wants to go back and jump beside her. He wants to reverse her fall so that persons become world become the two of them in an airplane suspended between departure and arrival. Then around him the mirage is on fire, monuments burn down to dust. He has no idea how much time has passed—perhaps years. He has no idea how to get back to where he used to be. Anyway he can't go back, he can't unsee what he now sees. Where the monuments stood lie bodies, corpses covering the ground. He walks through them, he hears cars passing by, he smells juniper trees . . .

I go to the bathroom and vomit. How did my novel get onto Sandra's computer, the part that I wrote, and especially the rest? The toilet spins and the water stays still. I vomit again and again. The daughter at the door and the plane and the mirage—feels as if it really did happen to me. As if what happened in those missing eighty-four days is that I went to my protagonist's bitter end and instead of crashing and burning, I found a city of attractions and I saw what they really were and I came out on the other side in **XXXXXX** in someone else's story. But that story isn't finished. There's more time missing. Charlotte is still out there. I flush, and wash the vomit off my face, and in the mirror I see what Sandra must mean about hell: My chin has grown sprouts, my eyes have grown bags, my haircut has grown eighty-four days longer.

I've never needed much shaving, so the sprouts are all on my chin and sideburns, my lip has a thin fuzz. It looks like several different people's facial hair all mixed together. In the shower sits an old leg razor. I wash myself, and then the razor, and when I'm dressed again in the only clothes I have, I shave my face until I bleed. I stick little bits of toilet paper to the blood. I wonder whether failing Charlotte in my novel means I failed Charlotte in real life. Did I spend the last eighty-four days leaving her for the monuments of my imagination?

I find Sandra on her bed, talking into a tablet. On her floor are a bunch of Post-it notes—she must have torn them off the wall. They lay scattered like leaves around the tree that spawned them. She smiles widely, and at first I think she's talking to Yumi, but then she says, "Mom, I already emailed a reporter. My friend Olzmann's a lawyer. We will sort out everything tomorrow, I promise." She says, "Sorry that I couldn't get in touch for so long. Sorry that I worried you. It was a shitty thing to do. I didn't mean to." I back quietly out of the room. I searched Sandra's computer to know her better and only found another Matt.

"**XXX-XXX-XXXX**," I mutter under my breath, which is how the government knows her.

I set up my bed on her sofa, which is 300 percent more comfortable than mine, though I miss the stains. Why does discomfort comfort me? Is comfort just about what is typical? I am already Matt Chung, because that is the way I exist here. I haven't had a drink all day. I close my eyes—and as soon as I close them—or is it as soon as I open them?—I was in Boston.

WHO ARE YOU CALLING A STRAW MAN?

I knew exactly where I was: in the brand-new California king bed in my old apartment. I was dreaming. Or **XXXXXX** had been a dream. A middle-of-the-night hush surrounded me. On the walls hung two squiggly art pieces. I took them down now. Covering the windows hung smoke-colored curtains. I took them down too. When the walls stood naked again they whispered back, "I love you." Then I realized I'd just copied Sandra taking down her notes to self. I went across the hall to ask her whether I was dreaming.

Her room was empty. Her bed was unmade. Her closet open. Inside it one suitcase remained—beside a gap where the suitcase full of shoes had been.

The feeling of a dream was replaced with the feeling that part of me had never made it through to **XXXXXX**. Some part of me, like email and phone calls, couldn't pass through the jello. Though the rest of me was asleep in **XXXXXX**—with Sandra, who wholly belonged there—the nontransferable part of me was here in Boston. That was who I was now: the part of me I had left behind.

Why hadn't Sandra split in two? Maybe she did and I didn't know. Or maybe she didn't because she didn't go through a wall to get here, she drove through an earthquake.

I peed and took a look at myself in the mirror. I had the same face I used to have. The facial hair was gone. I wasn't surprised. What was strange had become typical.

I went to my bedroom to get the photo of Jenny and Charlotte and me, and I rubbed off the thumbprints with my thumb. But this time the act felt shameful, even vaguely threatening. Beside the photo lay my phone, plugged into its charger. I closed one eye and pressed the home button: My phone had only charged to 3 percent, and the date was the same as when we had gone through the wall. It was impossible, but highly likely, that time in Boston had barely passed. Then was now.

In my notifications were two voice mails from my ex-wife and a text from our child. Jenny was angry I had invited myself over to their house (which I hadn't, but was better than her knowing I had been in jail). Charlotte invited me to dinner. Tomorrow night. Mom won't say no bc I told her I'd already agreed to it. You know how she is about promises.

What could Jenny do? I imagined dinner with the detective and the detective's gun. I poured myself a glass of Chardonnay, the last wine Sandra had bought. Yet I didn't feel like drinking, it was just habit. Even my desire not to feel was disappearing. I took the glass to my desk, to check for the novel I'd found in **XXXXXX**. My computer was still busted. In this world my protagonist would never see through the world he longed for.

I dug through my closet for a box of things I had saved after my parents' deaths. In it was a list of places they'd wanted to see, titled "Buckit List." They were basically the same places my protagonist wanted to see, also the same places anyone wanted to see. As a foster kid I had puzzled over why the entire list was crossed off, since they never saw any of it. The last thing on the list (and the only thing that wasn't a place) was "have a baby." That must have been me, since it was circled. I used to think one circle among all those strike-throughs meant I had ruined my parents' lives.

I decided to write my own list. "Fuckit List," I titled it. I had racked up questions without answers—how to love better, how to see better, how to appear, etc. At one time I had been an expert test taker, which was about the process of elimination. Maybe instead of trying to understand my choices, I should have been using plug and check. The options were limited.

Fuckit List

1. *Become the other Matt*

2. *Avenge the other Matt*

3. *Change whatever circumstances lead a Matt to un-Matt*

4. *Burn murder/disappearance to the ground*

In the Looking Glass the guard lifted two pitying eyebrows. He was the guard I usually saw during the day, maybe he'd switched shifts. I understood his pity for me—our pity is always pity for ourselves—it was late at night and despite our positions we were both at work. He was a nice guy, this guard: Every morning and afternoon I'd been practicing small talk on him. I'd set a reminder on my phone to ask how his kids were doing—they were in high school at Boston Latin, a boy and a girl, and wanted to be a civil rights attorney and a politician, and the guard had joked several times that the school was called Boston Latin but his kids were about the only Latinxs in their classes. I pitied his immigrant heart, its willingness to postpone happiness generationally. I carried my own parents' postponements everywhere I went—exactly as they had wanted.

Tonight the guard didn't chat though. He opened and shut his mouth without producing any sound. I understood. We were all that tired. "I feel you," I tried. I thought I saw him shudder, which was a little harsh. I swiped my ID and got on the elevator.

The office cubes had not returned. The sign had not been satisfied, the Airing of Grievances continued. On my desk sat the cat half of the dog-cat, propped up on its two feet with the torn middle behind it. Stuffing peeped out of the tear. I didn't have any cat halves left—I wondered where it had come from. Probably Jenny had returned my gift. I couldn't see the homeless guy whose bench I had taken giving me his cat half back. The third option was a new stuffed animal, as if another dog-cat would appear (and get ripped apart) whenever I was without one. I petted the cat head, picturing the dog head in my pocket in **XXXXXX**.

On my office computer I downloaded a bootlegged pdf of *The Story of Hong Gildong* and printed out all 118 pages. Out of curiosity I also googled "Matt Chung murdered." Still nothing. While the pdf printed I wrote a resignation letter that I could sign by hand and drop in interoffice mail. Stealing my daughter's strategy I wrote that I had already instated Yoonha, so there was no going back. I asked for my partial paycheck to be sent to Jenny's address.

For the first time—at least for the first time consciously—I was disappearing myself. And it felt surprisingly good, troublingly good. I was disappearing not through failing to appear but by dismantling the appearance of my life.

Once I had logged out I spread the pages of *Hong Gildong* over the floor where the cubicles used to be, forming neat rows. The story was as gripping as when I first read it. It was the story still told over and over in K-drama: that of a person who fights their entire life to escape the fate of their birth. You live two lives in one, because up until the moment you take responsibility, they are the same life. In other words: you only know you are living two lives when you destroy one.

213

I stepped up to the sign and put on my boss voice one last time, in order to fire myself: "This is the Airing of Grievances, round two. I am the me that's alive when I am dead. I am Matt and yet Matt I am. I am the leftover me. For which Matt does a Matt long? Which I is the eye with which I see?"

As if in answer the elevator dinged. "Sir," the guard asked, staring at the sign and the papers all over the floor. "Mr. Kim?"

I hadn't realized he knew my name. I sat on page 104.

"Are you okay?"

Just above my head I seemed to hear heavy breathing, loud breaths coming down on me. When I raised my eyes nothing was there.

"This some kind of team-building thing?"

"I'm okay. I'm resigning. I'm just airing my final grievances."

He didn't move.

It occurred to me that I was resigning from being Matt Chung in one context and yet becoming Matt Chung in another. My pits grew sweaty.

I moved a few pages to the right, but the breathing still came from directly above me. I moved a few pages more: the same. "This might sound strange," I said. "Or maybe it won't sound any stranger than I look . . ."

"Man," the guy said, holding his head.

"But do you hear someone breathing loudly?"

His eyes pinched like he was about to cry. "Man, this is too much for me. I hate this job. I just thought I would check on you, you looked really damn sick—sorry for the language—really sick. I thought maybe I'd call the ambulance, maybe it'd be the right thing to do."

Sick was one way of looking at it. Maybe it was sickness to know, intuitively, that the breathing must be from Sandra's apartment, from Sandra mouth-breathing over me as I slept.

"Let's forget this," the guard said. "But you get yourself checked out. Sir."

I nodded. I needed professional care, and I needed to forget I needed it.

———

I drove to my ex-family's house with the breaths still coming down on me, and when they stopped I snuck again around the side of the house to the backyard. The footprints all over seemed suspicious, but I had probably made them the last time. Above me was the window the detective's chin had popped out of. I needed to find Charlotte's window if I was going to climb up the drainpipe to it. That was my current plan—not a great one, but I didn't know how else to love better.

I moved quietly, careful not to wake the dog next door, though maybe today it slept inside. I used my phone to zoom in on the ceiling fans. I had scared Charlotte once with the Korean belief that leaving a fan on while you slept would kill you, and she had refused to use one ever since, day or night. If I could find a fan with a lot of dust, I figured, I could find her room. I was leveling up my investigative skills.

Even with the zoom turned all the way up, I couldn't detect dust. Luckily the night was hot and the fans turned in every room except one.

I got a good grip on the pipe and tried to lift myself. I felt light. I felt strong. My feet left the ground—and then my arms gave way, and I landed flat on my ass. Two more tries got the same results. When had I gotten so out of shape? I needed to exercise—really I needed to go back in time and exercise. My intentions always came late.

Then I remembered that Charlotte had texted me and I could text her back. I texted her back that I was beneath her bedroom window. One minute and twenty-four seconds later she stuck her head out of the next window over. She must have gotten past the fan thing. I waved, and she rolled her eyes and pointed at her wrist. I hadn't woken her though—her hair was still sprayed in place. I motioned for her to come down.

As soon as her head retreated I panicked. No footsteps pounded this time, nothing indicated her descent. I had a kind of old-Matt feeling that she had disappeared. I would go up that hill in Somerville and dig under the statue of the white soldier and she would be there, underground. My body itched all over.

"Dad," someone whispered beside me.

I shouted in surprise.

The dog barked.

"What the f," Charlotte said. "Why did you scream like that?"

Upstairs someone groaned. I grabbed Charlotte's hand and pulled us back against the wall. Just like last time. The detective's chin popped out of the window just like last time.

The dog kept barking.

"Don't worry," I said. I pulled her along the edge of the wall to the far side.

"You look really weird," she said. "Is it the dark? What are you doing here?"

When we got to the corner I said, "What if I can't make it tomorrow?"

"You could have just texted. You didn't have to come here in the middle of the night."

A voice called down, "Charlotte, is that you?"

I thought I heard Jenny say, "What is she doing up?"

I ducked around the other side of the house.

But no one followed. When I poked my head back around the corner my daughter stood calmly in the center of the yard where they could see her. She had no reason to fear them, of course. She waved and said she was just looking for something that fell out the window by accident. She had the flashlight on her phone turned on.

I walked slowly back to the road and up the sidewalk to my car. My daughter had sacrificed herself for my sake. Even if only on a small scale.

When I got home Charlotte had texted: You really looked weird out there. Like you were turning into a shadow. Why are you so gross?

I didn't know what she meant. I texted back: When did that detective start living with you? She didn't respond.

———

I sat on the milk stains on my couch and thought, *Why am I so gross?*
What would other Matt do? WWOMD? W_____ Weapons of Mass
Destruction. White Weapons of Mass Destruction. Word Weapons of
Mass Destruction. If the first step was admitting you needed help, the
first first step must be knowing you needed help.

Finally I called my old college roommate, who had become some
kind of neuroscientist. He was probably getting ready for work. He had
always been an early riser, a heavy coffee drinker, a devout believer in
facts. Our dorm room had been full of open books with pencils in their
pages. He had transformed himself from the nerdy guy who got stuck
with me as a roommate because we were both Korean into a big-shot
scientist. I watched it happen little by little. He acquired the habits of a
scientist, and then he became those habits, as if you could turn the sun
into an orange just by saying it enough times to make everyone believe
it. Early in my marriage I let him scan my brain, and that ended our
relationship—the moment you let someone see into your brain your
love for each other is over—but those results still existed somewhere.
Those results said for sure whether something was physically wrong with
me or colloquially wrong with me.

He answered on the second call. "My cell says this is Matt Kim,
but it isn't, right? Especially not at four in the morning? Especially not
at four in the morning after a decade of no contact?"

I had the time difference wrong. I had forgotten where he'd moved.

I apologized, I asked about his family, I was sincere and wished I
had been sincere before. Maybe I had made a mistake not wanting to
know what I could only know about myself from science. Jenny had
wanted me to do the scan and hated that I never got the results, she
wanted to get an official label, seek official support.

I heard him shuffle out of his bedroom. He was probably married
and didn't want to wake his partner. He had always been considerate.

"Is this really you?" he asked. "You sound different. Though I guess I must too. You know you were a real dick to me back when? I only picked up because I figured you'd keep calling. That's what kind of person you were."

"I was," I said. "I know that now. You were a good friend."

There was a pause.

"Huh," he said. "It's surprising to hear you say that. I guess that's why I wanted to know what was in that head of yours. I was always curious. Remember that brain scan you did?"

"That's what I'm calling about," I said. "Also to ask about your family and apologize."

"I don't have a family," he said after a moment. "You sure have changed."

We talked for a while about old times, he was still half-asleep, I was still taking responsibility. It was kind of nice. He even told me he wasn't a he anymore, he had undergone surgery to become a she. People were out there evolving without each other, with only a common predator to guide them.

"Congrats," I said.

"You know," she said finally, "you didn't have to ignore my calls. You didn't have anything to worry about. Though I guess you realized we all thought you might turn out to be a sociopath? It did seem a strong possibility."

"I was scared," I said. "I didn't want to know I needed help."

"That's why I wanted to tell you the results," she said.

"Because I'm a sociopath?"

"No way," she said. "You're a normal human. You just have a weird personality."

That news must have really exhausted me, because I fell asleep soon after that. I remember her saying, "You know, if we ever both have time," and the next thing I know I am back in **XXXXXX**.

REPORTS FROM THE FIELD

This is how I become the other Matt. I wake—or the part of me that made it through the wall wakes—and I am in Sandra's apartment, with Sandra, in **XXXXXX**. Because she has no food we breakfast at a nearby café, and in the middle she gets an email from the reporter she contacted. We buy new clothes and have a close call when the salesperson says he's definitely seen me before, though maybe he's just hitting on me. Then we meet the reporter for lunch in our new outfits. The restaurant is a French affair with an open, airy feeling that means the tables are far enough apart to have a private conversation. Waitstaff float around with water pitchers. The reporter is a skinny older white man with kindness wrinkles around his eyes, full pink lips, a receding hairline, and baby cheeks. It's a face that makes him seem like he does nothing all day but sit around and smile at things. Only after he gushes for five minutes about Matt Chung being alive do his eyes sharpen in focus and I catch the ruthlessness it takes to ignore a person's own story and tell their truth. He seems aware of this quality in himself, because he quickly averts his gaze. And yet he never doubts that I am Matt. His sureness makes me suspect myself—I feel something different than I have ever felt before. I feel doubly seen, as if when I wasn't looking

Matt crept in and now shares my body. I feel—*present*. How to explain? When there's a tragedy in a far-off place, most people go about their lives as if it never happened until they know someone who died in it. Matt Chung is someone I know who died and made the story of our life a tragedy to me. The reporter scribbles notes and fires off a few questions about where we've been and why we didn't contact anyone, the whole time giving the full extent of his professional and (it seems to me) personal consideration.

"We went on a long vacation," Sandra says. "A road trip. We left our phones behind. We wanted to travel without internet."

I wonder when she rehearsed this. And how she knew that Matt's phone wasn't on his body.

"You didn't tell your parents? Or even your friends? Your colleagues?"

Sandra says she was the one who didn't want to tell anyone, we had agreed to get away and clear the air, to make space for the two of us. In her story we solved our problems and have returned happier than ever.

The reporter writes all this down, but waits as if for Matt Chung to answer.

I say something about how sorry we are that our existence causes an inconvenience. The reporter belly laughs and slaps my arm. I chuckle with him. In other words truth has left the building, and the punch line is that the act of disappearing myself is what finally gives me presence.

Bad jokes are the gestalt of the earth.

Sandra pinches my leg.

"I have only one more question." The reporter leans forward. The room shifts, and I know he's going to say I'm not Matt. "This may sound strange," he says, "but I wasn't surprised you're alive. Do you want to know why? I never believed that friend of yours. Everyone else described you as responsible to an only fault. Your friend basically called you delusional. Plus he went out of his way to mention insignificant details, like what you ate together. That's what I would do if I was trying to cover a story's tracks. Usually people get the general scene the same and mix up details. Unless they're directly involved."

Sandra interrupts that she never trusted Matthew Salesses either. The reporter continues as if she hasn't said anything.

"I even—I hope it's all right—hired a private eye. After those other disappearances started happening too, something felt funny. I guess that makes it sound obvious. And that's when I called up folks from your hometown. I've been doing this for more than thirty years, and there's always someone who wants his grudge on record. But as I said you were like a unicorn. They all thought you were some kind of magical Asian."

This almost distracts me from the mention of other disappearances.

"Oh no," Sandra says. "You're a conspiracy theorist."

"Wait a second," I say.

Sandra sighs now, not even pretending this is going well. She literally taps her fingers on the table.

"What's the name of that private investigator?" I ask.

The reporter hesitates, but gives me a business card with the name and address. I pull out my cell. Suddenly, however, it seems like bad news that my phone is charged and working. The electricity buzzes in my fingers, the current strong enough to carry over from Boston.

"What is it?" the reporter asks. He bends over my screen. "Hey, I've never seen a cell like that. What's the model?"

Sandra waves a hand in my face and makes a low-pitched plea to snap out of it.

"How quickly can you get the article out?" she asks the reporter. "Will people actually read it?"

He shrugs. "Everything's online now. All we need are some photos, since I've already cleared it with my editor. I wrote almost everything last night anyway." He types something into his phone as he talks. When he turns the screen to me it says, Blink twice if you don't trust her.

221

Sandra's teeth grind. She says she has to go to another meeting, one I know nothing about. Though she has her own two lives. "I'll see you later, Matt." Her lips press my cheek.

I almost forget it's for show, it feels so good to be seen and touched and smelled and at last tasted.

———

The reporter and I take a cab downtown to a ten-story building in the center of what must be the business district. The entire thing belongs to the newspaper—either the economy or the entertainment is different here. It's another concrete construction, though it has more windows than the buildings farther out. Except for one floor that's an entire band of concrete, the others are all sunny office space. We take the elevator to the no-window floor, of course. It's the fourth floor, which my parents would have warned against. The Korean word for *four* is a homonym for death. We step into a huge, empty space with professional lighting and a green screen and stylish employees. Immediately a young black woman brings an outfit for me to change into. She seems to know exactly who I am: the other Matt. I wonder whether any newspaper in Boston could afford to hire her, could afford this entire space.

"You'll be fine," she says, noticing something in my expression.

I *am* fine. With no effort I am succeeding with the first thing on my Fuckit List: becoming Matt.

"That's the whole point of this shoot, right? That you're fine, not dead?" She smiles.

I laugh obligingly, a laugh I could not have pulled off months earlier. What *is* my problem—I am fine, why can't I be happy? I am human, why can't I be human? If everything seems so sudden, it's only because I forget that eighty-four days have passed. I went through a wall to get to where I am. To become Matt Chung I left behind a part of Matt Kim. My ex-family is still in Boston. I have made my sacrifices, so where is my salvation? Why can't satisfaction satisfy me?

A young brown man applies a thin layer of makeup supposed to "emphasize my lines" and tells me all I have to do is act natural.

"We'd usually do more," the woman says sheepishly, "but we want you to be exactly as you are. No photoshopping. We want people to recognize you."

The outfit she gives me is a typical sports jacket and a polo and jeans, what most people expect a writer to wear, only more expensive versions. Absurdly I miss my purple tracksuit. I wore it for the same reason: not to be seen as someone I wasn't, but to be seen as someone's ideal of who I was.

I ask quietly whether the stylist might have clean boxers too. "Not for anything creepy," I catch myself. "Sorry, that was inappropriate. What I mean is—I may or may not have been wearing this same underwear for the last eighty-five days."

This is no improvement.

Become Matt, I think. I re-apologize without adding anything.

"We're going to make it look like you're walking around any regular street," another young black woman calls over, sensing something going poorly. She must be the photographer. "And don't worry, I know how to light Asian skin."

I am Matt Chung when I stay silent. I smile and nod.

In the end the stylist does bring a pair of boxers, and I take them into the bathroom to change. In the mirror I cry a little, I don't know why. One minute I'm looking at a better me, and the next I need a makeup change.

223

PRESENCE AND ABSENCE

At first a photo shoot is a real ego boost. The photographer's not the only one perceiving me in my best light, a bunch of people gather around to praise me. They tell me I look like myself, Matt Chung. I turn left, and right, and with each pose they say, "This is the one," which must mean I am the one, since the poses are many. To feel present, I think, is to experience other people sharing your experience. My earlier apprehension leaves me. How to see better is unclear—but I like being seen. I like everything except when the photographer pauses and everyone gathers around a screen to look at the photos taken so far. Then I might as well not be there. "He doesn't look happy to be alive," the photographer says, when a minute ago she said, "Perfect. You're doing great." "You don't look happy," they say to each other. When the photographing resumes I smile harder than I ever smiled in my life. When it pauses, everyone's attention shifts to the screen, and where does my presence go? Somewhere between me and the pictures of me Matt Chung's glowing presence goes back to my dull one.

In the novel I wrote that never sold, the protagonist finds presence by losing his other options. He is what is left for him to be. That's how I feel now. I am limited by the process of my elimination. What others see in my disappearance is the appearance of Matt. In the end the shoot unanimously disappoints. The stylist takes the clothes back, but tells me to keep the boxers. I don't ask where she got them.

In the parking lot I remember that Sandra isn't coming to get me. The reporter lights a cigarette. He seems more suspicious of me now that I failed the photo shoot. "I know it's a pain in the back," he says, "to be under everyone's scrutiny for an hour."

This is what we are doing now, giving and receiving sympathy.

"Thanks for waiting it out," I say.

He nods. "I'm not a conspiracy theorist," he says, "but ever since I wrote that article about your gruesome murder, after your perfect life, I haven't been able to stop thinking about it. I've been wishing I could ask how you got this far, how you get everyone to love you."

It's like I am hearing my own desires for Matt in an older white man's mouth. I shake off the image of him as my adoptive father.

"Tell the truth I got a little obsessed with you," he says. "I never felt that way about a subject before. But the compliments . . . I actually couldn't use most of them, they were too unbelievable. You're like some kind of movie hero, working off your brother's funeral debts while volunteering for hospice and making valedictorian and all-state cross country? And to grow up even better from there?"

It still seems impossible to me too, that someone like me could have made other people so happy.

There's a moment of surprise when he sees my confusion. I smile. I try to funnel Matt into my mouth. And then he is—weeping. Really *weeping*.

When he can talk he whispers, "I feel like I can tell you. Can I tell you?"

But he's already saying it.

"I'm having personal troubles, my boyfriend and I—"

For a moment I see who he must once have been, when he embraced that ruthlessness in his eyes. He shivers. I put a hand on his shoulder, trying to accept the love he thinks he has for the me he thinks I am. *Note to Matt Kim,* I think. *You have to take responsibility for who you used to be in order to be who you are.*

"If I can make you happy," I say, "I'll be glad to try."

The reporter lives in a nice brick row house between two not-as-nice brick row houses that must make his property less valuable. His shutters red and the brick whitewashed. It's a lot stuffier and fussier than I expected. The kind of house you can draw with only a triangle and a square. "My partner gets home early," he says. "Around four. He's a language arts teacher. He does most of his prep at home. We've been seeing each other for over twenty years." He talks quickly, as if unused to reporting on his own life. But the last thing he says slows time: "His name is Phil Collins. Felipe Collins."

"Ha. Ha."

"What's so funny?" he asks seriously.

"You know—Phil Collins, the singer . . . Plus I know another Phil Collins."

He shrugs. "It's a common name."

There's nothing left to remind me. It's shameless and unfunny, so it must be fate.

Suddenly the thought of fate warns me that the reporter's street is eerily quiet for the middle of the day. Why hasn't this registered with me? It's impossible, though likely, that I followed a white stranger to his house without telling anyone. How could I forget Matt's chopped-up body? Sweat beads under my armpits.

I knock wood, then remember I got this habit from Yumi. If I die in **XXXXXX**, will anyone look for me? Will anyone from Boston—Jenny, Charlotte—be able to find my grave? Maybe I will automatically return there. I wonder why I think that.

The reporter brews some kind of flower tea that blossoms in its clear teapot. I excuse myself. My leg bumps a side table. The reporter pretends not to notice—which only makes me more nervous. It doesn't cross his mind that I might be able to disappear from him. I try not to limp until the bathroom door shuts. Then I massage my shin. I text Sandra the address, and she texts back:

> That guy was telling the truth. There HAVE been other disappearances. And get this . . . ALL ASIAN PEOPLE.

I shut my eyes.

The phone buzzes again: GET OUT.

That may be difficult, I write. I may have to go through a wall. BTW sorry I pulled you through with me.

She doesn't reply. I wait a while to be sure.

I keep failing to do the third thing on my Fuckit List: *Change whatever circumstances lead a Matt to un-Matt.* I walked right into this un-Matt situation. Do I tempt fate or fate me?

It's not a murder mystery, I remind myself, it's a love story.

When I come out the tea is in full bloom. "Don't go in there for a few minutes." I feel somewhat smart about this line. The reporter makes small talk, telling me how he started at the newspaper. He pestered an editor with letter after letter, he visited her office until she just wanted to be left alone. It sounds like typical harassment. She gave him a throwaway assignment, and he made the most of it, writing a sharp, critical opinion piece that was sure to piss people off. The controversy got him a regular column. Eventually he graduated to the kind of profile he did on Matt. I think about how to defend myself, maybe throw hot tea in his face. He says when he started profiling people, he wanted to be generous, but it was hard to turn off his old criticisms. He kept looking for something wrong with his subjects, and he had to teach himself to kill off his own perceptions, which was difficult enough, but now he can't call them back.

This is what kids call a humble brag and what murderers call explaining their plans to their victims.

"So what's wrong with me?" I ask, taking the bait. I pour some tea and hold the cup ready to attack.

The reporter shakes his head. "I made myself stop thinking like that. I thought I'd be happier. But now I don't know how to trust my reads on people, even my boyfriend, even myself."

Something squeaks. I look toward the door, but it's my body nudging the table.

"Too sentimental," he says. "Sorry."

Maybe we need to throw away our impressions altogether. I drink the tea. I empty the pot into my empty cup. When the pot is dry I pull out the flower inside. It drowns in the air.

In my pocket I find the dog half again and pet furiously.

———

The reporter's boyfriend parks the sexiest car I've ever seen. He must teach at a private school. We watch through the window. The instant the engine shuts off, the reporter's mood shifts. I pet the dog half and wonder how to jump through a window *without* dying. But this is another circumstance that leads to un-Matt, a circumstance I need to avoid.

From the sexy car steps a short white-passing guy in his fifties. I look down to make sure I haven't turned into a short white-passing guy in his fifties too, but I haven't. I don't feel relieved. Felipe Collins is the kind of man who wears a tie with a long-sleeve polo shirt. A red tie and a red shirt, with tan slacks and pointy tan shoes. He's the kind of man who's always embarrassed me, like I haven't quite understood the rules.

The reporter shuffles his feet beside me. He doesn't wave. His boyfriend doesn't wave. The reporter squints at me with desperation, pleading for help.

I'm ready to dump my tea on Phil Collins and, when he doubles over in pain, ax-kick the back of his head. But as soon as he touches my hand I sense at once why the reporter asked me here. I sense something obviously askew with Phil Collins. Something unidentifiable on the surface level. He is in exceptional shape, his polo lumpy with muscle, his handshake extra firm to moderately hostile. He flashes a smile like a torch to a barren tree. But what I sense isn't that aggression. It isn't anything public. It's like something inside him is blocked. I can feel the blockage.

He yanks his hand back quickly, yet I am sure of what I felt. I am sure, because I have felt my disappearance. Instead of a crack in a wall, the blockage is a wall where there should be a crack. Phil Collins has something he wants to protect, his own box full of toys, and he put it somewhere hard to get to, somewhere maybe not entirely real or not real to other people. But I have been to that invisible place. I have felt its boundaries. I can feel his wall, it's like the surface of a glass bubble. If I can only get my fingers on that surface, I think, I could pop/crack it.

"This is the guy I told you about," the reporter says.

"The one who came back from the dead?" Phil Collins asks. "The one who could do no wrong? You look pretty normal."

I thank him for saying so.

The reporter asks how Phil Collins's day was — he teaches at an exclusive Catholic high school. His students have typical rich white kid problems, the problem of figuring out what they want when they can have anything. As he talks his bubble seems to expand and contract, breathing in and out whenever he does. The whole room seems to breathe in and out, expand and contract. Soon I barely notice anything else, only the bubble breathing. Phil Collins goes on about how one rich white kid with two parents and a nest egg did something to another rich white kid with only one parent and a nest egg—there's always someone to bully—and I breathe along with the bubble, matching my rhythm to its rhythm. I picture a hand reaching out of the top of my head and resting on its surface. The bubble expands and contracts, my hand rises and falls. I place the "hand" of my mind on the slick, cool surface, and I run the "fingers" of that hand all over it . . . No cracks. No way in. Not a single blemish.

My phone buzzes my concentration. I pat my pocket quiet. The conversation has stalled without me noticing. I apologize and check my phone. Sandra wants to know whether I'm still there, here, where I am. The time between this text and her last text is fifty-two minutes. I text back that I'm thrilled to announce that I'm not in danger after all. (Though what is the nature of danger if you're supposed to know when you're in it? Danger is a state of intention.)

I don't text that last part. Instead I text fish emojis, then lizard emojis, then monkey emojis, then people emojis—I'm evolving. Sandra texts back a shoe.

"Staying for dinner?" the reporter calls.

I need to hurry. It's almost five, and I need to sleep soon if I want to wake in time to meet my ex-family for dinner in Boston. (As I understand things.) And yet I don't want the reporter to lose faith, not in his partner and especially not in Matt. If I let down the image of Matt, I would be my own disappearer. *I* would be the circumstance that leads a Matt to un-Matt—what a joke.

I ask Phil Collins what it's like to teach the next generation, stopping myself before I mention Charlotte. What really matters in the Schrödinger problem is: do you love the cat? Phil Collins's theory is to teach his students to understand the language of their own oppressing, maybe he's a good teacher after all. With the "hand" of my mind I search again for the surface of his bubble, somewhere inside of him. I feel for the blocking point. I push every bit of my presence into that "hand," I concentrate on making it real. And then it is like my real fingertips touch the real surface . . . because I feel that the bubble has more give than I imagined, a rubberiness that absorbs my force when I try to pop it.

The bubble breathes in, breathes out. It breathes in, and as it expands, my fingers rise with its surface. It breathes out, and as it contracts, my fingers fall with its surface. It breathes in again, and I get an idea of what to do. I recall how, during the Airing of Grievances, each of my team's airings started with the grievances before them, building on each other so that the sum total seemed both too much to take and a list of the ways we *took it* together, even as we *took it* alone. And the next time the bubble breathes out, I go in with it and try my best to hold my ground. The bubble breathes in again, and as it expands, it pushes my "hand" back, but this time not as far. It breathes out, and as it contracts, I push in a little more, closer to the imaginary center.

With each cycle of breaths, the surface stretches thinner and thinner, as thin as it can take. The tension between the bubble and me makes my "hand" quiver. Some part of me keeps telling me to stop, to go to sleep and eat dinner in Boston with my daughter, before it's too late. But another part of me says: this is love. Going past the point of no return. I've gone through a wall, so what's a bubble? I wonder, if the other me had gone through the wall to Boston and become me, whether Charlotte would have loved me more.

Finally I feel my hand go into the bubble, I feel the bubble engulf it. If I am still in the reporter's living room, it is only in the past—my present self slips inside the blockage. I am part here and part there, part then and part now, as if Boston is a kind of practice.

———

The inside of the bubble isn't like the space between the walls. It's like a giant circular room. I stand in the center of that room or a projection of me stands in the center of that room. The walls all around are covered in projections of Phil Collins. The projections are kind of like art prints, but they don't neatly decorate the walls, somehow they tangle around each other as if they are simultaneously two-dimensional like the pictures we know and three-dimensional like huge strands of thread. I get the sense that they once moved freely about the room, that they are stuck in place now, each one caught in the others. It's like they *want* to move. Something stops them from doing so, and the result is that the room grows more and more frustrated, unable to order itself.

I am both my "hand" and the projection of me in the room. With my hand I try to move the pictures into focus, pull them one by one from the single mass until they are individual moments. From my place in the center of the room I watch for connections. A boy, his father pinching his cheeks until he cries, asking why he's so light-skinned—the boy as a man meeting the reporter, drawn to, of all things, the shape of his eyebrows—the boy-man wanting to teach boys to unlearn manhood—the man feeling unsafe in his own classroom, his last sense of power slipping away—the boy held underwater by his brothers, taught to hold his breath—the man told off by the head nun—the mother always praying while the boy tries to ignore his name—the boy lifting weights until the father's muscle becomes his. I turn the pictures this way and that way, aware that I am a part of their appearance, that any appearance is also a disappearance. They are here because I am here, beholding them. The oldest pictures seem the easiest to sort and the more recent pictures the hardest, like the bubble encloses each one of them. I have to pop each bubble individually in order for the picture to fall into place among the others. I have to untangle them as individuals in order to untangle the lot. As the mass loosens and becomes parts that are each whole unto themselves, those wholes rejoin each other until the room is spinning and sorting itself.

The reporter circles the couch, muttering, shaking his arms with his cell phone in hand. The light is on. The sun has set. We sit across from each other, Phil Collins and I, staring into each other's blank faces. Who knows how long we have been like this?

"Oh, thank God," the reporter says when I look up at him. "What the hell happened?"

What happened? I feel a part of Phil Collins within me now—like a desire to exercise though I hate exercising—and I feel a part of me missing, probably within Phil Collins.

I don't tell the reporter this. I don't tell the reporter the last time I gave someone relationship advice he killed himself and his girlfriend blamed me. I tell the reporter that I tried to help Phil Collins see himself—"Like hypnosis," I hear myself saying, "you didn't know I could do that? Don't worry, it's fine, I have to go now"—and I stumble out into the dark, unsure what I really did to Phil Collins and afraid that it wasn't me but the absence of me who did it. The last thing I remember is hailing a cab and saying the address to Sandra's apartment.

CHAPTER 6:
DISAPPEARING

THE BODY IS NOT A VESSEL FOR THE SOUL BUT THE SOUL

Something was different in Boston. As soon as I opened my eyes in the dark I knew this. As usual I could feel the bed beneath me, I could smell my own farts, cars drove past on the street. But I didn't turn on the light, because someone would have a pistol pointed at me, likely the boyfriend detective. I felt, if not my disappearance, its increased probability. I couldn't even remember falling asleep.

My phone lit up and briefly threw the room into shadow. No one shot me. I sat up and read: I said text if you were not coming, and then, from Jenny: Never contact us again. You are such a fucking fuck-up. Have a good life.

My phone said it was 10:28 p.m. I had missed dinner.

I could cross one thing off my Fuckit List: Becoming the other Matt was somehow another circumstance that led to a state of un-Matt. Go figure.

What I had now for options was:

Fuckit List

1. ~~Become the other Matt~~

2. *Avenge the other Matt*

3. *Change whatever circumstances lead a Matt to un-Matt*

4. *Burn murder/disappearance to the ground*

Was I, after all, such a fucking fuck-up? I was someone who slept in one universe while awake in another. I was someone who simply wanted to love his ex-family better. Was that so strange? I put my phone down before I embarrassed myself, and petted the cat half. I needed to meet face to face. If I could see how my ex-family saw me now, then I would know who I was to them.

I reconsidered my evolution in the light of the discovery that becoming a successful me meant losing myself. Does the success of a doppelgänger species depend on its loss of self? Does a member of a doppelgänger species sometimes mistake itself for poisonous? Poisonous species evolved bright colors, because predators evolved warning systems for bright colors. Safe species evolved the same bright colors, because predators evolved warning systems for poisonous species. What would a doppelgänger species be like if it wasn't hunted? The safety it evolves depends on the slow disappearance of what it would look like if the world were safe. Is its original appearance buried somewhere deep in its gene pool, waiting for its predators to die out? Or are predators actually what keeps safety from becoming poison? As with rabbits, a safe species with no predator quickly becomes dangerous to other forms of life.

I texted Jenny that I could explain and to meet me at her gym, I wanted to give her home court advantage. Plus her gym was open twenty-four hours, so I could wait all night if I had to—I would bring the cat half for company.

For some reason the desk person gawked at me, then made an obvious effort not to look at me. They rushed through the membership process. They had some kind of problem with my appearance, I didn't know what. This was typical. On the elliptical I used my phone to search for "how to solve a mystery when you're used to being the mystery." I read through a blog called *So You'd Die to Be a PI.* My legs churned, full of Phil Collins's urge to exercise.

The blog's target audience was white college graduates who still lived with their parents in the suburbs and who'd played all of their video games and now wanted to know the neighborhood's secrets. I read about how to go undercover even with people who knew you, how to tail a car down a quiet street, how to use the "deep web" to find buried records or sex tapes or other forms of identity. I read about how to take fingerprints properly and how to fasten handcuffs securely. All of the things Jenny's boyfriend would know how to do. Being a detective was the opposite of loving better: It meant knowing a hundred ways to turn presence into absence.

The cat half sat on my dashboard, vibrating with the machine, purring. While I read and ellipticaled I felt an unusual number of eyes on me—as if I was still taking photos as Matt Chung. Two bulkier guys sneaked glances whenever they thought I wouldn't notice, though they weren't full of violence, just anxiety.

Someone pulled the plug on my machine.

———

"What—the—Matt?" Yumi asked. I sighed a breath of relief. It was probably her night off and she hadn't followed me here to murder me. I remembered now that Jenny's gym was also her gym. She swam in the pool here, which was big and often empty. She wore a black tank top and black athletic shorts over her swimwear. I was happy to see her. Her hands rose into pushing position and fluttered in little circles.

"You have every reason to be angry," I said.

"Good Goddess," she interrupted, "you really look like you're disappearing now. How are you doing that?"

I was a little sweaty and maybe smelled bad. But I could tell that wasn't what she meant. She was worked up: Her face burned red and she gasped for breath. On the other hand we were working out.

"Are you—" she asked, twisting her hands. One twist left, one right. "I mean are you—a ghost?"

"Huh?" I said.

"Matt Chung?"

I stepped down from the machine, not sure how to explain what I was.

"Stay away," she said, crossing her forearms in an *X*. "Don't come any closer!"

Fair enough.

She bit the left side of her upper lip, then the right. She bit the right side of her lower lip, then the left.

God, I missed her.

"You must have some kind of sickness, is that it?" she asked. "You shouldn't go out to public places."

A sickness—somehow I left that out of my calculations. A sickness meant I could be healed.

"Did you infect Sandra too? What happened to her? Where is she?" She gathered herself with a shiver and prepared to say more. Whatever it was I would take responsibility. "She was supposed to move into my place, but I never heard from her. Did you do something? Her cell is disconnected. I went over to your apartment, no one was there all day, now at night you show up at my gym like a ghost . . . At least tell me why you look like that."

"I wish I had known how to know you," I said.

She coughed. She literally closed one eye and looked at me with the other, then switched. "Matt Chung?" she said again.

It was like she had gone back in time to when Sandra first showed up and confused things. She wore the same look the desk person had worn: a desire to escape, like the ants on me might spread to her. Finally she ducked as if I was about to hit her and scuttled away like that, low to the ground, shaking her head. She was entirely different. She had called me a ghost, but with her long hair flying behind her, pale and scared and searching for her other self, it was she who looked like one. I chased after her to apologize. She was so fast. "I know I screwed up," I called. "Can't we talk?"

In the end I returned to the elliptical, still harboring an urge to work out. No one else approached me. In fact the entire rest of the night people seemed to stay away. On the other hand: not many people exercised after midnight and before five a.m. and maybe those who did wanted to be alone. At the first sign of light I went straight to my ex-family's house. I knocked and knocked. Jenny took one look at me and dropped to the floor, screaming.

WHAT IS LEFT OF ME

First Jenny screamed, then she got up and pulled me inside. She threw her arms around me. How confusing after all of my efforts to love better. To receive love all you had to do was walk through a wall. Behind her the detective poked his head out of the staircase, and stopped dead. My ex-wife squeezed me, examined me, squeezed me, examined her hands. She gently pushed her finger into my chest. "You're—what?— you look like the kid in that time-travel movie, like you erased your birth and are flickering out."

How to translate? I seemed to recall a scene from a movie in which a boy holds a photograph and watches the image of himself disappear. But every time-travel movie has a scene like that—at some point the protagonist makes a mistake in the past and then spends the rest of the movie putting things back together so his present self will still exist. Movies always assume time is a straight line.

"I honestly couldn't make it to dinner—" I said.

"Stay for breakfast."

"—I swear on my parents' ghosts."

"Don't swear on anyone's ghost," Jenny said. "I said you should stay for breakfast."

Well. I was in real trouble if she would involve herself in my problems again.

For the first time in three years I followed her into the house. The foyer was as big as a room, with one shoe rack on the left and one on the right. They still took off their shoes, I had thought that habit would be the first to go. I kicked mine off. To the right was the living room and kitchen, which flowed straight into the dining room. Much of the furniture was familiar, the appliances were new. I found wood floors and wainscoting and a cross over every threshold. When had she gotten so pious? Seeing our old stuff, my brain clicked for a drink, but only by rote. I didn't feel thirsty—not even for water—not even after working out for nearly six hours. Which made me realize I had worked out for nearly six hours, an amount of exercise impossible for me. I was overlooking some crucial clue, something about observation . . .

The detective followed behind me. I turned and faced him, and he darted into the kitchen. I walked toward him, and he backed away. He seemed genuinely terrified. I walked past him and threw three slices of bread on a buttered pan. The smell calmed me. The detective swore under his breath. I cracked three eggs to scramble them the way Charlotte liked, and he touched my shoulder quickly, pressing my skin with the same lightness Jenny had, with one fingertip, like I was an unlabeled button or a Jenga block.

He pulled his finger back and held the tip up to the light. "W-T-F," he said.

A sarcastic voice behind him called, "Hello, *dads*," with the same irony Charlotte had used for me, but this time for both of us.

———

She wore a grape-toned oxford and a purple-striped skirt and sneakers with purple stars, neatly matched, quiet and studious and not at all desperate to fit in. She wore another new presence. Funny how we buy our clothes for bodies we wish we had. I could see the desperation my daughter hid only because I had already seen it in the elevator. I wondered how to tell her that desperation would never go away, even if she went through a wall into a world that actually believed in her right to exist. She had come out of her mom not needing belief to make her real—a perfect, loving being—into a world that kept trying to get her to believe that she wasn't real without it.

"Nice to see you wearing something appropriate today," said the detective, feigning surprise.

I strode toward him. At the last moment I veered and handed Charlotte her workbook. All three of us noticed him flinch. It was a pathetic triumph, a regression to an animal state. What the predator fears most is that he himself will become prey.

Just before I let go of her book, Charlotte laughed with me. Then, catching me catching her, her smile twisted into a smirk.

It nearly broke my heart, that effort to protect herself from loving me.

She flipped through the workbook, probably comparing her handwriting to mine, as I had done. I watched carefully, but the smirk didn't go away. I added two more eggs and another slice of toast. Jenny returned from wherever she had gone and eyed Charlotte's innocent outfit.

"I guess we can thank your dad for something, at least," Jenny said.

It took me a minute to figure out what. "You're dressed like that because of me?" I asked.

My failures to appear had given our daughter the idea to dress for success. The best failure to learn from is somebody else's.

Charlotte left the kitchen and wandered into the dining room. Silently I set the table at which we used to eat together—for three, then four, people. I plated the eggs and toast. I got three, then four, glasses from the cupboard above the same side of the sink as always. I poured orange juice for three, then all four, of us, and I waited for them to join me, trying not to cry into their cups.

Jenny sat first, on the opposite side from me. The detective moved his plate down to the far end and glared. Finally Charlotte chose the seat next to me, though she seemed to do so in order to avoid seeing me at all. She made faces at her mother. I felt their anxiety around me and I waited for our togetherness to make us happy.

"Ew," said Charlotte finally.

"Why don't you say grace?" Jenny asked.

"Me?"

"You. Charlotte."

Charlotte dug her fork into her eggs, then put it down again. "Sorry, God, for killing chicken babies."

"That's your favorite food," I reminded her. "And those eggs aren't fertilized."

"Mom?" She pushed the dish away. "What is up with him? Why doesn't he look alive?" She got up from the table, about to run off again—not through a wall but emotionally—then suddenly picked up her knife and held it in front of her with two slim hands. "I do kendo, Dad."

"That's not even Korean," I said.

The detective groaned and laid his fists on the table. Jenny lowered her head to the eggs and sniffed them, calm or pretending calm.

"Dear Lord," I said. "Bless our toast and eggs. Let us eat our grievances. Let us be *Homo sapien* to each other."

"*Homo sapiens*," the detective said.

"Let us dismantle our lives."

"Let us have cereal," Jenny said.

I forked egg into my mouth to show them it was good. I made sounds of intense enjoyment. I had practiced making these eggs every day for the last three years.

"What was I thinking?" Jenny said. "This is a disaster."

My fork dropped. All three of them jumped at the clang. The sun kept rising and rising, because the earth kept spinning in place.

"Are you dying or something?" Charlotte asked. "Is that why you were such a mess the other day? Is that why you couldn't be at dinner or even text that you wouldn't be there?"

She would be late for school soon. Soon the light would drag me back into **XXXXXX**. How to explain? I couldn't be there for dinner because I had never been there. I couldn't be present for Charlotte because the presence I knew wasn't what I wanted for her. I wanted to love better, but I didn't know how to dismantle a life that was disappearing. Like my daughter, I had been so many people for so many other people—I adapted, I evolved—that my first thought upon any new encounter was, *How should I appear?* I feared disappearance even as I chose it, I feared disappearance *because* I chose it. And when I finally found out who I could be, I found out I shouldn't be him, because he was brutally murdered.

"Please put down the knife," I said. "Killing your father isn't literal."

The detective rolled his eyes.

That wasn't what I had intended to say.

"Please," I said. "Let's live."

"She doesn't like eggs anymore," Jenny said. "She's vegan."

Charlotte nodded.

Well. I had never liked eggs either.

Jenny cleared the plates. I got up to join, and she shook her head. "Give her some cereal and do the dishes with her. I'll call the school and my office that we'll be late. Pull yourself together."

"I'll stay too," the detective said. "You know—just in case."

Didn't he have enough cases? What was the crime I'd committed? He needed to stop investigating us: To love better was to love without arresting anyone. To calm down I looked out the window. Nature was out there acting natural. My breaths slowed, my muscles loosened; still my heart pounded. A bird landed on the grass and pecked away. Immediately other birds alighted. The first bird flew away, and they all flew away.

I had given everyone in the house half a dog-cat except for the detective. I wondered now whether I should give him the cat head in my pocket.

A clap rang out, and my heart stopped.

"Hey," Jenny said. "Wake up!"

I never slept anymore. What she called waking up must be not an action but an interaction.

———

The day Charlotte pushed me out the emergency exit of her school, I didn't just go home. I had waited until recess and then sneaked back to spy on her. I watched her boss her friends on the playground. To become popular she hadn't become the class clown, that role wouldn't work in her favor. Instead she became cruel. She had her way with her friends, threatening to excommunicate them if they didn't follow her. She claimed she was the only one loyal to their friendship. She acted like a pope making up the rules of their faith. I knew that if I introduced myself, it would indeed ruin her, that her power relied on a constant show of godliness, of the ability to be a universe unto herself. She had to look like she didn't need anyone else. Suddenly she caught my eye through the fence, and for the sake of her humanity I pretended to be passing by. I had taken responsibility that day—I had meant to dismantle my life—I had gone into my cave and eaten nothing but toast and eggs for nearly a thousand days. What had I done wrong?

———

I filled the kitchen sink with soapy water and soaked my hands in its warmth. The soap smelled like cucumbers, one of my favorite smells. It reminded me of our old house, which was still my house. Charlotte dropped her cereal bowl into the basin. It glanced my wrist, and I

247

pretended it hadn't. She was almost as tall as me now, I hadn't noticed on the hill where it seemed natural for height to fluctuate. "You're sure you're not dying?" she asked. "And don't say something dumb like we're all dying."

"Not yet," I said, smelling our loving past. "I'm still trying to figure out how to be alive."

"You can say that again." She tapped my arm with two fingers, then brought the fingers to her lips and made her smoking-gun gesture. "If you're not dying," she said, taking out her phone. "I have stuff to do."

Her fingers zipped over the screen. Stuff. I leaned over her shoulder.

"It's none of your buttness," she said.

I scrubbed the dishes slowly, to make the present last.

When I finally caught a glimpse, she seemed to be chatting in a language I didn't recognize, on an app I had never seen before, too cool for school.

"Make America talk again," I said.

"Lame."

"It looks like that app is in beta."

She paused. Her eyebrows seemed to think and then remember that I used to have a job that could understand. "I'm testing the US version," she said. "It's a friend's program in Egypt."

"You speak Egyptian?"

"Dad," she said. "That isn't a language. Unless you mean hiero-glyphs." She swiped her thumb over her screen and put the phone back in her pocket. "You're so clueless. Let me give you some advice."

"I'm eager to hear it," I said.

"Never mind." Her phone buzzed, and she took it back out again.

Why would eagerness stop her? It reminded me of the game we used to play, when I would try to figure out why she felt how she felt. I would ask her emotion, and we would trace its origins. The goal was to find meaning. She felt angry, because I had treated her like a baby, which was about injustice, etc.

"I've been clueless since before you were born," I said. "Even before your grandparents died, I guess. I've been thinking that was when I changed, but maybe I was always like this. Like I didn't know what people saw when they looked at me, what they wanted or how I should provide it, they seemed to see someone else, I was invisible—" I didn't know why the word *invisible* had come out, I had meant to say *bullied.*

She stopped typing, but didn't raise her head.

"I was invisible," I said. "After a long time I couldn't even see myself."

"I'm not like you," she said.

"You're not, that's what I mean."

She went back to typing. To avoid communicating in person she would communicate with someone thousands of miles away in another language.

I wondered whether that was why I had gotten into computers.

"Let's play the game we used to play," I said. "The emotion game. Remember? What emotion are you feeling right now?"

"Annoyed," she said. "Game over."

In my head arose the old video game screen that used to read: YOU HAVE DIED.

"And what are some other times you've felt annoyed?" I asked.

She didn't answer.

I thought about how I was feeling, like I wanted to go back in time. Not to be who I was before, but to go back as who I was now and do better.

"My emotion is envy," I said. "I envy the old days when we played the emotion game together."

"That's nostalgia," Charlotte said. "I envy you for feeling nostalgic about yourself when you were never that great to begin with."

Ha ha. Yet it wasn't nostalgia. "You envy me, but you don't want to become me," I said.

She made a humming sound like an old man's disapproval. It was a low vibration in her throat, which ajusshis made on Korean TV when they watched young people in love. Some reminder to the lovers that they were observed. She stopped typing and her phone buzzed on without her response.

She was thinking. Finally she stepped up and started drying dishes. I wasn't sure what had changed. I had almost finished the job. I slowed down even more, wet a glass, sponged vigorously, rinsed and put it in her hands.

"So you envy someone because you want them to change," she said, running a cloth over the glass. "Is that right? Is that why you've been stalking us?"

It was astounding. I had been her age when my parents died. I had thought I envied the white kids at school because they still had parents who looked like them. But that had never been the real reason for my envy. Why hadn't I understood then that I envied them because I wanted *them* to love better, because they received enough love that they shouldn't need to feel poisonous to feel safe?

I rubbed my pruned fingers together underwater. "When you were born I wanted to be a good dad, but I was too scared of being a bad dad to know how to raise you."

"What?" she asked.

I explained. At eight or nine I used to think of the future as thousands of doors ahead of me. I could open any one, and it would lead to other doors, and from there I could open a new door that led to other new doors, etc. As I got older I wondered what I had missed out on, what was behind the doors I hadn't chosen and behind the doors that those doors led to, etc. But when I looked backward, the only doors I could see through were the doors I'd opened. The only path I could see was the path I'd taken. I thought I had chosen those doors so carefully, to arrive at where I was, when in fact I would never have chosen any others. "When you were born," I tried, "you were born with a whole new set of options I had never seen before. I couldn't tell you where to go, because I didn't know where your options went. I could only tell you not to go where I had gone."

"My God." Charlotte pushed her fingers up under her hair like the teeth of a comb and fixed me with one of those stares that seemed more mature than I would ever be. "That's not an explanation. What are you even talking about?"

"I'm talking about you being half your mother and half me, in the kind of country we are living in and the kind of country we'll be living in three months from now."

"You want the advice?" she said.

I nodded and held my tongue.

"Don't be so dumb."

But that wasn't an explanation either, unless she meant I had been too silent in life.

I thought about adding "Don't be so dumb" to my Fuckit List. The entire list was things to do in **XXXXXX**.

Charlotte dried the last of the silverware and it shone in the light from the ceiling fan. I showed her my fingers, and she said I had "raisins." I had read once that our fingers prune in order to grip things better underwater, even though our ancestors' chances of drowning from lack of tools were slim. We evolved to survive our worst nightmares.

"If you don't play with toys anymore," I asked, "what do you play with?"

She said she wouldn't tell me because she didn't want me to bury it in the ground.

———

Before she left for school Charlotte showed me her room. The walls were white. She had a canopy bed that looked like something from a fairy tale. Beneath her window sat a row of stuffed animals that might all be bought on Halloween: vampires, skulls, ghosts, cute vampires, cute skulls, cute ghosts. She had her own computer, which she had built herself. With it she designed and sold things in a shared virtual reality. That was what she did now, instead of playing. She made virtual objects for which people paid real money. "So you can't bury them anyway," she said. In this virtual world, avatars could even commit virtual murder and go to virtual prison, though if you died, you could start over. Most people, Charlotte said, lived in their virtual lives the way rich people lived their real lives: in mansions with robot pets and lots of "sex stuff" and collectible items. The major difference was they could fly. Maybe that was all we wanted: to be richer and able to fly. Charlotte's avatar even looked vaguely like her and had a bedroom vaguely like hers. Somehow she had gotten the skin color and hairstyle and wardrobe all remarkably similar. Either that or, more frighteningly, she had made the avatar first and then made herself like it.

The items she sold she called "hauntings." They were one-time-use ghosts with which players could play tricks on other players. The ghosts could be seen by the player who bought them, but not by anyone else. The only rule, Charlotte said, was they couldn't kill anyone. She said if someone wanted to do that in the game, they had to do it themselves.

It was possible, though unlikely, that I was just another of this game's creations. The game was just another "My Novel" file, a story you started in one world and that took on a life of its own in another. Even fictional worlds had doppelgängers, why not? The current fad, Charlotte said, was to make a nonplayer character twin, who would live a simulated virtual life in comparison to your "real" virtual life.

"Doesn't it freak you out?" I asked.

"Isn't it awesome?" she asked.

"Listen," I said as she mucked around with her hauntings.

"Charlotte," I said.

She didn't respond.

"Can you reverse the hauntings and make them avatars?" I asked.

She asked why anyone would want to do that.

"What if the hauntings suddenly rose up against the people who bought them?" I asked.

She ignored me.

"If you don't see me for a while—" I said.

Jenny called from downstairs that it was time to go. Charlotte kept playing.

"If you don't see me for a while," I said, "don't think it's because I ran away again. I just need to take care of some things first. Turn my intentions into love. Make sense of my resistance."

She rolled her eyes.

"I mean existence." I touched the power switch, and she batted my hand away.

Jenny called up that she would throw the computer out the window, she would turn off all the Wi-Fi and use only the 4G on her cell phone. Charlotte sighed and logged out.

"What do you think?" she asked.

"It's kind of scary."

"It's a game, Dad."

It was a game, why did I keep forgetting that?

"Anyway I won't think that you ran away this time," she said. "But maybe Mom will." She shrugged.

I said that was as much as I could respect.

"Okay," she said.

"Okay," I said.

Sometimes okay was a great success.

ADOPTION

Back in my apartment I lay in bed ready to wake in **XXXXXX**. I had made it through the morning, Charlotte was off to school, Jenny off to the Looking Glass, the detective off detecting. I shut my eyes and waited for the jello to consume me or whatever happened. When I opened my eyes I was still in Boston. I shut my eyes again and tried to see myself in Sandra's apartment. The problem was her apartment was no different from mine. I counted to eighty-four and back to zero again. Sunlight poured through the window. I wasn't even tired.

In Sandra's room I looked around at all the Post-it notes, wondering why so much of her communication in Boston had been silent. What did silence offer that speech did not? When my mother was very angry she used to do everything she always did around the house, except without talking. She always won those fights, my father never knew how to handle the absence.

I went to the kitchen to make toast and eggs the same way I had made them for my family earlier that morning and the same way I had made them for myself for the last three years. I plated the meal carefully and imagined time collapsing, my daughter small and hungry and nonvegan. Then I dumped the whole thing in the trash. My stomach was empty and I didn't want to eat. Instead I lay on the couch on the milk stains. An hour later I played the electric keyboard, trying to work out a church hymn I liked. I hadn't learned hymns, since my lessons had stopped at my parents' deaths. The day I stopped going to church, our priest told Jenny she was blessed for adopting an Asian child, forgetting that he had baptized Charlotte or mistaking Charlotte for another kid. I was across the room and couldn't come to their defense. As usual I had been pushed off to the corner little by little as other people made space to chat.

I checked my phone again. It seemed to take a long time and a lot of effort to pull it out of my pocket. It was past eleven. I was still in Boston. I was awake: I had to wake. The light kept shooting through my windows at 186,282 miles a second. I didn't know what was happening to the me in **XXXXXX**. The breathing had started again and had been going on for a while.

I turned on the TV, and the KKK-candidate's face appeared. It was as bright and pocked as the moon. Why such fascination with him? The brightness of his face came from the reflection of many other faces watching him. What they saw wasn't really his presence, it was their own. What he had to offer was absence. If we couldn't dismantle the desire to see ourselves in him, then he was indeed our president.

The TV said it was noon now. My phone said it was noon. The electronic world, as we knew it, allowed only one deviation. To be or not to be. 1 or 0. Awake or asleep. Matt or Matt. Only in the superposition can I both shut my eyes or open them.

TO EACH THEIR OWN PROTEST

I am on Sandra's better sofa. Sandra's face hovers above me. I hear her actual breathing. Beside me is the same coffee table, only perhaps slightly smaller, as the coffee table she moved into my apartment. Beneath the sofa is the same rug, only perhaps slightly smaller. Across the room is the same big-screen TV, only perhaps slightly less big. The air smells slightly cleaner. The art looks slightly more appropriate. I feel slightly more relieved than I should feel to wake up as myself.

"You slept like crazy again!" Sandra says, which is how I know that I am alive.

"Am I fading though?"

"What?"

"Am I see-through? Like a jellyfish? A ghost?"

"Why do you have to be like this?"

One person's frustration is another person's right to exist.

"Seriously why? First you text that you need help, then that you are fine, then you turn off your phone? I guess I'm the idiot for worrying about you. I pulled you out of a taxi last night, just so you know. Passed out. The driver had to turn your phone back on and press your fingertip to it."

She says all of this with a lot of sharp arm movements. How to explain without using the words that fail me? That seem to start in one world and come out in another.

"As soon as the news gets bored with your resurrection," she says, "you have to get out of my apartment. Start looking for a place."

I bow. "I too," I say, "want to resign from the superposition of Matt."

But she isn't done airing her grievances. While I was with the reporter, she says, she had to go alone to the police station and convince the newspaper to corroborate a story it had yet to publish. After that she had to convince her mom that she wasn't either murdered or a murderer. Then she had to convince her mom she wasn't a heartless daughter trying to kill her one remaining parent by ignoring every call and email for three months. "She thought I was one of those people who disappeared after Matt died," Sandra says. "Seven, all Asian, without a trace. Or six now, I guess."

Sandra had mentioned the Asian part before. "Like tourists," I ask, "or Asian Americans?"

"What does it matter?"

It matters. I imagine them wandering around Boston or working in the Looking Glass now. Getting used to the change, normalizing it, or still trying to figure out why them.

"I've never seen my mom cry before yesterday, is my point—not even after my dad died."

"It's my fault," I say.

She nods.

There's only one thing to do: take responsibility for the disappeared. I ask Sandra where Matt's parents live.

Her face shrinks suspiciously. Lips pursed, she steps in front of me as if I'm about to slip away like a thief. "You can't tell them you're not Matt. You know that, right? They'll call the police."

Strange that I have to remind her no one would believe their story. On the other hand reality is the really strange thing.

I try to remember who told me the face has the most muscles of any body part. It has to express fear or disgust instantaneously—if a cute sabertooth tiger appears and your child looks to you, emotion is survival. Maybe my college roommate told me. Science tells us our faces move even before we know how we feel. Sandra's face is as hard and gray as stone.

Her legs bend, as if to sit, but no furniture waits beneath her. She drops into the squat of our ancestors. I smile as humans do to acknowledge each other's frailty.

This is why it matters if the disappeared are Asian American: To be Asian American is to risk a superposition, not one or zero but a set of probabilities under varied circumstances. It is to refuse dichotomy. It is to resist what's essentially a colonial separation: one world into two. A person can disappear simply by stepping out of the superposition into the gaze of an observer, and therefore a single universe. The simplest way to disappear, in other words, is to give up the discomfort of possibility for the comfort of definition. I tell Sandra that I read the notes she stuck to her walls, my walls, in Boston; I read the letters to Yumi; and I am as afraid as she is. "Why didn't you tell me how you felt? We could have helped each other."

Every day she was in Boston, Sandra says, she saw the world slightly differently than the day before, even though nothing about the world seemed to change. (Like the furniture, I think.) "It was disorienting. Each time I woke up the room looked a tiny bit different. I felt like a liar. Like I was lying to myself about how things are. Everyone else was telling the truth, and I was a liar. Yumi was the only one who seemed to understand then. You didn't even notice."

I squat too. We squat together in a cabbage patch a thousand years old in an ancient kingdom on the other side of the world. "Sorry I'm late," I say.

"I guess you haven't looked at me like I'm Yumi in a while."

I hadn't realized she caught that. Though I caught her looking at me like Matt.

She thumps her chest, hard. There's the little pop of a fart. She doesn't mention it. I realize she's never farted in front of me, nor I in front of her. All this time we've been trying our best to fit the ideal the other has of us. This is typical. What is not typical is our ideals have names and physical bodies.

"I farted," I say, as humans do to acknowledge each other's humanity.

"God," she says like another grievance. "I thought I smelled something."

———

Later I download the "My Novel" file to my phone while Sandra makes signs for some candlelight protest. (Though how will anyone read them?) Then I sit beside her and google "why do we feel envy?" One result is a film in which one white man admires another white man and things get creepy. The first man starts wearing the same clothes as the second man, gets a job in the same office, buys a house on the same street. But envy makes the second man anxious. The more the first man becomes the second, the more the second man tries to distinguish himself. He changes his fashion, quits his job, moves out of the state and then the country. It is just as Charlotte said: You envy someone in order to change them.

Art supplies range over the dining table. Sandra duct-tapes the side of a cardboard box to a mop handle. Her sign says: NO BODY GETS TO REGULAR MY BODY. On second look it's *regulate*, not *regular*. She tied her hair in a ponytail and she wears sweats and a bubble vest and, least typical of all, sneakers.

"Why don't you make a sign too?" she asks.

I try to think of something other than "The Airing of Grievances."

One finished sign reads, *LIFE STARTS AT PERCEPTION*. Another, *ALLY IS A VERB*. A third, *REVOLUTIONS R EVOLUTIONS*.

"Make America great again?"

"My great-grandparents were sold to a sugar company," she says seriously, "and got paid so little they could never buy themselves back."

"Sorry," I say. "I make bad jokes when I miss my daughter."

She fishes out a particular piece of cardboard. It's oval-shaped as if used to pack a mirror. "This is for you," she says.

MY OTHER EGO IS SUPER.

"Ha ha ha," she mouths.

I think: *They Delight Like Cat and Dog*. I think: *Where Id Isn't, There Shall Ego Believe*. I use a yellow highlighter to write, *LOVE IS COLLECTIVE, NOT CORRECTIVE*. All of these signs are countersigns, I think. All of these signs are puns. As if they can change the thing referred to by changing the way to refer to it. I have been speaking this language, the language of protest, ever since I first struggled to speak.

On the bus ride to the Chungs' house I decide I don't believe in the multiverse. If each observation splits the universe, a universe is worth nothing more than an eye/I. It's a dangerous kind of faith that makes free will God. It isn't human to make the world exist or not exist. In this one and only world, messy and circumstantial and shared, nothing is completely free from its opposite. You are not only who you are, but who you are not.

GHOSTS

The Chungs live in a ranch house on at least an acre of land, with a stone walkway and kitschy garden gnomes and wood paneling to look like logs, plus a scarecrow that must be seasonal decoration. The scarecrow wears a dirty white dress shirt and a panama hat. It seems to be missing legs. As I face it I think: *appear doppelgänger appear.* I think: how to be a better Matt. I think: it's better to tell the truth, but the truth is I impersonated Matt and he's still dead. As the bell chimes I think: *Don't be so dumb*, I should have brought a gift.

A balding ajusshi answers. He's shorter than I am, late-middle-aged, with a *U* of gray hair, deep forehead grooves, and gaunt, flappy cheeks. Behind him hovers an ajumma with a tight perm, puckered lips, large eyes sunk in skin like two small fists. They wear matching athletic gear as if to climb a mountain together.

With no proper greeting Mr. Chung says, "It's that person," as if he's translating from Korean. Mrs. Chung gasps and covers her mouth.

I want to explain my responsibility, but I no longer know what it is—because they are not Matt's parents, they're mine. They are my parents—not like doppelgängers, like themselves twenty-five years older. Like they aged naturally. Like they never died. On the back of Mrs. Chung's hand is my mother's scar, which she got sheltering me from a falling iron.

They should be ecstatic, or at least surprised, to see their son again. But instead they seem pissed. They don't embrace me, they stand where they are and glower. Only their shadows seem to reach out to me, as if they and their shadows exist at different times of day.

"Did you come to tell us who you really are?" Mr. Chung asks.

I wonder whether Sandra called ahead. But when I ask, Mrs. Chung says the newspaper sent them photos, and it is clear I am not their son.

"Who are you?" Mr. Chung asks.

Please, I pray, *let me go back two sentences, to before they said I wasn't theirs.*

"How can you do this to us?" Mrs. Chung adds in my mother's voice. "How can you call yourself a person?"

She means, how can I call myself Matt?

This feeling, that they know somehow that I am both Matt and not Matt, is eerily familiar. After my parents' deaths, when I came to live with my adoptive parents, I often had the sudden realization that I was a different person than I used to be. Each time I realized my old life was gone, it surprised me again—as if only a moment earlier I had been living with my parents behind the Chinese restaurant. Whenever I realized who I was, I mean, my parents seemed to die anew.

That was how I came to believe in the kind of ghosts my parents had believed in. Because if they were still alive, and I was still as Korean as other people insisted I'd always be, then my life with my adoptive parents was impossible—and if my life was real, as I knew it was, then my parents were ashes and I was supposed to act like a white kid. In this way, both my parents and whiteness became ghosts.

It was the same after Jenny and Charlotte left me. Each time I went to the toy shop, I went because I realized suddenly that I was alone. When I forgot my current situation, I lived as if Jenny and Charlotte and I were still together. In this way living my life and living a life with my ex-family came to seem mutually impossible. My problem was always how to reconcile two facts: the fact that you want only what you don't have, and the fact that what I want is to be myself.

I reach into my pockets. In the right is the dog half, which I can't seem to give away. I don't remember how it got there. I hold it out to my parents. It isn't much of a gift, and it's all I have. "I forgive you," I say. "Sorry I don't know what kind of dog this is. I know you used to like Pomeranians."

They don't accept. Their bodies stiffen with self-protection.

"Are you threatening us," Mr. Chung says. "Is this ripped toy a threat?"

What threat is forgiveness? On the other hand: forgiveness is forgiveness for something.

"In my life," I say, "you're *my* parents and you died when I was twelve." As usual this doesn't come out right, yet I press on. "I miss you. I have missed you for so long I even forgot what you look like. Thank you for reminding me. Thank you for being alive. Can't we love each other again?"

I offer the dog half a second time. Still they do not accept.

"Do you stop loving someone just because you're someone else's family?" I ask.

Their expressions are not promising.

Before they reject me again, I toss out more words, I try to think what they want to hear, what will make them happy. I find myself telling them that I will figure out what happened to their son, that this is what I came to say: that no matter what, even if I have to use my body as bait, I will get them justice for their love of Matt.

I don't embrace them, I don't invite myself in. I don't force on them who they are to me. Maybe I will regret this. My yellow yarn is probably somewhere inside, but I have chosen the second option on my Fuckit List: *Avenge Matt.*

"귀신," Mrs. Chung says. "Get out of our son's body. You let our son rest."

They think I've possessed him. They slam the door shut. I heel the dog half beside their broken scarecrow.

———

I'd rather not take the bus back, rather not see other people, but my ride share app shows no availability and the taxi app doesn't work. We may be too deep in the suburbs. The fall chill makes me wish for a tracksuit or the summer in Boston. The wind reaches under my lapels, coldly fingers my collarbones. Nature is kind of a creep. I follow my GPS back toward the bus stop, past larger and larger houses. The closer to public transportation the more private the properties. I have walked 451 steps when a stranger calls out to me.

It's an older white lady in a wheelchair, being walked by a dog. White people in tree-lined neighborhoods usually assume I'm in a gang or an Asian Studies department.

"Youngster," she calls.

It could be worse, etc.

That's when I see that the dog looks exactly like the toy I left outside my parents' house, a chipper little thing with two stripes on each cheek and fur as thick as sheep's wool around its neck and chest.

"Oh," the woman says when she catches up to me, "you're not young. You have a very boyish gait. Of course my eyes aren't that good no more. Have we met?"

"Matt Kim," I say.

"Matt Kim?" Her eyes roll back in memory. The dog circles its leash around my leg. "Kim—you're Korean?"

I untie her dog from me and try to pet it to get a better look. It growls. It still looks exactly like the dog half, except realer and alive. Though not as welcoming or friendly.

"I used to know a Korean boy named Matt," she says. "Very nice boy. He's about your age now. I think."

"Maybe it was me," I say.

She claps her hands like a child. The dog barks, once, as if to mimic her.

"Excuse me," I say. "I better get going. I need to get rid of this me. I mean I need to catch my bus."

"Yes," she says. "You must be him. I still never forget a face."

I'm about to go when the dog bares its teeth. I must have made a wrong move.

Behind it a white man appears on a jog, sweating and huffing.

"Stop that, Peter," the old woman says. "Sorry, he's a racist fucker."

Maybe I heard her wrong.

"What's going on, Mrs. Riley?" the jogger calls.

"The dog's being racist again. Now listen, this Mr. Chung needs to catch a bus. Can you help?"

I'm pretty sure we agreed I said "Kim." I didn't ask for help.

When the jogger gets closer he sucks in too much air and can't stop coughing. "Matt Chung?" he coughs.

"Not me."

To my surprise he throws his arms around me. He tells the woman the story of Matt Chung's murder, and they imagine a joyful reunion with Matt's parents. They completely ignore me, as if now I cannot *not* be Matt. The old woman scolds me for not reminding her who I am.

It all seems a typical encounter with the other, until the man calls a taxi for me and the woman clasps cash in my hand and apologizes for the dog. The two of them drag it away as it strains at its leash.

———

Instead of Sandra's apartment, which I am supposed to move out of, I give the taxi driver the business card the reporter gave me. To keep my

265

promise to Matt's parents I resume my investigation. On the way I text Sandra where to meet, if she wants to. Maybe she's already tracking my phone. The address leads to a squat concrete building at the end of a row of squat concrete buildings, like a strip mall for offices. I find the bathroom first, then the PI's door scraped up like a lot of furniture got forced through a too-tight space. Beneath the office number is another sign on another sheet of printer paper. It reads, *OUT OF BUSINESS*, as if I came for a toy shop, not a person.

But no. *Appear doppelgänger appear.* I am not giving up so easily. Even if there is nothing inside, I want to see the disappearance, at least, for myself.

I try to pick the lock with a credit card. I try to look through the blinds, then the keyhole. I try to recall the private eye blog's advice. Why do we lock our doors? Because how someone tries to gain entrance—a knock or a shout or an ax—tells us how to react.

"Open sesame," I say. "Open wall. Open crack. Open doppelgänger. Open for business."

Through the wood I hear a muffled hiccup. I barely believe it myself.

AN I FOR AN EYE

"I hear you," I say. "I heard a hiccup." I press my ear to the door. "No take-backs."

More muffled pops, then a burp.

I step back so that I'm directly in front of the peephole, my face recognizable. "I just want to ask some questions."

There's a short silence. The hiccups return faster, louder.

"Go away," a voice says. "You can't be Matt Chung—it's impossible."

"Please. I know you can see me."

"God, this is so embarrassing."

"Okay," I say. "I'm not him. I just pretended to be him to a newspaper reporter, and that reporter gave me your address. An article is going to come out that Matt Chung is still alive. I'm his avenger, and I need to know what to prepare for. And who killed him."

"Very funny," says the voice. "You need a pastor. Not a PI. Anyway read the sign."

There's another hiccup and a huff of exasperation.

"If I end up murdered too, whoever kills me will find your name and address on my corpse," I try.

That does something. I don't feel comforted.

"Cheap shot," says the voice.

"To me it's my life's worth."

———

The office is as bare as my apartment once was. No furniture, only metal folding chairs. As if the PI really did go out of business, but can't stop coming back. She's a petite black woman in her early forties or so, with a stylish undercut, dressed in black tights that bunch at her ankles and white tennis shoes and a green T-shirt that says "IF YOU CAN READ THIS, THAT'S PRIVILEGE." Something glints from her hand, a good luck charm maybe. She lets me in after a serious, cautious once-over, and gestures with her chin at the chairs.

"Don't judge," she says between hiccups. "Stress gives me indigestion."

"Occupational hazard?"

"None-of-your-business hazard," she says. "Long-lost twins?"

"Very long lost."

She rubs the object in her hand, possibly a dog-cat. She sucks on her upper lip. She doesn't seem to believe her own twin hypothesis, which means she is either a very good PI or a very anxious one. In other words she's not typical. The glint in her hand becomes a flip knife.

"I like your style," I say nervously.

"I'm not into Asians."

"Okay," I say nervously. "I guess I am."

She scoots the second chair until it's across from me, and sits with the flip knife in her lap.

"I'm not really a twin," I say. "I'm Matt, but from another—place. In that place I'm disappearing. I don't know why I keep appearing here. My current theory is that if I get revenge for Matt Chung, I'll be able to go back to where I was." When her eyebrows wrinkle, I add, "It's not the best theory, but it's my second try."

Her hands do some final calculation with her knife, and then she folds it up, cracks her knuckles, and sighs. It feels kind of pathetic to be suddenly demoted to unthreatening, to out of business, but it's her second try too.

"Is Matt Chung's death connected with all the other Asians who are disappearing?" I ask. "If that's what's happening with me, maybe I need to change my strategy."

The last two options on my list are:

3. *Change whatever circumstances lead a Matt to un-Matt*

4. *Burn murder/disappearance to the ground*

I'm clearly not doing a good job changing the circumstances of un-Matt, since I came here alone. Though this time I told Sandra beforehand. On the other hand: maybe I am closer to dismantling my life.

I panic and glance down at my nonrhetorical hands . . . they're still visible. I breathe a sigh of belief.

The PI fixes me with a kind of future pity. Like she pities me, but she doesn't expect me to understand that pity until later. "Look around you," she says. "I can't help you. Anyway I'm not a shrink. You need one of those or Jesus."

"Matt Chung—" I say.

"Is neither."

"But you came back here despite going out of business. You let me in when you didn't necessarily have to. You must have something you want to say?"

"I came back to get the chairs," the PI says, "since I'm poor. Also you threatened me."

She's right. I might be able to get into her bubble and see for myself—but the reporter's panic and Phil Collins's blank stare still bother me. Even if I didn't know what I was doing, I never got permission. Phil Collins couldn't even tell me to fuck off like the woman in The Cave. That day, after the one dudebro spat on me, I wanted to make them envy me, but my girlfriend wasn't there. Yumi's absence, I realize now, was why I sat with the crying woman. What a relief that she told me off, that she made me envy her anger.

"Why are you looking at me like that?" the PI asks.

My phone buzzes. Twice. I don't check it because she doesn't trust me.

"I won't get mixed up with someone like that Salesses guy," the PI says, a little frenzied.

How many times, I wonder, can you tail a car by appearing not to tail it or hide as a way to find someone or turn a friendly ear to your suspect before you lose your sense of security? (How many times can you hear "Go back to your country" before you lose your sense of country?) The PI's anxiety is like a second knife, always sharp and ready—her hands have learned to never be without a weapon. Maybe the job got to be too much for her. I read a memoir once by a spy who had to know before she entered any room all of the ways she could get out—maybe the PI had to keep too many exits open, leave too many cracks in her walls—I seem to slip through one of those cracks now (one man's exit is another's etc.)—almost unintentionally—and into something like a bubble, but not—something the PI wants to escape, but can't—a memory perhaps or a dream—and in front of me are two strange marbles—no, eyeballs—veined and severed—

My stomach retches on air, my breath rots, and I'm back in the PI's office. The PI sits across from me, still and alert. Her facial muscles tense and ripple across her skin. For a while all her surprise and anger and fear are in her stare, trying not to believe whatever she believes happened. Finally she gasps and asks me what I did.

I saw two undersized eyes, set on wax paper, with threads of flesh hanging off them. "Would you let me do it again?" I ask. "There were a child's eyes—in a box?"

"Matthew Salesses," she says, as if this happened to both of us.

Her knife flashes. The memory is already zooming out though—from the eyes to a box, to the box in a dumpster, the dumpster where Matt Chung's body was found, to a nerdy white man walking away from the dumpster, grinning at his own self-disgust, to a crime-fatigued neighborhood in the city of **XXXXXX**, where elsewhere, in a safe office building, the PI pulls her knife.

To be continued.

She lunges for me, but she's still only minimally mobile. She slumps to the floor, cursing, as if she too has a doppelgänger: Her energy drains from her. I have done this somehow, I apologize. The knife slips from her hand, and I pick it up and fold it into its shell, and apologize. I help her back into her chair, leave the knife in her hand, then sit back in my own chair, and apologize.

I wonder where Sandra could be if she's not going to come in the nick of time.

"You were inside my mind," the PI says, panting from the effort. "How did you do that? How come I can't move my body right? What are you?"

"I'm an estranged father," I say. "And there's no such thing as a mind, at least not separate from a body. Did you cut out those eyes with your knife?"

As soon as I ask I know that she didn't, I know why she's out of business, etc.

"I accept your judgment," I say. "I wish I could take back what happened. To be honest I don't really know how this—how what I am—works. I'm estranged from myself sometimes."

271

Her knife flashes a second time, I should have foreseen that. "That—memory," she says, flinching as if the eyes still watch us. "Can you get rid of it?"

———

On the way back to Sandra's apartment I stop at the animal shelter she mentioned in one of her notes to self.

The dog in the shelter on 3rd Street, will it still be there if I go back? I'd name it Sir Barks-a-Lot. Sir Barks-a-Lot would save the office with me. Would bite Dave in accounting . . .

Then later:

God, I just remembered Sir Barks-a-Lot was the name of the dog I had as a kid.

I had read that note over and over, because of her late remembrance. How memory fools desire. You slowly forget what is gone but never stop feeling its absence. For instance gaining one set of parents and wanting them to be the set you lost.

It's a pretty sizeable shelter, with probably a hundred dogs side by side each in individual crates. But even a no-kill shelter with more volunteer staff than a day care depresses me. In those crates I keep seeing myself and the other foster kids. How did the word *adoption* become so unironic? I remember how, when we fought for attention, my adoptive parents used to say foster care was about kids staying a certain amount of time, not about getting a certain amount of love. There was some study or other about how a child in foster care too short a time has little chance to adjust and a child in foster care too long becomes less and less adoptable. They get used to economizing love. I could adopt every single dog here, but could I really love them better?

As I look around I read the two messages that came through while I was with the PI. They're both from the reporter:

U have a curse or a miracle in u

We both quit r jobs n r trying 2 change r lives. Thx

Does he mean I *caused* them to quit their jobs or *helped* them to quit? *Thx*?

A young guy with a Brazilian accent waits by to answer questions. He knows many dogs by name. He tells me he should be in school, but he spends all of his time here. He recommends favorite dogs, secretly, since they aren't supposed to play favorites, they're supposed to match a prospective owner's wants. He says his picks are dogs lovable enough that you might move continents to be with them despite their American habits.

But I already investigated Sir Barks-a-Lot, checking photos on Sandra's desktop. The dog she had was a rescue greyhound—an animal done running for money. The shelter has two greyhounds, so I choose the one that has been there the longest. I write Sandra's information on the application. If we pass, the guy says, we can always foster-to-adopt, in case the dog isn't a match. I put my hand in my pocket, but it's empty.

ONLY THE HAND THAT ERASES CAN WRITE THE TRUE THING

When I woke in Boston it was the middle of the night. I had the feeling that time was somehow getting longer—or thinner—that everything was stretching out. As if I were pushing on the surface of time's bubble and it was about to give under the weight. I decided to wait until morning to see Charlotte, whenever morning came. I didn't want to wake her before she was ready.

In the meantime I had something to say to Yumi. I took a long shower and then drove to an all-night Wendy's for two double cheeseburger meals. I had been to Yumi's apartment only the once (and hadn't recorded the address) so it took me a while to find my way back. By the time I got there the car stank of meat. It was 1:46 a.m. Yumi would usually be up, but when I buzzed the intercom she didn't answer. I buzzed until I was sure she wasn't pretending—she hated repetitive noises, like Christmas songs. She ignored my phone calls. If she was at work, The Cave would close before I got there. I waited in the car for her return. The smell was unbearable, and after an hour I ate the first sweaty burger (cold), and after another hour I ate the second (cold and hard). I listened to an audiobook about a couple whose dog runs away, except it isn't their dog, it's their kid. They're just in denial. The one time I visited Yumi's studio apartment, I hadn't been able to concentrate. Her collection of dolls stood and sat everywhere, on shelves and tables and sometimes in original boxes. Some of the dolls were antique and in various stages of restoration, and I made the mistake of pointing out that she had quit medical school to doctor toys. The more dolls I found (one in the medicine cabinet!) the more I felt at a loss. Their nearness to life seemed more than my life. Yumi teased me by bringing a doll with her the next time we hung out, hiding it in the room and telling me it was in there while we were in the middle of things. She said my discomfort was about the "uncanny valley." "What you really fear," she said, "is death." At the bottom of the uncanny valley are bodies exactly like ours except not alive—corpses and zombies. It was true I didn't want to think about corpses and zombies having sex. But I was pretty sure dolls didn't freak me out because I associated them with dying. I associated them with a doll my adoptive parents brought home, about the size of a four-year-old, handmade by one of their friends "to look like me."

In the car I kept thinking about dolls and feeling this urgent need to exercise. I reclined and did sit-ups. The sun rose. Either Yumi was home or she wasn't coming home. Finally I drove to the gym, which maybe was the most likely place to find her anyway.

This time the desk person didn't even glance at me. Inside no one noticed me at all. They didn't avoid me like before—my presence didn't register. No one sneaked looks or averted their eyes. I tried not to think about what it meant that even my difference from them was different. It was exceptionally suspicious. I ran on a treadmill, but my suspicion kept growing. I started looking for clues.

Immediately what I detected was that I didn't know what I was doing, which was not a new detection—what was new was how fast it came. It seemed to come from the other side of the wall. It was someone else's intuition: the PI's. Her intuition said I could not reverse the circumstances of my murder/disappearance, only speed them up. I couldn't avenge the other Matt in Boston. My last option left was burn murder/disappearance to the ground.

I had to disappear disappearance, to murder murder, which seemed a lot like semantics. Like the problem with the problem was its meaning: you couldn't undefine a word with the word.

The other thing the PI's intuition told me was that Yumi was here, somewhere. Finding her seemed a lot more accomplishable. I searched for her at the swimming pool. I searched for her among the free weights. I looked through the windows into the empty rooms used for dance and yoga and pilates and tai chi. I searched the climbing wall and even the sports facilities, though she hated sports. I was ready to give up on intuition, when I heard my name called out, faintly. As if the person I was really searching for was myself.

I followed my name through the gym, getting closer and closer, until I heard it clearly. The voice belonged to Yumi. I remembered how many times Yumi had paused in the middle of telling me something. Those missed connections had come home to roost.

Yumi called my name and scuttled through the gym.

I almost caught up to her in the men's locker room.

The early exercisers started to come in, but she didn't care. Her voice shot down row after row of lockers. The gym had a lot of faith in its appeal—after all here what you consumed was lightness. This was not lost on me. The stench of feet and the horror movie vibe were not lost on me. I headed for where Yumi's voice would end up after she looped around, the trick I had used on Charlotte in tag. And then there Yumi was, sweeping her head left and right and calling me.

"Here I am," I said, my voice creaking. I realized I hadn't used it all night.

Despite her fear the last time, she didn't turn away from me or run off. She didn't even stop moving. I waved. She continued sweeping left and right, her hair swinging. Then she lurched straight toward me. I fluttered my hands in her face, but she didn't blink. Just before she walked into me, she made an almost imperceptible shift and stumbled by. She didn't look back no matter how many times I called.

———

When I got to Charlotte's school it was midmorning. I parked up the street and waited for recess. At first another class played outside, little kids pushed each other for the slide and screamed over the seesaw. To feel less pervy I looked down at my phone. I opened the "My Novel" file. The entire document was blank. I wasn't surprised, I was angry. I searched the internet until I found clips from three separate films with fading time travelers. Which one had Jenny meant? I googled my name and got the typical results. I was still online. Finally my daughter's purple-tipped hair appeared. It bounced up and down. She jumped rope. I walked up to the fence and called out.

She didn't respond. The PI's intuition had told me she wouldn't. I tried again anyway. Not one kid even turned their head.

"달," I called. "달." I circled the fence until she jumped maybe three feet from me, the rope nearly hitting the fence. I stood in her line of sight and made faces, stuck my finger up my nose. As she jumped she sang a song about how many boys had a crush on her. A boy came up and stuck out his tongue. She never lost count, but after another jump her eyes suddenly—at the speed of light—caught mine.

Or she side-eyed the boy.

I started up the fence, and the bell rang. It startled me so much I fell back on my ass. The kids ran inside. I couldn't be sure she had seen me or not.

On the way back to my car I heard a shout. Some commotion up the street. With nothing else to try I walked toward the sound. As I got closer a crowd gathered. It looked like an eviction, though for some reason the feds were there. The speed at which people multiplied reminded me of my neighbor's suicide, his ex pointing at me as if to say: if she suffered, everyone she knew should share the blame. Where did that many people come from? I didn't know. Anger ripped through the throng. Four white feds pulled an older brown couple out of the building. The woman screamed that their son was a citizen. "That's why we're not taking him," said one of the feds. It was an immigration raid. Someone in the crowd shouted, "How can you live with yourselves?" and, "A child needs parents," trying to enforce human dignity. Yet we all knew that what was happening was typical and that what is typical is justifiable to someone. If this was justice now, what would it be like when the KKK-candidate won?

The couple cried and shook, their bodies clenched, trying not to do the violence they wanted to do, trying not to make anything worse for their kid. Violence belonged to the ICE: Any pain would automatically become its to use. These parents were my parents too, breathing in other people's smoke. Their son, about to be left behind, was learning an important lesson. He was one of many enduring real disappearances for the sake of other people's existence.

I stepped forward—but what could I do without presence? As if by accident one agent jabbed an elbow into the man's ribs. I threw my absence between them, and a second blow landed on my no-thing. The pain in my ribs belonged to no one.

In the end the couple was taken. This was reality. The van sped off and left a little boy alone inside the house. We heard him crying, but he refused to come out. Whatever you called this fate—strange or typical, justice or injustice, nothing or something—a family had been separated. In that meaningful absence, that absence of meaning, we waited for history to record them. On the horizon the first changing light of sunset appeared. My entire day had passed in Boston.

CHAPTER 7:
THE MURDER OF
THE DOPPELGÄNGER

NATURE

Someone is knocking on Sandra's door. At first I think it must be a lawyer—"We can save you," they call, "your salvation is for sale"—but then I realize they must mean *soul*. Sandra doesn't answer, because she isn't there. She left a note on the coffee table that she would be gone for the day. It's already evening now. Not that she should worry about me. Here my body isn't fading, only my connection to other bodies is. I don't answer the knocking, because it's not my salvation. It's literally not my place to be saved, and one man's salvation is no sole sale.

Instead I come up with a plan. Either with the PI's intuition or my memory of a forum on searching the deep web, I turn on Sandra's desktop. The internet will end human wonder. In five seconds I have addresses to every place Matthew Salesses has ever lived. I print out the bus route and pocket the transit card Sandra made for me. Then I add to her note Matthew Salesses's current address. As a last thought I squeeze in: *Here is my resistance.*

Here is my resistance's state:

Fuckit List

1.   ~~*Become the other Matt*~~

2. *Avenge the other Matt—????*

3. ~~*Change whatever circumstances lead a Matt to un-Matt*~~

4. *Burn murder/disappearance to the ground*

The bus drops me at what during the day is probably a complete and ordinary street corner, but at night is somewhere a group of people would feel alone. I have a sudden vision of Matthew Salesses going through the wall each night to collect children's eyes from Boston. The reason the PI has gone out of business is because there are some unsolved mysteries you don't want to solve, and when you solve them you can't go back.

White dudes in hunting gear, carrying assault rifles on their shoulders, stalk the neighborhood in pairs. They all wear those red hats. I shut my eyes, my pulse doubling. *Don't be dumb,* I think. *Love better.* But on second glance the hunters are still there.

I speed-walk away from whatever adventure they're on, though I might be trading one murder for another. The only place I know in the neighborhood is Matthew Salesses's. I want to tell the hunters I'm not their prey, I'm from out of town/dimension. But you don't get to decide what eats you. The numbers on the buildings descend, **XXX, XXX, XXX, XXX.** I am almost there when the footsteps stampede. My back twitches with bullet holes waiting for bullets, and I run toward a three-story brownstone, most of its windows busted or cracked, some failed attempt at gentrification.

"Hey," someone shouts. It's a lie that life flashes before your eyes: What you see before you die is your death. "Do you know which way to **XXXXXXXXXXXX** Street?"

"Is this," I ask hopefully, "some kind of parade?"

"War games," the dude says. His friends wait for him.

Their hats say: "Make America Hunt Again."

"That's cool," I say. "I'm recording this, FYI."

For a while they keep standing there, staring at me and thinking. Then the closest one's lips curl up, a wolf's smile. "What's FYI mean?" For your individuation? He lowers his rifle, and I jump inside the building and shut the door behind me. Only then do I realize I exposed my back. I've never been so reckless. The lock was broken, when did I notice that? I hold the handle tight, ready to struggle.

The next one of them over shakes his head and nudges the one with his rifle out. I feel like I've seen this before a thousand times. But then they move on, not like they decide to spare me, like they reject me as a meaningful mark. Once they're gone I hang my head and knuckle the back of my neck.

Looking down like that I see, on the floor, dimly lit by a ceiling light—my face. Or Matt's face? Not in reflection, on a piece of paper. I also see Yumi's or Sandra's face. Plus six more Asian faces, a total of eight. They're arranged in a grid, like in that old TV show about a bunch of Bradys. Beneath the grid are the words OPEN YOUR EYES, WE EXIST. And beneath that: THE PEOPLE UNITED WILL NEVER DISAPPEAR.

How to explain? I can try, at least. Sandra made and distributed flyers, and someone in this building took one and either dropped it or littered. It did not come through the wall.

I recheck the apartment number I wrote on my hand. I climb the stairs two at a time so that my heart rate will feel appropriate. The third-floor exit opens to a long, pissed-in hallway. Doors line either side like in a creepy hotel. I wonder why the articles never mention the squalor. Matt really cut himself out of his photos to come here?

Behind one door a child screams, behind another people have loud but uninteresting sex, behind a third someone weeps and blares country music. It's enough to make the silent apartments terrifying. On the other hand I don't know these people—maybe these sounds are sounds of joy—nothing bad *has to* happen. At the door to Matthew Salesses's apartment I seem to hear the brick grinding its teeth, as if eating in its dreams. I collect my breaths, lining them up neatly in my lungs. "I am Matt Kim," I practice. "You killed Matt Chung, prepare to die." I try to clench my jaw in a confident, underwear-model way. But it's all too dramatic even in my head. I knock three times, and then something shakes my elbow and I rap impatiently.

Get out of here, the me on the flyer says. I realize I am holding it in my other hand.

Matt came to this door thinking someone he knew was going to die, not knowing that person was him. I feel a tug on the tip of my memory. I taste blood, having bitten through my cheek. What a smile I'll have. I touch the handle Matt Chung touched, and it gives like it remembers me. *I'm not him anymore,* I tell the door. But it won't let me be anyone else. If I enter, this place seems to be saying, I live or die as him.

I am in a place of soft, multiple sounds: the hum of machines, the low cast of TV voices, the rattling of pipes, a noise like someone munching a sandwich. A truncated foyer leads on one side to a kitchen and on the other side to a hall that must end in a bedroom or living room or den. A dull glow comes from down that hall, the glow I see by. The iron in my mouth tastes earthier, as if it's coming from deeper and deeper underground. If anyone heard my knocks, they would already have responded, I am sure. I breathe in through my nose and out through my mouth, remembering the few meditation classes I took with Jenny, where it felt stranger than usual to be the only Asian, since everyone kept looking to me as if I knew something they didn't. A lump of saliva wets the back of my throat, irritating because I can't cough it up. Every time I swallow it, it comes back. I wish I could use the invisibility I had in Boston now.

The tugging on my memory seems to come from farther inside. I count down silently from ten. At six it pulls me forward. My feet follow one in front of the other, with light steps. What leads them? As I drift toward the glow I realize what—it's the yellow yarn. When did it stop unraveling behind me? Was it here, in Matthew Salesses's apartment, where only the other me has been? Did I get here from inside or from outside?

The yarn pulls hard, until it's difficult to go slowly and breathe freely. I feel muzzled, leashed. I can't seem to draw air through the tightness around my throat. Even with the war game afoot I want to run back outside and take my probabilities. But then I know the yarn would keep unraveling, a constant reminder behind me of the way I didn't take.

It isn't a decision—the air is charged with fate. If I left, I would be a third Matt, and I can't handle another me. I walk down the hall, waiting to be struck with lightning. The walls smell like wet wipes at BBQ restaurants. I picture someone wiping them with one wipe after another, meticulous about erasing the traces of consumption.

From the far end of the hall floats the noise of channel surfing. Whoever's there doesn't yet know I am here. Or doesn't care. I whisper to myself, "In a world where one man finds out he is two men and one of them is murdered . . ." The hall ends at two rooms, one on either side. I stand in the middle between the two open doorways. In the superposition. How do I enter both at once? To the left is the TV. Pundits debate the pros and cons of a real wall to build along a symbolic border. The main question is: who will pay for it? The secondary question is: what will happen with the displaced wildlife?

What happens when people stop being polite, I think, *and start murdering?* But this is the question America's actually founded on. It's why we celebrate Thanksgiving. I remember Charlotte trying to go to school in the costume they gave her the day before Thanksgiving, with ketchup smeared all over her face. We wiped it off, we confiscated the bottle, but did we do the right thing? "It's good for her to know these facts," Jenny said. "But she doesn't have to show everyone else she knows them." We wanted to give her the superposition. Yet when Schrödinger's cat lives or dies what use is a superposition to grief?

To the right is a laboratory of some kind, with medical equipment of all shapes and sizes. IV trees and heart monitors and more I don't recognize. There's a human-sized table on which my body will be chopped up and burned. My heart pounds in my ears. A bloody mouth may be intimidating, bloody ears are not. My brain sends me pain signals from a future I don't plan to experience. I have my own plan, of revenge. I don't want to see formaldehyde jars preserving little eyes, little intestines strung up beside measuring tape. The yarn runs directly beneath my feet now. It turns right, into the lab. I turn left . . . and a hard, stick-like object smashes into my neck and collarbone.

NURTURE

A star of pain is borne in my neck—puns fail me. My hands go to the star and I crouch on the floor. Matthew Salesses stands over me, in red flannel pajamas, wielding an upside-down hockey stick, poking his tongue through his lips like a white Air Jordan or a human snake.

"Wait," I say. "Don't you recognize me? Doesn't this face look familiar?"

The stick wavers.

"It's Matt Chung's face," I say resentfully.

His tongue slides back into his mouth with obvious disappointment, and he flips on the lights.

Behind him, inside the TV room, is a small flat-screen, a beautiful leather sofa covered with a plastic protector, and a lawn chair with a bag of sour cream and onion potato chips. What I see is a life of bitter preservation. What he sees makes him furious. His jaw squares, and he strains to keep from squinting. It's the kind of look you get when someone you never thought would insult you tells you exactly what they think of you.

"Matt Chung," he says, barely restraining himself. "Matt Chung is dead—so who the hell are you?"

The neck he smashed is Matt's neck though. I spent an hour being photographed as Matt so that his death could be taken back. Who is Matthew Salesses to say otherwise, when I can't seem to convince anyone?

"You were supposed to be a friend," I say.

He hangs the blade of the hockey stick over his shoulder. I think back to my old taekwondo lessons, the ones I took to protect me from the kids who thought I could do karate. The most difficult thing to preserve in this life is who you are not. That's the part of you that disappears first, because it's the easiest to let go of. Those taekwondo moves are still in my body somewhere, if it has not indeed become Matt's.

"How did you even get in here?"

Shallow breaths hurt my neck less. "The door was unlocked."

He wields the stick again so naturally, like it's simply the nature of a hockey stick to be swung. "I don't want to hit you again," he says, wanting to hit me again, "but the door was locked. I checked ten minutes ago. I always check twice."

I touch my collarbone, feeling for a crack.

"Who are you?" His hands twitch.

The office door is shut now, he must have done it right before or after he hit me.

"I'm a ghost," I say. "An avenger. Christmas future."

There's a slight whistle as the hockey stick slices toward me. Out of instinct or muscle memory my arm pops up. I block the stick with my forearm, a shiver goes across my elbow and up to my shoulder. Though the bone holds. At first the blow almost seems independent of me, like it has the manners to leave me out of its pain. Then the convulsions begin.

The convulsions take the place of my arm, I can't seem to feel any arm otherwise. I belong to the pain, pain says only: *this is mine.* Maybe pain is my avenger, if I am Matt's. I'm already halfway back down the hall, crab-walking faster than I ever thought I could move on three appendages. Now would be a good time to be dispossessed.

Matthew Salesses doesn't follow. One side of his face quivers, half-apologetic. The other is still furious. With some effort he holds back the fury. He makes some calculations of his own. *Open your eyes,* I think. *We exist.* But then he resigns himself, which is somehow more terrifying than anger.

"I know Matt is dead," he says, "because he asked me to kill him. And sorry, but I think this means I have to kill you too." He lunges. The blade cuts sideways, he moves so fast. What saves me is the hall is too narrow and the stick hitches against one wall.

I don't have time to think it, but I think, *Matt wanted to* die? Matt *wanted to die? Matt* wanted *to die?* while he raises the stick again. I am in avenge mode, are we supposed to work something out? Matthew Salesses gets in position between the walls, ready to reattack, and I charge him. I lift a foot off the floor and fear fills me with purpose. To fear is an act of protest. I have been afraid before, but always with my fingers crossed, trying to fear at a manageable level. To really accept fear is to accept you can't live in this world the way you or it is. I come down on his knee, and it makes a sickening crunch, like stepping on a frog barefoot. He screams and chops at me twice, so fast. The blade catches my thigh—then his knee buckles and he jams the handle of the stick into the floor to support himself.

A charley horse spreads across my quad. My leg goes immediately stiff. But I have him off-kilter now, I surprised us both. The blood in my neck drains to my leg and forearm, the liquid in my ears dispels. The space in the hall grows bigger for me and smaller for him, I sense this. He puts the stick on his shoulder again, bracing himself with one foot against the wall. I am in fighting position. He looks at his knee and then at me, back and forth, like he can't figure out how I did it. His pity is gone now—there's just murder or vengeance. My only hesitation is suicide.

"Matt asked you to kill him?" I ask, watching carefully. "You mean you murdered him?"

There's a little movement, not in his face, in his ears. A bit of snot drips down, and he wipes his nose.

"You mean you murdered him," I say again, hurting him.

I know this look. He is a man I've known all my life, happier if he gets hurt along with you: an imaginary man who, because he is already suffering for his sins, can be absolved of them before he even commits them. I have known this man in myself. He still eats in The Cave every lunch break. I back up a little more, still holding my arm. But my body is aware now of awareness. My awareness vibrates in the palms of my hands, open to whatever way he moves.

"Matt was a fucking idiot," Matthew Salesses says, but it's to keep hurting himself.

I spring toward him.

This is what he expected. He waits and flicks the blade down onto the arm I'm holding at the same moment I get to him. Then the stick moves again, and I stagger to the side just in time to avoid a jab at my stomach. I prop myself against the wall and try not to throw up. He smiles that same self-disgusted smile. "I wish I didn't have to do this," he says. "Matt owes me double now." It's this sentence, the sentence in which he thinks my body owes him because it belongs to pain and he returns it to pain, that finally pushes me over the edge. In the space of that imagined debt my old senses are there again—I know how he will try next to hurt me. He will try to feel just and dignified. He waves the stick like a sword, and it's not a sword. So I step into his stabbing range and let him underestimate me.

What do I have for a weapon? *You always have the tools you need to defeat the enemy where you found those tools,* goes the logic of video games and of murder mysteries. God only gives you as much suffering as you can take, goes the logic of my adoptive parents and of suffering.

Matthew Salesses can't help himself, he jabs the stick at the bait. The blow glances off my ribs. The pain shouts, *This is mine, This is mine.* But I know how to dispossess it. If you see its greed, you can trap its hand in the cookie jar. The moment his eyes flicker I grab Matthew Salesses's hockey stick, confusing him. He wanted so badly to destroy his vision of Matt that he mistook the Matt he was fighting. I pull the stick toward me, he doesn't let go. He stumbles headfirst into the space between us. Using basic taekwondo I could raise my leg and ax-kick the back of his head. But—if Matt wanted to die—do I also mistake the Matt I am fighting?

I pull the stick harder, bring my disappearance closer, and then Matthew Salesses falls down on top of me and I pat his back, once, twice. He shoves the handle into the side of my head.

WHO KILLED VINCENT CHIN?

When I wake I am tied to a chair, my body bruised and aching. I have seen myself here before. We have seen our ends coming, they are always someone else's end first. Matthew Salesses has his back to me, his phone makes artificial clicks. On the TV is a program about mass animal kill-offs. Freak whale beachings and a species of elk that goes extinct all at once. I want it to be a relief not to see the news, but the news is: humans have changed the circumstances of death. This is the state of our lives: In order to live we must know what it means to us not to live. In order to survive whatever Matthew Salesses wants to do to me, I have to find out what he did to me. I concentrate, feeling for his bubble, tracing his pleasure toward the source of self-pity. For whatever realization the process goes more quickly this time, your typical bubble-bursting. I know somehow that what I am doing to Matthew Salesses will affect how I'm seen in Boston, but I have no choice. He turns to me, slowly, and begins to say something—I slip past his words or inside of them.

His bubble is like Phil Collins's bubble, a small space encircled by pictures. The main difference is the absence of darkness. The whole space glows. The only darkness seems to come from *me*—from the shadows I cast in every direction. I see by these shadows: They give form to light. As my eyes adjust I think about what I am looking for. I am looking for a me who would rather not exist than exist as me.

And without even a "touch" I am there . . . on the night Matt Chung died. The other me stands at the door, his same wide forehead, his same square chin. But it's not like looking in the mirror anymore, because I am not Matt Kim. I am Matthew Salesses now, letting into my apartment someone completely other than myself.

As Matthew Salesses I make coffee. As Matthew Salesses I serve convenience-store brownie bites. As Matthew Salesses I talk about weather and work. Matt says the city tourism bureau that hired him wants to use the word *dream*, like "The city of your dreams already exists" or "A dream you won't want to wake up from," but every line runs into the problem that a dream that becomes reality is a nightmare. He's thinking about quitting again—he asks do I still like being off-the-grid, do I miss being an official doctor with official doctor status and doctor money?

A doctor, he says.

As Matthew Salesses the doctor, the only unfamiliar part of this question is the phrase *off-the-grid*. It seems I have never heard that phrase before and don't know what it means. This produces a familiar anxiety. After a moment it's clear Matt wants to talk about something we have already agreed is off-limits. "I wanted to help people who often don't get helped," I say. "You know that. What I miss is—not being afraid to know the situation? Like, for example, yesterday this guy came in with a gunshot wound and refused to go to the hospital. I couldn't ask what happened, because I couldn't ask, 'Are you the only victim?' or 'Did you shoot someone else?' One day I might replace some guy's liver and then find out on the evening news that he killed someone right before the surgery."

Matt nods with inappropriate trust. Even as Matthew Salesses I feel like my friend is looking straight through me, he seems to be talking to someone else.

"Matt?" I ask. "You okay, buddy?"

"Listen," he says. "I've figured it out this time."

I drop my head in my palms. I know, as Matthew Salesses, what comes next. The whole time we were chatting he was only working himself up to this.

"I know how to get out of this world. I even left Sandra. I'm ready."

Sigh.

"This can't be my life," he says as he always does. "This can't be my life." His hands shake. They always shake. "There's more out there, beyond this life, I've seen it this time. I didn't realize I have to leave my body."

"Oh, body," I say. "Buddy."

"You're a doctor," he says, "so you came here to help people suffering. But don't you get it? All you can do is prolong suffering. Your patients get healthy, but they don't escape their situation, they're still stuck in this shitty life. Don't you ever get tired of all that?"

"Of life?"

"Like get out of the business of suffering and into the business of transcendence!"

The marketing lingo is the last straw. I gesture to the door.

He doesn't leave. This time, Matt says, he will do it himself. "I'll do it whether you help me or not. You can be a friend and a doctor—or you can watch me mess up and become a vegetable or something, and not even harvest my organs. You know I always finish what I start."

———

There's no reason to see the rest. What else could he do? What choice does Matthew Salesses have? Who should take responsibility? I tear myself out of his memory. I have already seen my naked body cut up into parts and burned beyond recognition. I only wonder whether the secret pleasure that Matthew Salesses took in his attacks started with

Matt's murder or whether Matt always knew what his friend was capable of.

The TV room stinks. I must have vomited. The bruises from the fight ache again with responsibility. I return to myself. A voice I know calls out: "Don't be dead. Don't be dead. Don't be dead." Humans are the only animals that think in the negative. A human touch alights, hurting and soothing.

Sandra.

Then an animal licks my face. But it's just the dog half. Sandra holds it in her hand.

Makeup is smeared over her face and hands and sleeves. Matthew Salesses's body lies inert on the floor in front of me. I am sorry, I don't forgive him. I was trying, of course, to save myself. This is not an excuse though, it's a desire. If I've crossed out all my answers, fuck it—I will love the questions better. I breathe again, feel my skin again, feel the air circulate invisibly, and the yellow yarn is there, leading into the lab.

I ask Sandra to help me walk. "There are medical supplies. We should take care of him too."

"I saw your note," she says. "Plus the shelter called me. It was a sweet idea, I just can't take care of a dog right now. I'll stick to the stuffed animal."

I don't ask her how she got the dog half. "Why did you come?" I ask. "No, never mind."

"You believed I would come," she said.

"I've always wanted to say someone was just in time."

She drapes my good arm around her and half drags me. In her heels she gets the supplies off the higher shelves easily. I ask how she feels, reassure her that I am fine. She says an ambulance is on its way for both of us. She looks around the room, and I can see her thoughts forming, but I give her time.

"Is this where he—" She won't say it. She wipes her eyes.

My neck burns hot, and I hold my head with my good arm. In this room Matt refused to admit he'd given up. I feel an angry love for him. He always wanted to escape the form of his body—he nurtured that desire in the dark like the Korean bear in the cave. Or maybe he wanted to go to his brother, my parents, he wanted only to call his family his family. We reach for stories because we need something to acknowledge our absence, because to love is to give what we don't have. I picture my daughter and her purple-tipped hair, holding a cigarette, standing on the line between smoking and not smoking. We are always on that line. Every line is what kind of person to be.

"I should have made more room for your grief," I say. "In Boston. You should have been able to talk to me."

She turns, asking whether I'm in pain.

"You don't want to come back with me, through the wall?"

She shakes her head. "No, I do not."

"There's bound to be another earthquake sooner or later," I joke. "Another name change. Another tunnel dream."

When she laughs I wonder whether I was joking after all.

In this room my body got chopped into pieces. In this room my yarn's unspooling ends. What happened to the other people who disappeared? I imagine joining them in some space between. Between past and future self, human and bear, murder and disappearance. We are always there, in a present without presence. We desire presence because we live in a world in which we never know what the present means. To look for presence is to stand in a perspective of absence. I sense something, in the wall, in the air, in my body, opening and opening. An opening a disappearance can be. I want to tell Charlotte this, that an open cave is a possibility, that an open wound is never dumb.

I take the flyer from my pocket and unfold it. Sandra touches the nose of the dog half to it, nods.

"Yes," she says. "It's us. The disappeared."

OPEN YOUR EYES, her flyer says. WE EXIST.

I'm not ready yet. What have I learned about loving better? Our resistance is our respect for existence. To know how we disappear is to know how to recognize each other. To know how to recognize each other's disappearance is to know how to appear. What I see now is the disappearance between appearance and appearance. How to love now is not a state but a union. Our body is not a wall between identity and politics. Our absence is a thing that exists. This is not typical, this is not an exception, this is not strange, we are not strangers—we are not—

we are—

we—

ACKNOWLEDGMENTS

Over the seven years it took me to write this book, my wife gave birth to our second child and was diagnosed with and died of cancer. This is the novel's context. I hope someday that my children can find in it the guidance that their mother and they have given me. Thank you.

Thank you also to Vivian Lee, this book's godmother; Kundiman, its ideal audience; Chelsea Lindman, who made it real before it was real; Kirstin Chen, first reader and first friend; Hafizah Geter, Kristin Lunghamer, and the entire Little A team; hero agent Ayesha Pande; hero writers Mat Johnson, Cathy Chung, and Laura van den Berg; my dissertation team of Mat, Amber Dermont, Chitra Divakaruni, j. kastely, and Audrey Colombe; Alex Parsons, Henk Rossouw, Adrienne Perry, and the rest of the UH CWP; and everyone I am forgetting.

The following people also helped me live to write this book: Roxane Gay, Brad Listi, Karissa Chen, Jimin Han, Kevin Vollmers, Margaret Rhee, Alex Chee, Ashley Ford, my family and in-laws, my coworkers at Coe. I wish I could send this book to everyone who donated to my wife's chemo fund; whether you see this or not, thank you so much.

Last, thank you to my fellow Korean adoptees, scholars of Asian American studies and literature, and Fourth Kingdom writers, and to all of the communities that have welcomed me and my work. Thanks for reading.

ABOUT THE AUTHOR

Photo © 2019

Matthew Salesses is the author of *The Hundred-Year Flood*, an Amazon bestseller and Best Book of September; an Adoptive Families best book of 2015; a *Millions* Most Anticipated of 2015; and a best book of the season at BuzzFeed, Refinery29, and Gawker, among others. He is also the author of *I'm Not Saying, I'm Just Saying* and the nonfiction work *Different Racisms: On Stereotypes, the Individual, and Asian American Masculinity*. Adopted from Korea at age two, Matthew was named by BuzzFeed in 2015 as one of "32 Essential Asian American Writers."

Made in United States
Orlando, FL
17 August 2023

36177029R00188